**He drew me into his arms,
right there in front of everyone, and leaned down.**

"Happy birthday, Molly."

Rick's lips ghosted across mine. He angled his mouth against mine and I opened for him. My eyes fluttered closed. Tentative, I met his kiss and felt electrified. I clung to him, completely unsure about what I was doing.

He drew away, just a little, took a shuddering breath and returned. I was pressed so close to him that I could feel how his heartbeat matched the ferocity of mine. I felt awkward and amazed and—

We broke apart, grinning at each other.

"Open my gift, Mol." He turned toward the fireplace.

I don't know why he lost his footing.

Rick's eyes went wide as he twisted, falling, his head bouncing off the corner of the stone fireplace.

I screamed.

With Curt's help, I rolled him onto his back. His blue eyes were open wide and unseeing. I pressed a shaking hand against his chest.

"Too late, dude," someone said. "He's dead."

All the colors around me bled away until everything was gray and covered in shadows. Above the dark, dead figure of Rick a ball of white light pulsed. It glittered, like starlight, and emanated comforting warmth.

Rick's soul.

I knew that I had to capture the light before it took the journey into the afterlife. Rick needed it to live. All I could think about, focus on, was catching it and sticking it back in.

I had no tools, no magic spells, no perfect way to fix what death had broken. All the same, while Curt pounded on his friend's chest, I stepped around him, knelt at Rick's side and grabbed his soul.

◈◈ THE ◈◈
REAPER DIARIES

UNDEADLY

Michele Vail

HARLEQUIN®
entertain, enrich, inspire™

Recycling programs
for this product may
not exist in your area.

ISBN-13: 978-0-373-21046-6

UNDEADLY

Printed in U.S.A.

"To die will be an awfully big adventure."
~J.M. BARRIE, *PETER PAN*

MOLLY'S REAPER DIARY

Holy Crap, What Happened to My Life?

So, my...um, friend gave me a diary for my sixteenth birthday because, apparently, it's a necromancer tradition. I guess he did some internet research and found an archaic reference, which is kinda cool. It's nice that he wanted to give me something meaningful, even if it was a book with a bunch of blank pages in it.

Anyway.

I'm glad he gave it to me. Because I want my life to mean something, and it's so weird now! The night I turned sixteen, everything changed. Big-time. And you know what? If this kind of crap happens to anyone else (and it will) then I figured they might need a real guidebook...it's sorta like Reaping for Dummies.

Yeah. Reaping.

We'll get to that. But first, you gotta understand how everything started.

Here's a little history...

It is said that Anubis fought a great earth-chattering battle with his uncle Set, the God of Chaos. Anubis's legacy was to rule the Underworld and Set was all, "Nuh-huh. I want to rule the Underworld."

So they had this huge freaking war. Set stole some of the reapers that Anubis was the boss of—and wow, did that piss him off!—

so then, the reapers were fighting each other and the humans were all, "What is this crap? Reapers suck!" And there were plagues and famine and people dying for no reason, and the reapers were too busy blasting each other to do their jobs.

It was a mondo ick mess.

Finally, Anubis went deep into the Underworld and got some bad-ass magic. We're talking magic so ancient and powerful, it wasn't supposed to leave the world of the gods, like, ever.

But he got it anyway and used it to capture Set. He imprisoned the god in the bowels (Seriously? Ew!) of the Underworld, and then he banished all the disloyal reapers into this place that was like limbo, I guess, only way, way worse. And no one but Anubis could get there. Or something like that.

Anyway, Anubis was so upset about what went down, and he felt so bad about all the humans who'd been hurt, that he changed the rules about death and reaping and junk. (That's a god for you.)

He was like, "Sorry, humans, my bad. Here's some magic." Okay, it was *sorta* like that. He was worried that his reapers might get more ideas about mutiny or whatever, so he split a reaper's power into five magical abilities, which matched the five parts of the soul. (Did you know there were five parts to a soul? Heka 101, peeps.)

And he bestowed these five *heka* gifts upon some fancy schmancy nobles because Anubis is a snob. Most gods are totally noses up, you know? That's what being immortal and all-powerful gets you.

So, he's like, "Hey, I'm giving each of you one of these gifts, and you can use them to control parts of being dead." It was like an end-of-the-war party gift for all the survivors. Here's the down-low:

ka Heka – Reanimates dead bodies using a teeny tiny part of the soul called the *ka*. (Pretty common ability these days.)

Ren Heka – Calls forth and communicates with earth-bound spirits. (Lots of necros can do this one, too.)

Sheut Heka – Creates and commands soul shadows. A soul shadow is sorta like the top layer of the soul, peeled away. (This power is rare, and a total no-no. Anyone unlucky enough to be born with this ability is whisked away by the government. Well, that's what the internet says, so it must be true.)

Ba Heka – Supposedly, ba heka necromancers can bind souls and keep them from entering the afterlife. (No one in modern times is known to have this gift. Or maybe they're hanging out with the sheut hekas in a government lab.)

Ib Heka – Sees into the heart of the soul, and knows the person's true worth. (Necromancers who have this ability usually go crazy, or become hermits, or sometimes, they start cults. A few have been serial killers.) Very, very, veeeeery rarely, a necro is born who has two gifts. The last one recorded was Leonardo da Vinci. Explains a lot, right? No known human has ever had all five gifts. It's almost impossible, because a human with that kind of power couldn't handle it. We'd implode, or something.

Supposedly, Anubis watches all the humans who are born with *heka* gifts, and if they use their magic well and don't act like douche bags, then he offers them a reaper job after they die. It's like anyone who's born with death magic is training to be a reaper in the afterlife.

Just so we're clear, reapers are dead.

At least, they're supposed to be.

No one really knows how the whole reaper thing works, this is just the stuff they make us learn in The History of Necromancy, and it's called "theory" or "mythology" or "wasting an hour of my life every day."

These days, people use reaper powers to enslave ghosts, make zombies, and basically cash in. If Anubis doesn't like what humans ended up doing with those gifts...well, he hasn't done anything about it. Maybe he doesn't care. Maybe he's down in the Underworld having parties with gods and souls, and is all like, "Humans? What humans?"

Oh. And there's this really, really, *really* old wall relief in some temple in Egypt dedicated to Set that says, "He will break his bonds and rise again to take his revenge. Death will come to the world and the living will be no more."

Total suckitude.

Molly Bartolucci

Mrs. Dawson's English Class

10th Grade

Ghost Gin

In 1898, when Signor Guglielmo Marconi was inventing the wireless telegraph, Mr. Michael Ruddard decided he'd rather focus on undead communication.

Ruddard discovered the energy of the human spirit could be captured. His experiments led to the creation of the Spirit Extraction, Encapsulation and Restraining engine, otherwise known as SEER. Informal terms for the SEER are otherworld portals, S-traps and ghost gins.

To those caught by the ethereal fingers of the engine, it was called eternal enslavement. Why pay live humans when a SEER produced free labor by raising the spirits of workers already dead? *This is supposed to be a descriptive essay, Molly, not a persuasive one. Stay on topic.*

Psychics were hired to keep the ghosts working and some necros specialized in locating other spirits. At first, only rich people could afford SEERs. Like most other tech, the gins were eventually made smaller and more affordable. These days

nearly every house is haunted. *You're wandering away from your main subject, which is about the invention of the SEER, not about the ghosts.*

Dead rock stars go on tour, sports teams with spirit

players take championships and supermodel apparitions

strut the catwalk. But one problem with ghosts was that they

couldn't be photographed or filmed. Hollywood invested

millions into researching how to fix the issue, but so far, no

one has come up with a solution. Meanwhile, theaters made a

killing because audiences paid big bucks to see their favorite

dead actors performing on stage.

SEER machines aren't perfect. Some have failed

completely! Can anyone forget when Monty Klein wrenched

himself free of his SEER on "Night Life" and dove into his

live cohost? He made Johnny Moreland stab his own eyes with

pens! Everyone totally saw that show. And you're going to tell

me ghosts can't hurt people?

Where's the ending? Needs work, but good start. I suggest adding more detail about the psychics, which are an important element to modern-day SEERs.

Right now, your essay barely rates a C. You usually do so much better work than this! Please see me after class to talk about how else you can improve this project.

CHAPTER

1

"Necromancy has existed for as long as we have. Most historians agree, however, that it was the Egyptians who perfected the art of raising the dead. No other culture can boast that their zombies built such magnificent monuments. Consider the Temple of Karnak, the Sphinx and the pyramids at Giza. All gifts from the children of Anubis."
~HISTORY OF NECROMANCY, VOLUME II

"THIS IS THE THIRD TIME!" GROUSED MRS. WOODBINE. SHE slapped the arm onto the counter with a meaty thunk. I looked at the flabby, gray-skinned limb with its sausagelike fingers then at the jowl-faced woman who squinted at me through her bifocals. She wore a purple jogging suit that was too tight and amplified her chunky form. The top jacket was unzipped, revealing old-lady cleavage, which made me want to yark. Seriously. Wrinkled boobs were not pretty.

"Hello, Mrs. Woodbine," I said. *Must. Resist. Sarcasm.* "I see Mr. Woodbine has lost another limb."

Another Friday afternoon in hell, thank you. As usual, I'd come to work straight from school, which was only a couple blocks away on the other side of Warm Springs Road. Our house wasn't too far away, either. We lived in a typical Las Vegas house (think beige, Spanish tiles and zero-scaping) on Grimsby Avenue (ironic, right?), which was on the other side of Green Valley High School. I worked for my dad, every afternoon and on the weekends. I got paid, which was good. But I also had less of a social life than most girls my age. Try *no* social life.

Except for tomorrow. Finally, it was my sixteenth birthday, and I was having a big party. At least I hoped so. Lots of people had RSVP'd, including Rick Widdenstock. Even though he was just a sophomore like me, he was the quarterback for the Green Valley High School Gators. Did I mention Rick's hotness? We'd been flirting for the past couple of weeks; yesterday *and* today, he sat with me at lunch. Gena and Becks, my two best friends, had found other things to do, even though we always ate lunch together. That was why they were my best friends—because they knew when to bail. And they didn't even mind about all the zombie stuff. Most normal people were weirded out by my necro powers. Necros were all over the place, you know? But there were only a handful who attended my high school, and most of them were too dark and angsty for my taste. Plus, I didn't look good with kohl on my eyes and my nose was too cute to be pierced.

. Mrs. Woodbine jerked on the leash she held in her free hand, which was attached to the neck of her husband, Mortimer. He shuffled to the counter, his empty gaze on the floor. Like most zombies, he looked gray and hollow-eyed. His clothes hung loosely on his thin frame. His gray hair stood up in stiff tufts and his skin was flaking. His lips were crusty; his teeth blackened. Had Mrs. Woodbine even bothered to skim the state-issued guide *The Care and Feeding of Your Zombie?* No wonder parts of her husband kept falling off. Sheesh!

We were required to give every new zombie owner the guide at the end of the four-hour course. Hmph. *The Moron's Guide to Not Getting Eaten by Your Zombie* might've suited Mrs. Woodbine better. Zombies required care. You had to comb their hair, cut their nails, oil their skin, brush their teeth and give them weather-appropriate clothing and shoes. Even though I was a *ka heka* (zombie maker) in training and I knew zombies weren't really people (sorry, but they're not), I still felt a lurch of pity for the thing that used to be Mortimer Woodbine.

"It's the same limb," Mrs. Woodbine said. "Frankly, I'm tired of having to bring him down here. Big Al's low, low prices certainly don't translate to *quality* work."

I bristled. My dad, Alfonso Bartolucci, was what you'd call

larger-than-life (though that's not the description some people would use). He owned and operated Big Al's Zomporium, and despite the cheesy name and Mrs. Woodbine's opinion, we were a decent operation. My mom had been a ka heka, too. She'd walked out on us when I was ten. After she left, Dad hired a guy named Demetrius to be the Zomporium's ka heka, and he was teaching me and Ally. Demetrius was a cool dude. He was as black as coffee grounds, old as dirt and he still had a smear of a Jamaican accent. I liked him a lot.

But the zombie-abusing Mrs. Woodbine? Not so much.

"Hel-*lo!*" Mrs. Woodbine screeched, snapping her fingers in my face. I blinked, my thoughts skittering, and resisted the urge to slap her hand away.

"Teenagers today! I swear to God! You're all worthless." She huffed at me, turkey neck quivering, as she poked the arm. "Did you hear me? This is the third time his damn arm has fallen off."

It ka-illlled me, but I smiled. "Let me see what we can do for you."

"I want a discount," she said, her flat brown gaze flashing with triumph. "A big one. You're lucky I don't call the Zombie Safety and Inspection Service on this place!"

You're lucky I don't whap your big stupid mouth with Mortimer's arm. I slid the pathetic limb off the counter then picked up the phone. I buzzed the cell of my sister, Ally, who was supposed to be organizing the storage room but was probably making picket signs for Citizens for Zombie Rights. Ally and her friends had created the group last year after watching a *Dateline* exposé on zombie abuse.

She's such a dork.

"What?" she spat.

Ally didn't care much about social graces, diplomacy or keeping her mouth shut. That was why I was manning the customer care center and she was stuck rearranging all the crap in storage. I didn't necessarily like everyone who walked through the doors, but I knew how to be polite. Most of the time.

Ally sighed in that dramatic, you're-making-my-brain-melt-with-your-stupidity way that always drove me nuts. I wanted to ride her about making idiotic protest signs instead of stacking toilet paper, but I didn't dare misbehave in front of a customer. Not even cranky, gnarly ol' Mrs. Woodbine. Nonna Gina had ears like a reaper and a rolling pin we called "lightning fury." Our grandmother was unafraid of whacking our butts with it. That was how she'd raised our dad, and he was *still* afraid of the rolling pin.

"Mrs. Woodbine has an issue with her zombie," I finally said. "Would you mind keeping her company while I take care of Mortimer?"

"That hag is back again?"

I smiled at the hag. "Yes. So, can you come up?"

"Gawd!" She snapped her phone shut.

A moment later she stomped out of the door situated behind the customer care desk. Her scowl zeroed in on Mrs. Woodbine. Ally was fourteen, tall and gangly, still flat-chested and had braces, too. She had the best hair—long, silky chestnut waves with auburn highlights, but did she care? No. She also liked to wear baggy clothes in blah colors. Even though I would never admit it to her (not ever), one day she'd be gorgeous. Y'know, after she lost the metalwork, got some boobs and developed some fashion sense.

"Mrs. Woodbine," she said. Her voice held a hint of accusation. "Would you like some tea while Molly takes Mortimer for repairs?"

The woman was caught between reacting to my sister's less-than-friendly tone and the seemingly polite question. Finally,

Mrs. Woodbine nodded. "I would love some tea. Did your grandmother make any cookies?"

Sometimes I wondered if she broke Mortimer's arm on purpose so she could chow down on the almond biscotti Nonna baked fresh every day for customers. Luckily, my grandmother saved the *buccellati*-fig cookies for us.

Ally gestured toward the seating area and Mrs. Woodbine hurried toward the side table that held dispensers filled with three kinds of herbal tea and two large platters of Nonna's treats.

I rounded the desk, holding poor Mortimer's arm, and then grasped the hand of the arm still attached. It was like gripping crusted leather. I felt another surge of anger at Mrs. Woodbine's poor zombie management skills. "C'mon, z-man. Let's get you fixed up."

We entered the same door my sister had flown out of, and she sent me a glare, and hissed, "Hurry!"

"Do you want to take the zombie to Demetrius?" I asked.

Ally eyed Mortimer, and I got the distinct feeling she was imagining some kind of jailbreak. Knowing her and her nutso friends, they probably had a plan for that kind of thing. "Never mind," I said. "I don't want to get grounded because you're planning zombie intervention."

"Whatevs. Just go already." She looked down her nose at me, and then she perched on the stool behind the customer care desk. Her glare tracked Mrs. Woodbine as the woman filled a plate with cookies.

I kinda hoped Ally would do something mean to Mrs. Woodbine, but even Ally had her limits on rudeness. Probably.

I took Mortimer down the hallway, which had one door on the left (employee bathroom), two on the right (supplies, storage) and one at the end (*sahnetjar*).

Sahnetjar was the ancient Egyptian name for the place where they made mummies and zombies. Necromancers still used the term today, probably because it sounded all fancy and mysterious.

As I led the zombie to the sahnetjar, I felt another pang of pity. I don't know why Mortimer hadn't put an Advance Zombification Directive into place. Lots of people had an AZD—and sometimes, their relatives would still try to zombify them. Dad read anyone the riot act who tried to circumvent an AZD—and sadly, a lot of people tried.

A memory pattered me like cold rain. I was in the lobby watching Ally color because I'd been directed to "Look after your sister." Seemed like I was always watching her, and I was always caught between feeling protective and resentful. Pretty much the way I felt about my sister now.

Dad and Mom were arguing about a customer.

"You shouldn't have done that, Cyn. You know how I feel about AZDs."

"But he offered a fortune! And his wife's dead. Zombies don't have feelings, Al. She doesn't care."

"I do! We honor the wishes of the dying. You give his money back and you de-animate Mrs. Lettinger."

"You're such an asshole, Al!"

I missed my Mom. I probably shouldn't, given that she basically gave us all the finger and took off. What kind of mother abandoned her family? When I was ten, I figured it was something I had done. Something I said or did. I cried and cried, and so did Ally. Dad did everything he could to make us feel better. And then Nonna left New York and came to live with us. Eventually, life got better.

Anyway.

I know my parents tried to keep their fighting away from us, but…yeah, that didn't exactly work out. I remember that things were always tense, especially right before Mom left. So, I don't really miss what Ally calls the Angry Times.

Still. The thing that I remembered most about my mom was that she was spontaneous. I think my dad would call it irresponsible, but he's a lot on the serious side. Being a single dad is hard on him. He worries. Mom didn't let stuff bother her. She laughed a lot. And she'd do silly stuff like break out into random dancing, or a game of chase around the house, or sometimes, after I'd gone to bed, she'd crawl under the covers and wrap her arms around me and sing softly.

I don't know why she left. Dad didn't exactly know, either, so what could he tell two grieving daughters who'd been abruptly, inexplicably, abandoned?

Well, you know. Not that Dad doesn't crack a smile, or anything, he totally does. It's just different, I guess. Dad raised me and Ally—well, he and Nonna did. It was a good life, maybe a little stifling with all the rules about curfew, homework, job and boys. Still. Dad taught me to whisper my prayers to the dead every night, whether they were zombies or not. Some souls choose to move into the next plane of existence, but some don't, you know. Souls can get trapped in this world. If you die, and you don't move on, then your soul remains bound to this plane and your spirit can be…er, acquired.

Yeah. You can be attached to a SEER machine, which FYI, is way worse than being a zombie. Zombies are just animated corpses. We need only one teeny tiny part of the soul, the *ka,* to make that happen. A soul doesn't need the ka. It's like a spleen, or an appendix, or wisdom teeth. But if you're attached to a SEER machine, then your spirit energy belongs eternally to whoever owns it. And if you think people are mean to zombies, you should see some of the stuff spirit slaves have to do. The worst part is that they're sentient energy. They know what's being asked of them, and they have to do it. At least zombies don't know when someone is demeaning them. Spirits have about the same kind of rights as zombies—as in, none. Courts keep ruling that death negates the civil rights of the previously alive. That goes for spirits and for corpses.

Any jerk can have a SEER machine and spirit slaves. But there's something worse than being stuck to a SEER. You could end up a soul shadow. I totally read about this on the internet. A *sheut heka* can trap the soul, peel off the sheut and... Ew, I know, right? A sheut is the darkest, most awful part of you, sliced away from morals, conscience and empathy. So you're like zero-calorie evil, you know? That's why it's illegal. I don't know why there are laws and junk about it nowadays, because as far as I know, there aren't sheut hekas around. There haven't been for, like, *centuries*. I've never seen a sheut, but Dem says some exist. Leftovers from way back when there were sheut hekas all over the place. And he says that sheuts can only manifest in the darkness. *Shadows need shadows, Molly. Dark needs dark.*

Sometimes, Dem is weird.

*Any*way...like I said, a lot of people opted for an AZD and chose cremation. Signing a piece of paper saying you didn't want your corpse zombified didn't mean thieves wouldn't steal your freshly buried body. Black-market zombification was big business. Bodies were stolen, shipped off to crappy zombie-making factories and then sold to people who did not read literature regarding the humane care of the walking dead.

Zombies didn't have souls. Okay, *most* zombies didn't have souls. Every so often during a transition, a deadling would wake up with its memories, personality and humanity intact. Probably because the ka heka messed up and put the whole soul back in, or something. Only, a dead body is still a dead body, you know what I mean? Yeah. Gives me the shivers, too. Even though necromancy has been around since forever, it was really the ancient Egyptians who figured out how to separate the soul into the *ib, sheut, ren, ba* and *ka*. To make a zombie, you kept the ka inside the body and released the other parts to the afterlife. Only the ka was needed for reanimation.

It's kinda complicated.

Zombies work mundane jobs and understand simple commands; they don't need to sleep or to eat, either. Okay. They don't *need* to eat, but they love sticking things down their craw. They have unceasing hunger even though they don't require food. Part of raising the dead includes creating an appetite suppressant. That costs extra, and you gotta reenergize the magic annually, which is why some people chose zombie supplements instead of necro-incantations.

Not feeding a zombie isn't like not feeding your cat. He. Will. Eat. You. And your cat. People who forget to pick up a case of Ghoul-AID sometimes don't live to regret it. *Capisce?*

Finally! I reached the end of the hallway, which took forever because Mortimer wasn't exactly good at the walking thing. I unlocked the door, waited sixty years for the zombie to shuffle inside and locked the door again. When you're dealing with zombies, security is important.

We were standing in a tiny foyer. Calling it a foyer was stupid. It was just a little white room with a couple of plastic chairs. I let go of Mortimer's hand. This was the only way to get to the sahnetjar, and I still had another door to unlock.

"Stay here."

Zombies don't often respond, but when they do, they groan. I've never met one that can actually talk, although Demetrius says they exist. Sometimes, I think he likes yanking my chain. A talking zombie? For real? Yeah, right.

Mortimer stared at the ground, looking like the most pathetic zombie ever. I sighed as I headed toward the door at the other end of the room. I wasn't much for my sister's whole save-the-zombies effort, but I had to admit I wouldn't mind seeing Mortimer put to rest. I'd bet his wife ran him just as ragged when he was alive. At least now, he didn't know it.

I tucked poor Mortimer's leathery limb under the crook of my arm, pulled my keys out of my pocket and unlocked the door that led to sahnetjar.

I heard a noise behind me. Startled, I turned and found Mortimer just inches away, his jaw cracking as his mouth opened impossibly wide. I dropped the keys (duh), backed against the door and held out his severed arm like an old, bent sword.

Then Mortimer tried to eat me.

CHAPTER
2

"The only way to survive a zombie attack is if you see it coming. Running won't do you much good since zombies have the unsettling ability to jump long distances. They're also strong, unintelligent and conscienceless. If one attacks, the best thing you can do is go for the kneecaps. Once it's down, you have to remove its head. No, really. Zombies are relentless, especially when dealing with the Hunger."
~WORST-CASE SITUATIONS, PARANORMAL EDITION

I DREW ON MY POWERS. MAGIC TINGLED IN MY HANDS AS I aimed them at Mortimer. A ka heka was the most common kind of necromancer and I was only in training, but even so, I still had some control over zombies.

Too bad Mortimer didn't know it.

He grabbed me with his one good arm and jerked me into his stank embrace. Whew. He probably hadn't been washed since he died. Okay. I could handle this. So what if he was strong? And smelled as if he'd been rolling around in poop?

I aimed my magic at him again. Black sparkles drifted down like lazy snowflakes and melted away.

That was bad. My heart skipped a beat, and icy fear dripped down my spine.

Mortimer's horribly large mouth descended…and panic exploded. I struggled harder against him, but it was like trying to wrestle with a marble statue. His teeth clamped onto my shoulder. *Ow!*

Pain and terror clawed through me. Oh, my God. I was gonna get eaten by a zombie. Before I turned sixteen. Before I had my party. Before Rick kissed me.

Then I was yanked backward.

"Bamo!" cried a new voice, much stronger and deeper and more Jamaican than my own. Demetrius! Relief tangled with my hysteria.

The zombie stopped attacking and cocked his head as if he was a cute cocker spaniel instead of a dead dude in the grips

of the Hunger. Demetrius dragged me through the door, shut
it and barred it. He whirled me around.

"You okay, child?" He took the zombie arm, and for a
second, I didn't let go. Then I realized what I was doing and
gave him the limb.

My shoulder throbbed and my shirt was ripped. I looked
down in shock. "He bit me!"

Demetrius led me to a table and lifted me by the waist.
For an old guy, he sure was muscular. He pushed the material over my shoulder and peered at the wound. He walked to
the medicine cabinet on the other side of the table. I thought
about Mrs. Woodbine scarfing down all that biscotti while
her husband had been trying to scarf *me* down. Bitch.

Demetrius returned with a jar of ointment that looked like
black tar and smelled like puke. I crinkled my nose.

"Where's the other stuff? The ointment we sell to our customers? Ugh! What is that?"

"'Dis de good stuff. My own concoction. Gonna heal the
bite in no time." He rubbed the cold, greasy gel into the
place where Mortimer's disgusting teeth had gouged my skin.
"Zombie bites are nasty business."

A bite or a scratch doesn't turn you into a zombie. I mean,
I know every zombie movie ever made says different. Gah!
Who thought of that ridiculousness? Soooo unbelievable. *Any*-
way. Zombie mouths are filthy and filled with germs and all
kinds of ick. An untreated bite could get infected quickly, and
boom, you're lying in a hospital bed breathing through a tube.

"You know *bamo* isn't exactly a necro incantation," I said.
Not that you needed words to perform magic. Sometimes,
using a word or phrase was helpful to get the focus going, but
if you had any heka gift, you could access it pretty easily and
without acting like you just graduated from Hogwarts.

"It's Jamaican for 'go away,'" said Demetrius, his lips splitting into a gap-toothed grin. "You know it's not the words, but the power you give them." He glanced at my torn shirt. "Go home and change. I'll deal with Mr. Woodbine."

"Okay." At least my dad wasn't here to fret over the zombie bite. If he'd been around for Mortimer's attack, I'd be on my way to an emergency room right now. Dad panic was like, ten levels above regular people panic, so good thing my dad was up in Reno checking out locations for a second zomporium. Unfortunately, he'd promised that he would be back tomorrow. For my b-day. Sigh. He'd said he wouldn't interfere with my party, but I wasn't sure he'd be able to stay away. He was itching to play songs from '80s movies soundtracks. Oh, yeah, I'm named after Molly Ringwald. In particular, because my dad totally crushed on her. Ugh. I'm telling you now that if he plays anything from *Pretty in Pink,* I'm throwing myself off the roof.

"Do you want me to call da Empress?"

That's how Demetrius refers to Nonna Gina. Like everyone else, he has a healthy respect for my grandmother. It isn't just the rolling pin, either. She just has a way about her. A scary, obey-me way.

I shook my head. "I'd rather walk home than get into a car with her."

In Nevada, you have to be fifteen and a half to get a driver's permit. I'd counted the days until I was officially 15.5 and went off to get my permit (under parental protest, I might add). I'd finished the required driver's education courses over the summer and kept a clean driving record. After all, I had to drive with Dad or Nonna, which was as fun as it sounded. As in, not.

But on Monday, I would go get my driver's *license.*

Woot!

It was only three weeks into the school year, and soon I'd

have my own ride. Well, Nonna's ride. She had this huge boat of a car that she didn't drive very often, mostly because she didn't see so well anymore and hit stuff like mailboxes and curbs. I'd saved up some money, but nowhere near enough to get a decent car. Rick Widdenstock had turned sixteen over the summer. The first day of school, he'd arrived in a new black-and-silver Mustang. That car had just upped his hotness factor. I'm aware of how shallow that makes me sound, but hey, I can live with it.

Demetrius helped me off the table. "If the wound's not healin', you tell me."

I nodded. A zombie bite was nothing to blow off. I'd just have to figure out a way around the stink. I looked toward the barred door and saw the shadow of Mortimer flickering against the frosted glass. "What are you going to do to him?"

"Put him to rest, child. Like he want."

I frowned. "He's a zombie, Dem. How can you know what he wants?"

Demetrius shook his head, and I felt like I'd disappointed him. Hey, I paid attention during our lessons. I just didn't remember anything about zombies having feelings or thoughts. 'Cause they don't.

"You don't know everything yet, child."

Well, duh. "Mrs. Woodbine is gonna be pissed."

Anger slashed his expression. "Don't you worry. I deal with her." He patted my non-injured shoulder. "Go on now."

The sahnetjar was made up of several rooms. Zombification took time and skill and there were stages to the process. The room we stood in now with its gleaming silver table, wash area and cabinets was used for assessment. The other rooms included the materials needed for each part of the zombifying. So far, Ally and I had been allowed to train only in the first stage, which was the part where we took out organs, rubbed the body with *netjer*—also called natron—wrapped it loosely with linens and prepared it to receive its *ka,* what the ancient Egyptians had called the life spark. Soul work is tricky. The zombification process has to be completed within seven days of death. After that, there is no getting the ka back to reanimate the body.

Sheesh. You didn't think it was *easy,* did you?

Like all necromancers, Ally and I had been born with heka gifts. Probably because Mom was a ka heka. Dad didn't have any powers. He was just a regular guy.

Mom wasn't much on actual instruction. She didn't like us being in the back rooms, and she didn't really talk about the magic or the process too much. But Dem was a zombification master. He taught us how to draw on the magic and use it, usually with already-made zombies. Ka hekas can control the ka (um…duh), so we can control zombies. Usually. Sometimes, I wondered if Mom would've showed us the cool things we were learning from Demetrius.

We had a back door that led to a loading dock, where we took in supplies and bodies. The bay was closed, so I went out the side door. Then I realized my keys were on the floor with Mortimer. Crap. I couldn't lock it. I dug in my front pocket for my cell phone to call Ally to do it. Then I realized I'd left the phone, along with my purse, at the front desk.

I hesitated.

I did not want to see Mrs. Woodbine, especially not after she found out her husband was done for. Plus, I'd have to explain to Ally about the bite and she would call Dad and he would freak and do something parental like call an ambulance or the National Guard.

No, thanks.

If I hurried, I could get home, use the hide-a-key, change

clothes and come back. Ally wouldn't be thrilled to get stuck
in the customer care center, but she'd deal.

Vegas didn't have seasons. It was hot most of the time,
though it cooled down in the winter months. It had snowed
only once in my whole life, and that lasted all of two days.
September had brought lower temperatures, but it wasn't jacket
weather. I had nothing to cover my ruined shirt or messed-
up shoulder.

I strode out of the parking lot to the stoplight. It took forever to cross Warm Springs Road. If I'd been wearing sneakers
instead of my fabulous black ankle boots, I would've jogged.

I walked past a shopping center and then I was clipping
down the sidewalk that ran in front of the school grounds.
The school was set on the other side of a large parking area.
The sports arena was up on the left. I was almost to the edge
of the structure when I heard my name being called.

"Hey, Molly!"

I looked over my shoulder. I'd just crossed the entrance to
the school parking lot, and Rick's Mustang had just rolled up
to exit the lot. He leaned over the center console and peered
at me through the open passenger-side window.

"Wanna ride home?"

My heart skipped a beat. I sniffed and grimaced. The salve's
awful smell was still evident, though its stench had lessened.
And there was the matter of my ripped shirt. Still, there was
no way I was giving up a ride in Rick's Mustang. Or—and
here's my shallowness showing again—the potential to be seen
in Rick's Mustang.

I opened the door and slid inside. Oh. My. God. New
car smell was so delicious. Everything was clean and shiny.
I glanced at Rick and saw him check me out. Then his nose
wrinkled.

Heat surged to my cheeks. "Sorry," I said. "I had an accident at work."

"Are you all right?" he asked.

"Yeah. It's just that the medicine is kinda...fragrant."

Wouldn't my English teacher, Mrs. Dawson, be proud? Rick grinned, which made me feel warm and squirmy. His blond hair was cut short, his face all angular like a movie star's. He even had a little dimple in his chin. "No big. I just finished football practice and the showers are under maintenance or something. So I don't exactly smell like a petunia."

"Petunia?"

He grinned. "My mother runs a flower shop. It's almost enough to get my dude card revoked."

I laughed.

He seemed pleased that he made me giggle and offered another melt-alicious grin. "You live on Grimsby, right?"

I nodded. He looked at me with one eyebrow cocked. "Seat belt."

I put it on, embarrassed that he'd had to remind me. "It's the 'rents," he said. "You wouldn't believe all the rules I have to follow to keep my ride."

"Was blood sacrifice involved?"

He laughed as he flipped on the signal and made a right onto Arroyo Grand Boulevard. "Almost." He glanced at me. "You have to deal with any of that...you know with your powers?"

"Nah. We drink blood only on Thursdays." Rick's eyes widened and I smiled. "Joking."

He chuckled, but I was aware of the tension in his body. I'm a necro, and part of the gig is an über awareness of people's body language and emotions. I think Rick was a little weirded out by my gift.

It wasn't like there was a shortage of necromancers in the

world, but most people were born without any reaper gifts.
Being a necro doesn't make anyone really special, though.
Everyone has to learn about necromancy, about zombies and
SEER machines, and even Ancient Egyptian history (required
course, like math and science). But it's not exactly a big deal
these days, not like it was waaaaay back. So, reading about
necromancy is like reading about the Titanic and World War I.
The necros on board that Titanic couldn't stop it from sinking,
but they used their zombies and death magic to help people.
And World War I? The American zombies were the reason
we saved so many lives on the frontlines.

Anyway. Some necros take themselves too seriously, and
wear black and act mysterious. I tried to be normal, but some
people were still weirded out by the whole "she touches dead
people," thing.

Whatevs.

I wasn't too surprised when Rick knew which driveway
was mine. He lived in the same neighborhood, although in a
bigger house with a killer pool, and we saw each other occasionally. Usually with me walking to school and him catching
a ride with his friends, waving as they drove past.

We sat awkwardly for a moment. Then I smiled and said,
"Well, you know. Thanks."

"No prob." He looked at the house then at me. "Your dad
home?"

"Nah. He's in Reno." I looked at Rick (sooo cute!) and realized he was waiting for something. For me to…*oh*. My pulse
leapt. "You…uh, wanna come in?"

He turned off the car and slid the keys out of the ignition.
"Sure."

I looked at my empty house and felt my stomach hitch.
We would be alone in there. Squee! I was really glad that my
uncle Vinnie was at the Zomporium helping Demetrius with

the less-than-savory tasks of zombification. Vinnie had been my dad's older brother and he'd died when I was three. He'd helped Dad start the business and wanted to help even after his death. Mom was the one who'd zombified him. She might've sucked as a mom, but she'd been a Class A zombie-maker.

Vinnie was a good zombie, but sometimes I wished I remembered what it was like to have him as an uncle.

I picked up the fake rock hidden in the Angelita daisies that lined the sidewalk up to our house. The rest of the yard was zero-scaped—you know, volcano rocks and cacti. We'd planted the daisies and the fortnight lilies along the walkway because Nonna really liked them. She missed having a garden like she had back in New York. I almost made a comment on them, so Rick would know I was sorta flower savvy, but it seemed like a lame move.

I slid the key out of the bottom of the rock, unlocked the door and then put it back. Rick watched this all without comment. I didn't want to explain why my purse was still at the Zomporium because I didn't want to admit to the zombie bite. Hopefully, he just thought I was some kind of klutz and whacked my shoulder or something. I'm glad he hadn't asked me for details. If my gift freaked him at all, he'd probably bail if he knew I'd almost been zombie chow.

"C'mon." I led the way into the house.

Rick followed, shutting the door behind him. "I need to change," I said, looking over my shoulder. I caught Rick checking out my ass. *Thank you, jean gods.* "You want something to drink?"

"What do you have?" His voice sounded a little rough, but I wasn't sure if it was from being caught gawking or from lust. Yeah, I said the *L* word. Necro, remember? His eyes were dilated, his breathing had shortened and a delicious tension filled his muscles. Oh, yeah. He was definitely feeling attracted to me. It's the body language thing, you know? You have to pay attention to the details, especially when you're reanimating a corpse. That's a Dem-ism—and I've only heard it 3,000 times or so.

The front door opened into a small foyer. Three feet forward and you were in the living room. We had a sectional, a big-screen television and lots of bookshelves. The patio doors led to the backyard, which sadly had no pool. If you kept going to the right, you'd see the dining room and beyond that, our kitchen.

The hallway to the left of the foyer led to the downstairs bathroom and the master bedroom (that was Nonna's). The stairs led to the other four bedrooms and another guest bathroom. My room connected to Ally's via the third bathroom. Yeah. That made getting ready for school the opposite of pleasant, especially since both of us hated mornings. And sharing.

I led Rick into the kitchen and pointed at the fridge. "Take whatever you want. I'll be right back."

"Thanks."

I started to walk away, but Rick looped his fingers around my wrist. He looked at me, his eyes sparkling. "Don't be gone too long."

"Promise." My belly squeezed in excitement. Dad would be so un-thrilled to know I was alone in the house with a *b-o-y*. Not that he would have to know. Ever. Rick dropped my wrist, gave me another grin and I suppressed the urge to skip through the house.

In my room, I took off my shirt and assessed the damage to my shoulder. It didn't look too bad. I got a washcloth and wiped some of the goop off and then smeared what was left across the teeth marks. Yuck.

I got out my precious bottle of Dior Addict, which I saved for special occasions, and squirted it along my neck and collarbone. Then I spritzed my wrists. I picked out another shirt, my teal flutter-sleeve with a V-neck, and put it on. It looked pretty good with my jeans. I took a second to brush my hair, which I wore long and straight. It was a boring shade of brown, but I had hazel eyes, which kinda made up for the witchy locks. I also freshened my makeup. Luckily, I had decent skin and didn't need too much coverage. I wore peach blush on my cheekbones, lightly lined eyes with a smidge of mascara and gloss (Dad put the kibosh on colored lipsticks).

Then I brushed the hell out of my teeth. Just in case.

Finally, I came downstairs, heart racing. I wasn't sure what to talk about with Rick. We were in a couple classes together, but we didn't usually run in the same circles. I'd been kinda surprised when he started hanging around me more at school. I wasn't the only one who'd noticed, either. My friends thought it was way cool, but Mina Hamilton, head cheerleader, perfect princess and Rick's ex-girlfriend, did not. She'd been giving me dirty looks, making snide comments within earshot and "accidentally" pushing me aside when sashaying down the hall. Her mean-girl attention scared me worse than dealing with hungry Mortimer. Surviving a zombie attack was easy; getting out unscathed from a Mina attack was not.

Rick was standing in the living room, staring at our book-shelves. He held a can of 7UP and he took a sip as he studied the shelf filled with necro books.

"Hey."

He turned, checked out my blouse (and okay, my boobs) and smiled. "Hey."

He put the soda on the coffee table and stretched out his hand. Heart pounding, I took it and he drew me into his arms.

Holy. Freaking. Anubis.

"You're very pretty," he said. I smelled mints and the tang of 7UP. My heart beat faster still and my knees went all mooshy.

"Thanks," I whispered.

His blue eyes darkened. His tongue darted out to wet his lips. Remember when I said I had no social life? Dad had rules about me and boys—as in never the twain shall meet (another point to Mrs. Dawson). Sixteen was the magic number for dating. And driving. And everything else.

"You nervous?" he asked softly, his face dropping closer to mine.

"No."

"Liar." He chuckled.

I didn't answer because silence was better than admitting he was right.

He drew me closer and I realized how muscular he was. He was six inches taller than me, too, even with my two-inch boot heels making up some of the height difference.

"I really like you," he said.

"I really like you, too."

"Good." Then he lowered his lips toward mine—

"Ex*cuse* me?"

I jumped out of Rick's arms and whirled around. I knew that thick accent. Dad only pulled out the Bronx voice when he was trying to intimidate. He made it sound like he had mob connections—which he sooo did not. He'd lived in Las Vegas longer than he ever had New York.

"Dad!" I pasted on a smile as frustration (no kiss) warred with embarrassment (so busted). Dad had the worst timing ever. "This is my friend. Rick Widdenstock."

My father wasn't much taller than I was, but he was built like a bull. Barrel-chested and muscular with slicked-back dark hair and amber eyes that took in everything, he did kinda look mob-ish.

"How ya doin', *Rick?*"

Rick pretended my dad hadn't scared the crap out of us.

He crossed the room and held out his hand. "Nice to meet you, sir."

My father pumped Rick's hand. He was impressed by good manners. Me, too, actually.

"My little girl, you know, she's not sixteen yet."

"No, sir. But I'll be here tomorrow night to celebrate her birthday."

"Just see that you celebrate it with your hands in your pockets, *Rick*."

"I have every intention of kissing Molly, sir," he said. "I've waited for her a long time."

I almost fell over. A long time? I didn't think he'd noticed me until two weeks ago. And that was only after he'd broken up with Mina—and they'd dated all last year. Maybe he was just laying it on thick for my father. Although his announcing he wanted to make-out with me probably hadn't made Dad all that happy.

But it sure did me.

"I appreciate honesty, Rick. But watch the hanky panky, y'hear?"

"Yes, sir."

"Walk your young man out, Molly," said Dad. "I'll wait for you here."

Terrific.

Rick might've been cowed by my father, but he'd hidden it well. He'd made a stand, too. He took my hand and we walked outside together. We leaned against the driver's side door, close but not touching. I wouldn't put it past my dad to be looking out a window and scowling at us.

"You must really want to date me," I said, realizing as the words left my mouth that I'd made a huge assumption. I mean, kissing me was one thing, committing to dinner and a movie every weekend was something else. That was dating, right?

"Yeah," he said softly. "I really do."

"Why?" I asked. I didn't feel like anyone special, and I certainly didn't fit in with Mina and her crowd.

"You're pretty, smart and funny. What's not to like?"

I pretended to think about it. "True." I looked up at him through my eyelashes. "So why should I date you?"

"Because I have a kickin' ride, I'll pay for every date and…" He leaned down and whispered, "I'm a very good kisser."

"I'll have to take your word for it," I said primly.

He laughed. Then he put a finger to my lips. "You'll see tomorrow night."

Disappointment crowded my stomach. "Tomorrow?"

"When you're sweet sixteen, Molly Bartolucci, I will kiss your socks off." His lips melted into that oh-so-sexy grin, and I grinned back, butterflies jumping and fluttering.

I stood in the driveway and watched him leave. He waved at me then drove sedately down the street. I turned to go back into the house, prepping my story for Dad.

He was still in the living room. He'd pulled a picture off one of the shelves, the last one we'd taken before Mom bailed. When he looked at me, tears glittered in his eyes.

"You look just like her."

Dad didn't really talk about Mom that much. For a while, there'd been a hole in our family, but eventually it closed up. She'd left, and we'd survived. Still. This was weird. I'd been expecting the chewing out of my life, and he was getting all sentimental. I sucked in a breath and said, "We weren't doing anything. He just gave me a ride. I had to change clothes—"

Dad put the picture back and waved off my explanation. "Demetrius called my cell and said that Whacko Woodbine's zombie bit you." His gaze dropped to my shoulder. "You okay?"

"Yeah, Dad."

He nodded. "Good."

I put a hand on my hip and frowned at him. "Who are you? And what have you done with Al Bartolucci?"

Dad chuckled. "You think I don't know about you and boys? Oh, I know. You're a good girl, Molly. But you're gonna be sixteen and you wanna date. I get it. And that guy, Rick, he's all right."

"And the zombie bite?"

"Demetrius is a world-class necromancer," said Dad. "He says you're gonna be fine, so you are." He opened his arms and I walked forward to accept his hug. He kissed the top of my head. "You're very special, Molly. I know that. You gotta lot of things to do, you know? I'm real proud of you."

For some reason his words weren't comforting. His body was tense, and I felt the sorrow woven in with his pride in me. He wasn't telling me something—and I knew it was important. And it made him sad.

I leaned away from his embrace and looked into his eyes. I didn't know if I'd be able to bear it if something happened to my dad. I already knew life wasn't fair—if it was, parents wouldn't leave. "Daddy, is something wrong? Are you sick?"

He looked surprised. "What? No. No way. I'm just wallowing because you're a young lady now and you're making me feel like an old man."

I felt the truth in his words, but I still knew that he was holding back something important. Something I wasn't gonna like.

"C'mon. We'll go to the Zomporium and rescue your sister."

"I think you mean we'll rescue Mrs. Woodbine."

Dad laughed. "Yeah. Ally will eat her for lunch, that's true. But that woman deserves it. I should've never taken her business."

"What's done is done."

He looked at me, another flash of sorrow in his eyes. "Yeah," he said softly. "What's done is done."

CHAPTER
3

"The Greeks loved a good oracle, though they were not the first culture to embrace the art of prophecy. For millennia, necromancers have approached the Oracle of Anubis to find out their life's purpose. Not every query is answered nor is all news heard welcomed. However, unlike the questionable nature of the Greeks' oracles, the prophecies told by Oracle of Anubis might as well be written in stone. A necromancer is always at the behest of Anubis's will."

~HISTORY OF NECROMANCY, VOLUME II

IN THE DREAM, I WALKED THROUGH A TUNNEL CARVED OUT of rock. Ahead, I saw lights flickering and my footsteps quickened. Unrelenting black followed me, shadows that seemed to chase and growl, as if trying to stop me from going forward.

Torches lit the small, circular room, which was hewn out of the reddish stone and painted in bright hues. It looked like a picture from a history textbook. The incense was thick, but its odd scent wasn't unpleasant. The only statue on the altar was Anubis, god of necromancy. I walked to the small wooden table and stared at the painted idol. Slowly, I reached out and touched it.

The statue felt warm. Alive.

"I present to you Molly Inez Bartolucci," whispered a low, feminine voice. "She comes before you to be judged worthy of your gifts." Then, like the white smoke of the incense, the voice faded away.

I wasn't sure what was going on. I'd never been to any place like this. I had a small altar to Anubis in my room and every day, I said a prayer and made an offering. Dad taught Ally and me about honoring Anubis, even though Dad wasn't a necro. He said we should always respect the gods and offer our gratitude daily.

I was still in my pajamas, and I was trapped in a place I had no idea how to leave. It was only a dream. Right? But…but if it was a dream, how did I know that? *Wake up, Molly.*

"Be still, daughter." The booming voice bounced off the chapel's walls and vibrated in my chest.

"Anubis." I fell to my knees, more from fear than in supplication. Still, it had the same effect. I felt the death god's approval.

"Your task will be great, daughter. And at times, the burden of your gift will be heavy. I have looked into your heart and judged you worthy. You are a child of Anubis, chosen of my gifts. Are you willing to accept my bidding?"

"Yes," I said, because I was afraid not to agree. Hel-*lo*. God of the Underworld. The Reaper of all Reapers. I don't think you're allowed to say no.

"Of course you can say no," said a voice that was closer, softer, but no less commanding. "Those who serve me, serve willingly."

I hadn't realized my eyes were closed, but they were. I didn't want to open them, but then I felt a gentle hand cup my chin. So I opened my eyes.

The man sitting next to me cross-legged wore a T-shirt and jeans. He was barefoot. He had skin like a café latte and his almond-shaped eyes were as dark as the night. His long black hair brushed his shoulders.

Huh. Anubis was cute. Not my type at all, though. In fact I felt a little…repelled. Probably because he was a god and all.

"Trust me, Molly, I'm not cute." He laughed. "This is just the form I'm taking now."

Whoa. Anubis could read my thoughts. I blushed. "Sorry."

"I'm quite old…say, around infinity. Cosmos, spiritual energy, psychic nuances…it's complicated."

"Oh. Well, if it's more complicated than algebra, I'm out." He laughed. "Got it."

He took my hand and turned it over. Little lines of black

sparkles followed Anubis's finger as he traced patterns in my palm. Heat followed the trails.

"What are you doing?" I asked.

"Giving you the gifts you will need for what challenges lie ahead. You're choosing to serve."

"Yes," I reiterated even though he hadn't really asked a question. I was scared and not at all sure I could do what he wanted, and the whole *challenges* thing did not sound fun. "Um...what challenges?"

He looked at me, and his wise-beyond-the-ages expression held amusement. "It will be revealed as you go. Think of it as a life puzzle, something I've given you the ability, intelligence and talent to put together. Patience, wisdom and fortitude are what you'll have to cultivate to prevail."

My stomach clenched as I realized the weight of his words. "What if I can't do whatever it is?"

"I believe you can." He pressed my hand between both of his. His dark eyes held mine. "And so must you, daughter."

"Molly? Wake up!"

Ally's screeching voice echoed in the cave. Anubis winked at me, and disappeared. For a moment, I sat alone in the cavern, and wondered what the—

"Molly!"

"Ugh!" I pried open my eyes and found Ally leaning over me. The curtain of her brunette hair tickled my forehead.

I blinked up at her. "Jeez. I'm awake already." I glanced at the digital clock. 1:06 a.m. I sat up in my bed and she crawled in next to me. She wore Happy Bunny pajamas. The top said I Deserve All My Stuff. The rude pink cartoon character was one of her faves, which figured. My sis was, in a lot of ways, Happy Bunny.

She tossed a small wrapped gift in my lap. "Happy birthday."

I grinned. After Mom had bailed on us, I'd started the birthday game. I woke up Ally on the exact time and day of her birth (3:03 a.m. on November 4), and gave her a present. She surprised me the next year, on my birthday, by doing the same. It was a tradition we'd created and stuck by—no matter how much we irritated each other.

I plucked off the tiny bow and tugged at the taped edge. "Have you seen *Deadlings?*"

What had she taped this with? Super Glue? I glanced at her. "No. Is it a movie or something?"

She sighed. "*Deadlings and the Cursed Ones* is one of our necromancy books. It's not on the shelf. I wanted to look something up—"

I stopped picking at the tape. "What?" I asked sharply. Ally was too smart for her own good. Her plans created mondo trouble. I mean, they always worked, but again…*mondo* trouble. I wasn't getting grounded again because of her. Shall we discuss the zombie dog incident? Yes, animals can be zombified—but it's illegal. Animal souls are different from people souls. Animals brought back are usually vicious and can't be controlled. More than one pet owner has ended up injured or dead because they took their precious fluffywuffykins to a black market zombie-maker. And having dead, vicious dogs appeals to certain criminal types. But does my sister pay attention? No. At the tender age of twelve, Ally had come across a zombie Doberman chained in a yard and talked me into rescuing it. And by rescue, I mean being chased and almost eaten.

Somehow, someway, I always got blamed (she's persuasive, all right?) because I was the older sister who should "Be the example, Molly, not the afterschool special." Sigh. Well, I had bigger things at stake now. Like cars and boyfriends.

She shrugged, her gaze skittering away. "Just something for the club."

"Like what?"

Rolling her eyes, she plucked the gift out my hand and used her fingernail to rip open the side. She handed it back. "Nothing, all right? Club business, which means not your business. Just open your stupid gift already."

"You're so sweet," I muttered, ripping off the paper. It was a shiny red box. I opened it. Nestled inside was a slender, delicate-looking bottle with the ankh, the symbol of life and the soul, emblazoned on it.

"It's perfume," she said. "I ordered it special from this necro website. It's called Soul, Baby." She looked at me. "Dumb name. But it smells good. And you like that kind of stuff."

"Ally...it's wonderful."

"Dad helped me buy it for you."

I didn't know what to say. Ally could be annoying, cranky and generally a jerk...but sometimes she got things right. Really right. I had to admit I felt a bad case of the warm fuzzies.

"Oh, and BTW, you're welcome for bringing home your purse and cell phone. After you left me to deal with that hag from hell, I should've tossed it all into traffic."

"I already said thank you," I said. "You want it written in blood or what?"

Ally grinned at me. "Well, I did get to see Dem and Nonna take her down. But not before she ate her way through a plate of cookies. I saw her stick a bunch in her tote, too."

"Meh. Parting gift," I said. "Good riddance." I closed the box with a snap. I rubbed the top of the lid and chewed my lip. "I had a dream...um, about Anubis."

Ally peered up at me. "You had an Anubis dream on your sixteenth birthday?"

"Yeah," I said. "I know, right?"

She was quiet for a moment. "You remember what Dem

told us? About how Anubis would visit some necromancers in their dreams?"

"Sure."

"On their sixteenth birthdays?"

Something inside me went cold and still. "That kind of stuff doesn't really happen anymore."

"Are you brain-damaged? It just happened to *you*. You really don't like school, do you? We're talking about this in my eighth-grade Necro 101."

"I remember that class. Sorta," I said, feeling defensive.

"In the sixteenth year of a necromancer's life, parents used to take their kids to the Oracle and ask to know their paths. If the child had an Anubis dream, it meant they were chosen to do something important."

I stared at her. "Hel*lo,* have you met *me?*" I vaguely recalled Dem telling us that during one of our necro lessons. Ally had a brain like a computer. She remembered everything in excruciating detail. Suddenly the gift in my hand felt like a huge weight. My heart felt heavy, too, as if too burdened to keep beating. I took a deep breath. "Do you really think I had an Anubis dream?"

Ally shrugged. "Well. Maybe it's psychological. I mean, people don't consult oracles anymore, right?"

I eyed her because she sounded almost soothing. And Ally trying to comfort was so not her style. "Aw, man. They do, don't they?"

She stared at me, obviously debating, and then, like always, her honesty won out. "Yeah. Some necros still consult oracles. They're built into the temples, Molly. Lots of necros honor the old ways."

Foreboding crawled through me. We both sat on the bed, the silence thick.

Ally said, "You think Mom misses us?"

It killed me to hear the longing in her voice. She'd had the least amount of time with Mom; she was barely eight when Cynthia Bartolucci hit the bricks.

"Sure she does," I lied.

Ally didn't seem to take comfort from my words. "I used to remember what she looked like. Her scent. Her laugh. It gets harder to think about her." She sighed. "She's never coming back."

"I know," I said softly.

She swung her legs off the bed and stood up. She took a couple steps and then looked over her shoulder. "I bet the dream means nothing. Why would Anubis pick you to do anything?"

Since genuine curiosity laced her voice and not the scoffing tone she used when she thought others beneath her intellect, I didn't throw a pillow at her head. Her gaze looked worried, too. And that kinda freaked me out. Ally wasn't a worrier. A plotter, a planner, a pain in the butt, yes, but definitely not a worrier.

"True," I said, waving my hand as if it could push aside both our doubts. "Besides I don't want to do anything that will ruin my manicure."

Ally snickered. Then she bounced off, going through our adjoining bathroom into her own room.

I fell back against my pillow, clutching the perfume box in my hand. It took me a long time to go back to sleep.

MOLLY'S REAPER DIARY

A Short History of My Life and the First Lesson of Reaperhood

So, I already wrote about the history of reapers. And I figured maybe I should write about the history of me. Well, not in a *Lifetime* movie kind of way. The first sixteen years of my life aren't exactly riveting. Here are the highlights:

I was born.

Then Ally was born.

Having a sister two years younger than me is annoying...except when it's not.

Uncle Vinnie died when I was three.

Mom left us when I was ten.

Nonna moved in and taught us about cooking and fear. (Hello, rolling pin.)

I started zombie-making training.

I survived my freshman year of high school.

I am currently enduring my sophomore year of high school.

I got my driver's permit.

I turned sixteen.

I had an Anubic dream.

Like I said, riiiiiiiiiveting. I hope that my future holds more exciting adventures, even beyond driving and dating. I did just accept Anubic's offer of extra gifts, but I had brain fail in the dream.

So here's the first lesson of being a reaper in training.

Ask questions.

I haven't known Anubis long, but I don't think he'd mind if you posed a query or two about what to expect when you agree to serve him. Here are few questions, you might want to ask:

WHAT DOES SERVING YOU MEAN EXACTLY?

HOW DO I KNOW WHEN IT'S TIME TO SERVE YOU?

WHAT'S THE TIMEFRAME FOR SERVING YOU? IT IS...UM, FOREVER?

DO I GET VACATION DAYS?

WHAT GIFTS DID YOU GIVE ME? AND WHAT AM I SUPPOSED TO DO WITH THEM?

ARE THERE PERKS INVOLVED WITH SERVICE TO AN IMMORTAL GOD? SUCH AS FREE CHOCO-

LATE, A DAY PASS AWAY FROM MY SISTER OR GETTING OUT OF SCHOOL EARLY?

WILL THERE BE HOMEWORK?

Feel free to personalize these questions as they suit your birthday dream conversation with Anubis. Meeting Anubis is usually a time-sensitive matter, so keep your questions precise and be prepared for answers that will totally bum you out. If you don't have time to ask him about homework...the answer is yes.

There is always homework.

One more FYI...

You will be afraid. That fear will sit like a cold, dark lump in your stomach, and it will grow tentacles and clutch at your heart and your brain, and choke your thoughts and emotions until all that exists is pain and exhaustion and terror.

My advice?

Embrace it.

CHAPTER
4

"The Oracle predicted Set's return, and that the god of chaos would ruin the world. Even though humans had reaper powers, they would not be enough to defeat Set. Anubis refused to abandon his human children again, and began to choose the worthy to receive more of his gifts. Throughout centuries, a secret sect of warriors with the strength, abilities, magic and skills trained, every generation, to go into battle against Set. Among them was the Chosen—a singular warrior who would channel Anubis's powers to defeat Set. This champion was known as the kebechet."

~THE CHAMPION AND OTHER TALES OF ANUBIS, AUTHOR UNKNOWN

I SPENT MOST OF MY BIRTHDAY DAY WORRYING ABOUT THE Anubis dream. And getting ready for the party. Gena and Becks came over early to help me decorate and get the furniture all situated. They were appropriately horrified by my Dad's ancient stereo equipment, but Becks took over the task of burning cool music onto CDs.

We had fun, especially when Nonna started bringing out the food. We had to taste test, you know? And the closer party time got, the more excited I got and the less I worried about Anubis and dreams and Oracles.

I said less, all right? No matter what conversation I was having or what food I was eating or what music I was listening to or whatever…the Anubis dream and what it could mean stuck in my brain like a tiny, sharp thorn.

I didn't want to be worried about it. I didn't want it to mean anything. But somewhere deep inside, where my fears and ghosts lay hidden, was the truth.

Anubis had chosen me.

It was just after 7:00 p.m. We'd strung up paper lanterns across the eaves of the porch. Cans of soda and water bottles were crammed into a couple of ice-filled coolers, and Nonna had outdone herself with the food. A long table outside was filled with appetizers and mini desserts, and we had trays set up around the living room and kitchen with similar treats. The partygoers spilled out through the open patio doors.

Ally was hanging out with her Citizens for Zombies friends, probably painting signs and writing speeches. Uncle Vinnie was with Dad. Even though my uncle was a zombie, Dad still treated him like a human. They watched TV together every night. I could hear Daddy's television turned way up, probably to drown out the noise of the party. Nonna Gina was out with her quilting club. I'd never seen her quilt, but she always came home from her "meetings" in a really good *grappa*-induced mood.

The CDs that Becks had burned were playing and so far I'd kept Dad away from the sound system. He'd been bummed that he'd been unable to sneak in the soundtrack to *The Breakfast Club* (which, BTW, has only one good song on it...well, one good song if you're old and like that kind of thing).

Presents were piled on a table near the fireplace. Everyone seemed to have ponied up a gift and I couldn't wait to plow through those babies. I wondered if Rick would bring me something (oops...my shallowness was showing again) and what it might be?

He hadn't arrived yet, though a lot of kids were already in the living room. Some were dancing; others were rambling out the open sliding glass doors and down into the yard. I saw several kids light up cigarettes near the back fence.

I turned around and headed into the house. I prayed my Dad wouldn't come down to snoop, because I would die if he got all parental.

When I came back inside, Becks grabbed my arm and dragged me into the kitchen. Rebecca "Becks" Fortwith had been my friend since seventh grade, when we had the same English class and bonded over our mutual horror about *The Grapes of Wrath*. I mean, John Steinbeck is all right, I guess, but reading about the dust bowl and farmers in Oklahoma was kinda boring. And he didn't mention zombies at all. Not like

Zombie-cide 1932 by Hayden Smith. He went into ugly detail about starving farmers cooking and eating their zombies. And the families who ate zombies went crazy, or died, because hel-*lo* you can't eat zombies. Even though necro magic arrests decomposition (well, mostly), zombies are still corpses and so, are yucky. Anyway, that's why Oklahoma banned zombification. If you already had a zombie, then you could keep it. And even now, zombies accompanying visitors to the state had to get special passes and couldn't stay longer than thirty days. Oklahoma is so weird.

"This. Is. Awesome," said Becks.

"Yeah?"

"Oh, *yeah*," she said, offering me a brace-filled smile. Becks was the tallest girl in school and her height made her self-conscious. She was always slouching. She had gorgeous blond hair and these big blue eyes, and creamy pale skin. Her parents let her wear makeup, but she hardly needed any.

"Where's Gena?" I asked.

"Talking to Mason." She waggled her brows, but I could see the flicker of envy. When you're taller than most boys, they don't really talk to you much. But there was also the matter of Becks being completely gorgeous, and that was probably extra intimidating to guys. At least, that's what Nonna said. "Beautiful girls need confident boys," she'd said. "Not so many of those around, *bella*."

"He doesn't really seem like her type," I said. Mason was a little too angst-driven for Gena, who was the perkiest non-cheerleader you'd ever meet. Mason was in the drama club and took it way too seriously. If I had to hear one more of his lectures about "the craft of acting," I would kick him in the shins.

"She's attracted to the damaged ones," said Becks. "She thinks she can fix them."

"Mason isn't broken," I said. "He's just serious. He never smiles. It's strange."

Becks smiled. "Says the girl who makes zombies."

"Ha." I took her by the shoulders and looked up into her eyes. "Truth. How does the party rate on the Mina scale?"

"Hmm," said Becks. "Too early to tell, but the arrival of football players, the cool music and the to-die-for food…yeah. It's heading toward a solid six."

I nodded. The Mina birthday scale was hardcore. Here's the deal:

Last May, Mina Hamilton had had a blowout for her Sweet Sixteen. Not only had she gotten a snazzy Corvette, but her parents had allowed alcohol. Sorta. They left the house for the whole night and let Mina and her friends do whatever they wanted. That's the gossip, anyway. I wasn't invited, so I don't know what really happened. I just lapped up the rumors along with everyone else.

"You can let go of me."

I was still clutching Becks, so I let her go. "Sorry."

"It's cool. I know you're dying to see if Rick made it yet." She grinned at me. "Go on. I'll do a food and drink circuit, make sure everyone's stuffing their faces."

"Thanks." I walked through the living room, scanning for Rick. I felt like I'd swallowed a sack of rocks. What if he didn't come? What if he was teasing me about that kiss? What if—

Chills crept down my spine.

Ever since I'd woken up from that fitful rest, I'd felt different. It was a subtle feeling, though. More like a hushed expectation—you know, like that creepy silence before a bad storm. Nobody had said I looked any different, and I hadn't noticed any manifestation of über powers. I wasn't sure that Anubis *had* granted me gifts—I mean, the dream seemed so fuzzy now. But maybe they hadn't kicked in yet. Or maybe I was way too concerned with dreams and destiny.

Still, the chill didn't dissipate. To my left, I saw a flicker of black. When I turned to look, nothing was there. But I could *feel* something. Someone. Frowning, I stepped into the empty space…and felt as though I'd fallen into a snowdrift. It was like standing in the Arctic Circle.

In the blink of an eye, I saw a boy leaning against the wall.

His eyes, the amber color of Nonna's sun tea, filled with surprise. For a second. Then his expression blanked.

I looked him over, head to toe. His chocolate-brown locks brushed his shoulders. His face was angular, his lips a slash of angry red. His T-shirt, jeans and sneakers were all black. Usually, one-themed looks totally didn't work, but for him… yeah. Black was the new hot. He crossed his arms, which showed off his muscles big-time. It also tightened his T-shirt to reveal the flat plane of his stomach. He couldn't have been much older than me…maybe a year or two. Was he a senior? I didn't remember ever seeing him before.

"Who are you?" I asked.

"You can't see me." The voice whispered over me. I'd been around enough zombie-making magic to know how it felt. And his command held magic. Oh, no, he did *not*. What kind of necro-idiot tried to use his mojo on a living person? Did I look like a corpse? No, TYVM.

"Hel-*lo*," I said, irritated. "I'm looking right at you."

One chocolate eyebrow rose. He studied me, taking in my red short-sleeved cowl-neck top, faded blue jeans and black peep-toed shoes. Hmm. Was I imagining it, or was his gaze lingering on my cleavage? His eyes meandered back to mine. "You're new."

"*I'm* new? I'm standing in my own house, where I've lived my whole life."

He looked at me, one eyebrow raised, his gaze assessing. "Definitely new. And mortal, too."

"Mortal?" I asked. "You mean like every breathing human being on earth?" Sheesh. I didn't know him, but that didn't mean much. Some of the people I'd invited had brought along friends who attended different schools. I couldn't quite get over the weirdness that he seemed perplexed by the fact I was an actual human being. He peered closer, as if doing so might give him a better view of my so-called mortality.

"This is…unexpected," he said.

He was kinda creeping me out, especially the way he was looking at me—as though I was some kind of science experiment gone terribly wrong. I put my hand on my hip. "So, who are you?" I asked.

For a moment, he looked like he wasn't going to tell me. Then he said, "Rath."

"Rath?" I know I looked skeptical because…c'mon. Rath? Who names their kid *Rath?* "I'm Molly."

"Molly. Never met anyone like you. You're odd."

My mouth dropped open, and I was so stunned by his comment, I couldn't make with the words. Then Rath looked around, his expression tense. "This is my show tonight, rewbie. Got it?"

What was he talking about? And what was a *rewbie?* The derisive tone he used suggested he wasn't calling me a pretty gem. I snapped my mouth closed. "My house, remember?" I pointed to myself. "Birthday girl."

"Well, I'd say happy birthday…" He shrugged. "But it's not gonna be particularly happy."

"Rude much?" I asked, stung by his prediction.

"Truth is truth, brown eyes." He eyed me. "How about I just say congrats?"

"Gee, thanks." I layered on the sarcasm, but he wasn't fazed by it.

Rath cocked his head, his gaze going distant. "Finally." He tapped my nose. "Watch and learn. And don't get in my way." He moved past me, taking the glacial air with him. I found myself standing alone near the foyer, shivering. Watch and learn *what?* I had no idea what the guy was talking about. Too bad that in his case, cute meant cray-cray.

The front door opened. The rocks that had been tumbling in my stomach sank all the way to my toes and anchored me there.

Rick stood in the doorway.

And beside him, possessively clutching his arm, was Mina Hamilton.

Rick had brought Mina? My heart kicked into overdrive, and I felt my face go hot. So. Embarrassing.

Rick shook off Mina's curled fingers and walked toward me, grinning. He looked happy to see me. The tight feeling in my stomach loosened. He reached me in three long strides and handed me a wrapped gift. "Happy birthday, Molly."

"Um...thanks." My gaze went over his shoulder to Mina. To make my party sooo much better, I saw her two best friends, Danette and Kylie, lurking behind her. Terrific. Rick's gaze met mine. He mouthed the word *sorry.*

Mina and her minions approached, scorn in their gazes as they assessed my house and my guests and my party-in-progress. I felt lame. Really, really, horrifyingly lame.

"Nice party," said Mina, her voice filled with contempt. She slung her arm over Rick's shoulder. "Remember my Sweet Sixteen, Rick? Remember that present I gave you?"

Rick's face went red. He pushed off Mina's arm. "Go home," he said. "You weren't invited."

Mina was obviously stung by Rick's response. Her blue

eyes snapped with fury. She glared at me, looking all beautiful and rich and vengeful. "Is that true, Molly? Me and my girls aren't invited?"

Her voice rose, and the room behind me went silent. The music suddenly seemed too loud. I cleared my throat. "You're welcome here," I said. "It's cool."

"See, Rick?" she pointed out in a saccharine-sweet voice. "It's cool."

She pushed past us and her hags-in-waiting followed her. On the up side, Mina being at my party meant points in the popularity column. On the down side, she would probably do something nasty, or at least humiliating, and I would have to throw myself under the school bus to escape the fallout.

Not that I'm being dramatic or anything.

"She just showed up at my house. I tried to shake her, but she followed me here. I'm sorry, Molly. I know Mina isn't always...nice."

Try never.

"You dated her for a long time," I said, unable to keep the accusation from my tone. "She can't be all bad."

His face went red again, and I realized that Mina had been a full-service girlfriend. Another wave of embarrassment heated my cheeks. I knew about sex, okay? And I knew that kids my age had sex. But I wasn't ready to do it. I had to tell Rick, because if he was just trying to get in my pants, then we were over before we'd begun.

"I can't be like her," I said softly. I stared at the present. It was thick and rectangular. A book? Disappointment pricked me. Rick had gotten me a *book?* "I'm not... I won't..." I looked up, unable to say what needed to be said.

He looked around, then took me by the elbow and steered me through the kids to the fireplace. It was the only space that didn't have people crammed into it. I put the book among the piled gifts and then turned toward him. "Rick—"

"Mina and I are over. I don't want her or her poison." He drew me into his arms, right there in front of everyone (including Mina…nyah, nyah) and leaned down. "I like *you*, okay?"

I nodded.

"Don't You (Forget About Me)" by Simple Minds started to play. Dad! He'd gotten that damned song into the mix after all. Rick smiled. "Wow. This is old school, Mol."

He held me closer and I lay my head on his shoulder as we swayed to the music. Someone turned off the living room lights. The lamps on the end tables were on, but their muted glow barely pierced the darkness.

Still, I could see Rick lean down, his nose almost touching mine. I'd brushed my teeth twice and refrained from food and drink. Because I wanted our first kiss to be perfect—you know, without Doritos taint.

His lips ghosted across mine. My belly pulled tight with excitement. I was chest to chest with him. *OMG.*

"Sweet Molly," he murmured. He angled his mouth against mine and I opened for him. My eyes fluttered closed. Tentative, I met the gentle thrust of his tongue. I felt electrified. I clung to him, completely unsure about what I was doing.

He drew away, just a little, took a shuddering breath and returned. I was pressed so close to him that I could feel how his heartbeat matched the ferocity of mine. I felt awkward and amazed and—

The lights snapped on. I opened my eyes, blinking, horrified that Dad might have come down to check up on us crazy teenagers and freaked to see me lip-locked with Rick.

"Mina! No!" Rick tried to push me out of the way, but he ended up projecting me right into Mina's path.

The full contents of the punch bowl showered me. Red liquid splattered my face, hair and clothes. Ice cubes fell down my shirt and spun off my toes. Some of the sticky sweet drink dribbled into my mouth. Shocked beyond words, I could only stand there like an idiot.

"Damn it, Mina." Rick's expression was murderous. He looked like he wanted to hit her. I just wanted to melt into a puddle of shame.

"Oops," she said in a bored tone. She let the plastic bowl drop to the floor. She flicked an icy glance around the room. No one laughed, which was a blessing. Usually Mina's cruel humor got all kinds of chuckles—at least at school. But even though the music played on, every conversation had stopped. People were looking at me, at Mina, or at the floor.

"Smile for YouTube," said Danette. That's when I noticed that both of Mina's friends were using the video cams in their iPhones to film me. I swallowed the knot in my throat and felt hot tears gather in my eyes.

"That's enough," said Rick. He moved to stand in front of me. "Get out."

"This party is a yawn fest." Mina swung her blond hair over her shoulder. "We're outtie."

She and her minions spun on their Prada heels and pranced out. The front door slammed, echoing above the soft drone of the music. Rick looked down at me, fury and regret warring in his gaze. "Mol, are you okay?"

I managed to nod.

"Aw, man. Is the party over?" I couldn't pin the voice, it had drifted from the back of the room. People stirred, looking at me. Some started putting down cups, picking up purses, turning toward the door.

"No way," I said, moving past Rick. I pasted a smile on my

quivering lips. I really wanted to cry, but I wouldn't. Mina couldn't have my tears. "I just need to change."

I sensed the hesitancy, the awkwardness.

"C'mon!" I said, nervous that people would leave. Then Mina would get exactly what she wanted. Me, humiliated *and* abandoned. "If you go, you'll miss out on Nonna Gina's triple-chocolate cake. And homemade ice cream."

Stupid, right? So totally stupid to bribe partygoers with cake. I was glad Dad hadn't made a surprise appearance. Then the party really would be over.

"I'm staying," said Rick. He grasped my arm, not seeming to mind that it was covered in punch. "I'll clean this up, Mol."

Cake had nothing to do with keeping my guests here. Rick was just as popular as Mina. Probably more so, since he was likeable. He was staying. His friends, the jocks I'd seen in the backyard earlier, would stay. So, everyone would stay.

"I'll be right back," I said, not quite able to meet his eyes.

Then Rick leaned down and kissed me again. I was sticky and gross, but his hands cupped my face and his lips melded with mine. People laughed, whistled and one joker yelled, "Give her the tongue!"

We broke apart, grinning at each other.

Kissing me had been the perfect thing to do.

When I turned to go to my room to change, Gena and Becks rushed over and met me by the stairs.

"Ohmygodwewereoutsideandtotallymissedkicking—"

"Breathe, Gena." I put my hand on her shoulder. Her eyes were wide and she was panting as if she'd just finished a marathon.

"We didn't know Mina was here. We were outside talking to Mason and his friends," said Becks. "I can't believe that bitch threw punch on you!"

"Sucked," I admitted. "C'mon. I have to get cleaned up."

I ran upstairs to my bedroom, and my BFFs followed. I gave them the quick rundown, then I jumped in the shower. While Gena and Becks concocted ways to make Mina pay for her crimes, I got ready as fast as I could.

Ugh! Every minute that ticked by rattled me. What if Rick decided to leave? And everyone left with him? I got so paranoid I sent Gena and Becks downstairs twice, and both returned with reassurances that everyone was still hanging out. I blew dry my hair, did a quick makeup job and wiggled on another pair of jeans and a V-neck T-shirt that was tight but not nearly as nice as the cowlneck. I hoped I could get the punch out of the material. Stupid Mina.

"Would you go down first and make sure we still have plenty of food and drinks?" I asked. "I need a sec to just breathe, you know?"

"No prob," said Becks.

Gena gave me a hug, then she grabbed my shoulders and stared hard at me. "Are you sure you're okay?"

"As long as Rick is still here, I'm perfect."

She nodded, and she and Becks left. I stood in the middle of my bedroom and took deep breaths to steady my nerves. Rick had kissed me! And I hoped that he would kiss me again. My stomach squeezed, and I grinned. Then I threw open my bedroom door and yelped.

Rath was leaning against the hallway wall, directly in front of my door. His arms were crossed. His amber eyes assessed me. An odd tingle coursed through me, which freaked me out because, hey, I really needed to save my tingles for Rick.

"You all right?" he asked gruffly.

I bit back the urge to say, *Why do you care?* Instead, I shrugged and offered, "Yeah."

"He did a cool thing. Your boyfriend." He frowned, his gaze somber. "It sucks. But you know the deal, right?"

What sucked, exactly? Mina throwing punch on me? Confused, I stared at him. He didn't seem compelled to say anything else so I said, "Deal. Right. Um, okay. Thanks."

He nodded. The air felt freezing again and I knew it was because of him. He walked down the stairs ahead of me and disappeared into the crowd of kids milling in the foyer.

I was relieved to see that people were still here. Most had drifted out to the backyard. Some were in the kitchen, and a few people lingered in the living room. Rick and one of his pals—um, Curt, I think—were chatting near the fireplace. The punch spill had been cleaned up. You could barely see the puddle spot on the carpet.

"Thanks for taking care of the mess," I said. The punch bowl was gone, too. A couple sat in Dad's recliner, the girl slung across the boy's lap. They were drinking out of red plastic cups and giggling at each other. Then they started kissing. I looked away, my face going hot.

A couple girls I knew from English class were piling up paper plates with appetizers and cookies. They were engrossed in a conversation that had something to do with Taylor Lautner.

"What Mina did was not cool," said Curt. He was a big guy—definitely on the football team. "She's such a bitch."

I wasn't sure how to respond, so I just smiled like a deluxe moron and stared at the carpet. Luckily it was a rich shade of coffee brown and stains didn't show up easily. The stickiness might be a problem, though. Nonna Gina tended to notice things like that.

Curt flashed me a grin then clapped Rick on the shoulder. "See you, man. Later, Molly."

He headed outside. I think he was one of the smokers I'd seen, but maybe not. What kind of athlete smokes?

"Open my gift, Mol," said Rick. He turned toward the fireplace.

I don't know why he lost his footing. Rick's eyes went wide as he twisted, falling, his head bouncing off the corner of the stone fireplace.

I screamed.

I hurried to Rick, my stomach roiling when I saw the blood dripping from his temple. I heard Curt cussing as he rushed back in and we knelt on either side of Rick.

I heard a whisper in my ear. *Sorry, brown eyes.*

Rath? I felt a stab of gelid air, but he wasn't around—not that I could see. No. All I could see was Rick. The blood was from a superficial cut near his temple.

"Rick?" I whispered. With Curt's help, I rolled him onto his back. His blue eyes were wide and unseeing. I pressed a shaking hand against his chest. I couldn't feel his heartbeat. I was afraid to put my ear against his mouth.

No. He wasn't...

The couple who'd been sitting in the chair now hovered over us, peering at Rick. Curt started doing chest compressions. Panic flecked his gaze. He tossed his cell phone at me. "Call 911."

"Too late, dude," said the guy from the chair, who was staring at Rick in morbid fascination. "He's dead."

CHAPTER
5

"Oh, love! Why hast thou abandoned me?
Over the stillness of my lover's body, I weep
She moves again, but she is not mine
Death steals the heart…and Anubis the soul…"
~FROM THE POEM "ABANDONED LOVE" BY REID MICHAEL

My hands shook so badly that I dropped the phone. The girl shoved aside her boyfriend, scooped up the cell and dialed. As if from a long distance, I heard her tell someone that there'd been an accident. The rest of the conversation faded from my hearing. I felt like I was falling into a dark hole, and it was getting darker and smaller as I descended.

Then I felt something within me pop, spark and glow.

The colors around me bled away until everything was gray and covered in shadows. Above the dark, dead figure of Rick, a ball of white light pulsed. It glittered like starlight and emanated comforting warmth. As I watched, it turned a very light blue, the color of sky, and started a slow rise upward. When I looked up, I saw a blue oval of light and I heard… sounds I couldn't quite describe. Music, but it was a mixture of voices and instruments, and even that didn't quite explain the splendid noise. I didn't understand the melody, what the sounds meant, but the now-dancing blue orb obviously did. It wanted very much to go up there.

The light was Rick's soul.

I'd never seen a whole soul before. Sure, I'd seen the ka, which looked like a sparkly blue worm, wiggling into the heart of the zombie. Ancient Egyptians used to believe that the heart was the seat of intelligence and emotion, and that the ka was the spark of life. They'd sorta been right. Inserting the ka into a dead person's heart was the key to reanimation.

"C'mon, dude!" Curt yelled. Desperation made his chest compressions clumsy, and sweat dripped from his brow.

I knew that I had to capture the soul before it took the journey to the afterlife. Rick needed it to live. All I could think about, focus on, was catching it, and sticking it back in.

I had no perfect way to fix what death had broken. All the same, while Curt pounded on his friend's chest, I stepped around him and grabbed Rick's soul.

It felt warm and soft, like the fur of a kitten.

Then the soul began to separate.

What the——! I had never seen the other parts of the soul before, just the ka. But it appeared that soul parts were all the same shape and color. And those five wiggling blue strands clutched in my sweaty fist were the difference between Rick alive…and Rick dead.

One strand wiggled free. I couldn't catch it, and it zipped upward, darting into the oval of blue from which still emanated the strangely beautiful sounds. A second one slipped through my fingers, and I watched it escape, too. No! Damn it. The three remaining strands fought against my grip, but I held them tight. Three parts of a soul were better than none. I swallowed the knot of fear clogging my throat. *What are you doing, Molly?* Ugh. Now the soul strands felt like long, cold, wet ribbons, and they struggled fiercely. I sensed their struggle against returning to their human vessel.

I didn't care. His soul, what was left of it, was going back in. I knelt on the floor. Curt was still pushing right underneath Rick's rib cage, and I slammed Rick's soul parts against Rick's chest, right where his heart should be. "Go," I said, desperation in my words. "Just get in there!"

The strands sank into his flesh and disappeared. I didn't know how I'd managed to do such a crazy thing. Usually, I just took the ka, and I had to use a special incantation to see it—a soul wisp that I directed into the heart to begin reanimation.

The blue oval of light and the music vanished. The color of the world returned as though someone had flicked on a light switch. The gray was gone, and I found myself sitting next to Rick, my hand pressed on his chest.

A second later, Rick sucked in a deep breath and opened his eyes.

"Holy shit," said Curt. He glanced at me, his gaze relieved. "I've never seen that move before, and my mom's a doctor. You have the touch, Mol."

"I...I didn't do anything." Tears dripped down my face. He hadn't seen me put back Rick's soul. No one had. Only necros could see the magic we wielded—and only trained ka hekas could see the ka. No one else had entered the colorless landscape with me. How had I gone there without anyone noticing what I was doing?

"Holy crap." The words came from Becks. Gena stood beside her, and they both turned wide gazes to me. I didn't understand the expressions on their faces—part amazement, part WTH.

"What happened?" My dad pushed through the kids who'd gathered in the living room. The wail of an ambulance cut through the thick silence, and suddenly, everyone started chattering.

"He hit his head," I said, my voice sounding far away. The room started to spin, and I felt sick to my stomach.

"Mol?" Becks leaned down. I couldn't quite focus on her face. In fact, she looked really blurry, like I was looking at her image in a mirror smeared with Vaseline.

"I'm okay, Molly," said Rick. He sat up on his elbows and gave me one of his wicked half grins. "Just got knocked out. I'm fine, Mr. Bartolucci."

The front door opened, and medics rushed in, but all I saw was Rick alive... Not dead. Not a zombie. Alive. Because of me.

I heard Gena gasp, and saw Becks lurch toward me...

Then the world turned upside down and went black.

I woke up in my bedroom. My mouth was dry, really dry, and had a metallic taste, like I'd been chewing on pipes. An ache throbbed in my temples, and my body trembled. I grabbed my cell phone off the nightstand and groaned. Almost midnight. I'd been out for hours. What the heck had happened to me?

"How did you do that?"

The stern male voice startled me into full alert. I yelped and rolled off the bed, landing on my feet. The phone slipped out of my hand and plopped onto the carpet.

"I'm not gonna hurt you," he said impatiently. "Would you relax?"

I lowered my arms and located the source of the voice on the other side of my room. Rath leaned against the wall, one leg propped up, his arms crossed. My heart stuttered in my chest, and the spike of adrenaline soured my stomach. I pressed a hand against my throat and stared at the intruder.

"How did you get in here?" I demanded. My voice squeaked, which made me sound so not threatening. I blew out a steady breath and put my hands on my hips. "Seriously. What are you doing in my room?"

"Waiting for an explanation." He eyed me, a mixture of fury and curiosity in his gaze. "You're not even dead yet and you're reaping?" He shook his head. "No reaper I've ever met has been alive. And no reaper has the ability to return a soul. So what the hell are you?"

I opened my mouth to answer his question and realized it

would be stupid to give him any information. Especially since I didn't exactly understand what he was asking. He obviously expected some kind of weird revelation about me, like, "Hi! I'm a soul wrangler! And I like unicorns!"

Whatevs.

I was trying really hard not to freak out. I mean, I'd done something impossible to save Rick. And then I'd passed out. 'Cause I know how to par-tay. Ugh. And now Rath was hanging out in my room as though he did it all the time. I felt weak and nauseated…and scared. For a lot of reasons, but the main one was having some hot, angry dude staring at me like I'd committed murder or something.

"Get out," I said, "or I'll scream."

He snorted. "Oooooh. Scary." His eyes met mine, and an electric thrill shot through my chest. His manner seemed to soften, just a little. "What did you do, Molly?"

"Gah! Fine! I'm a necro, okay? I know how to make zombies. Sorta. I'm in training. So when I saw Rick's soul, I just… grabbed it. And squished it inside." Most of it, anyway.

He pushed off from the wall and straightened, keeping his arms crossed. His expression turned serious. "You *squished* his soul back into his body?"

"That's what I said." My knees felt wobbly, so I moved to the end of my bed and sat down. I sucked in a breath, then blew it out slowly. I felt a little steadier. I glanced at him. "I've never done that before. It was weird." I glanced up at him. "You keep talking about reapers. Like, *reaper* reapers."

"You are the oddest girl I've ever met," said Rath. "You have no idea what you are. Or what you can do." He studied me as though he'd found a new specimen of insect, and then he shrugged as if it didn't matter. But I knew better. Something dark and cold slithered through me. I wrapped my arms around my waist, trying to stave off the feeling.

"What do you mean?" I asked.

"You're not that thickheaded," he said impatiently. "Obviously you're a reaper."

"Am not," I said without any real heat. "No way."

"You are what Anubis makes you," he said, arrogance edging his tone. "You agreed to serve him, didn't you?"

How could he know what I'd promised Anubis? I glared at him.

He raised his hands in mock surrender. "Ease up, brown eyes. I had the dream on my sixteenth birthday, too. I was called into service, the same as you. And I accepted it. Embraced it."

I went cold. My throat knotted. "You… Are you…you know, dead?"

"Duh."

"You don't look dead," I said.

"Reapers can see other reapers. We can be corporeal when necessary."

I tried to assimilate that information, but my brain almost melted. "So, you had the Anubis dream…and then you died, didn't you?"

"Not for three years," he said. He smiled grimly. "Car accident. On my way to pick up a pizza so I could get through an all-night study session. I had a big test on necro history." He shrugged. Then he looked at me hard, *judging* me, and he shook his head. "I don't think you have the chops for this, Molly. Death has purpose. It has meaning. And you screwed it up for Rick when you let him live. You think that's a good thing?"

"I think it's a *great* thing," I said. "He's not supposed to die."

"Yeah," said Rath. "He is. Only now? I can't reap him. Whatever you did, it's like you superglued his soul in there. Don't think for a minute you did that kid a favor."

Tears gathered in my eyes, but I blinked them back. Rath was just jealous that I could make souls return to bodies. He didn't have that ability and it pissed him off. I didn't want to admit I heard truth in his words, and that guilt was burrowing inside me like poisonous snakes. I knew, deep down, I had done something unethical, even though giving Rick his life back seemed like the right choice to make. Wasn't saving someone better than letting them die?

"You didn't think stealing a soul and sticking it back into the body was wrong? Really?" His gaze riveted to my face. "Are you so blinded by your own wants that you couldn't let him go?"

"Wouldn't you do the same?"

His gaze shuttered. "Had I the ability to save the ones I'm supposed to take, I wouldn't. The afterlife has rules. Everything in this world and the next has rules, damn it." He shoved a hand through his hair and then sighed. "There's more to life than malls and cute boys. If you want any hope of utilizing those powers of yours, you'd better grow up, and fast."

I was tired of Rath's lecturing. He set my teeth on edge with his attitude. What business was it of his what I was? Or what I did? Why would a reaper even show up at my house?

Oh.

Oh, crap.

"You came here to kill Rick!" I stood up. The sudden move made me dizzy, and I listed to the side for a second before righting myself. "You jerk!"

"I don't kill people," he said, his brows slashing downward. "Reapers untether the souls and then guide them through the Shallows." He looked at my expression and sighed. "It's the gray, Molly. All the color disappeared, right? That's the Shallows. One part of it, anyway."

"I didn't see you," I accused.

"Because you locked me out," he said, his voice low with fury. "I don't know how, but you pranced right into the Shallows and made it impossible for me to get to Rick's soul."

Bile rose as I realized what his description meant. I *had* been in the Shallows. That…that weird thing had happened inside me, like a big, heavy lock falling off and a door swinging open to release a monster. Everything had gone gray and cold and strange, and all I'd seen was the color of Rick's soul.

I didn't say anything else, because I didn't want to be told again how bad I'd messed up. I watched him stare at me while I tried to process everything he'd said. It became a game of silence.

And he won.

"I don't want to be a reaper."

"Too late. You don't know anything, do you?" His sarcasm scraped me like razors. "Necros are like reapers lite. The five powers of reapers were divided and given to certain bloodlines in the human populace. It was supposed to help keep the balance. The reaper wars forced Anubis to take action, you know? If you're just a ka heka…well, you shouldn't be able to grab a soul from the Shallows and put it inside its former residence."

The reaper wars? I searched my brain for info and came up with nothing. We'd recently covered the mythology of reapers in my Necromancy History class. No one really knew much about reaping, just like no one really knew what happened after death. It's not like any necromancers had died, become reapers and then returned to the world and said, "Oh, yeah. Here's how it all works."

I didn't want to talk to Rath anymore. My world had shifted in a way that was unfixable. I was striding down a path chosen for me, without a map or a way to avoid pitfalls.

Rath smirked at me, but worse than that was the genuine sympathy lurking in those eyes. Not even his arrogant expression could hide it. He knew something about me, about my life, maybe even about my destiny.

Sweet sixteen, my ass.

"I'm really a reaper?" I asked Rath.

He shrugged. "You accepted Anubis's offer, right?"

Yeah. But you'd think he would've mentioned the whole *you'll be dead soon* part. "You're really dead?" I asked.

"Didn't we go over this? It's part of the reaper gig. In order to do your job, you have to be able to travel into the Shallows. Only dead people can do that. And you, apparently."

Why hadn't I asked Anubis more questions?

"Don't look so down," drawled Rath. "This is only the beginning, brown eyes. Welcome to reaperhood." He put two fingers to his forehead and saluted. Then the air went cold and he disappeared, fading like the wraith he was. Huh. You know, it just wasn't in me to be any more freaked out.

Instead, I was getting pissed off.

Frustration boiled through me. I barely resisted the urge to scream. Instead, I stomped around and muttered for a couple minutes, but giving in to my temper didn't make me feel better. I finally threw myself on my bed and sprawled on my back, staring up at the ceiling.

Booooooring. I sighed, got off the bed to retrieve my cell. It was closing in on one in the morning. I had no idea what had happened after I fainted. Had Rick been taken to the hospital, or had he gone home? How long had it taken for everyone to bail?

I flipped out the cell's keyboard. My fingers hovered over the keys. Should I text Rick? I wasn't sure. What would I say? *Sorry you died at my party, but hey, I saved your soul. You're welcome.*

I slid the keyboard back in. Then two seconds later, I slid

it back out, chose Rick's name in my contacts and texted: You okay? I clicked Send before I chickened out.

Crap. That text was awful with a side of lame. Why hadn't I said something less sucky? Argh!

I saw I had texts from Becks and Gena. I texted them back to let them know I was all right (depending on your definition, ha), though they were probably asleep.

I put the cell on the nightstand, then groaned and stuffed a pillow over my face. Oh, Mina was going to be *super* happy. Not about Rick bashing his head on my fireplace, but about my total party fail. I could just hear the whispers down the hallway at school on Monday.

Mina emptied the whole punch bowl on Molly, and she just stood there. Moron.

Did you hear that Molly's fireplace nearly killed Rick Widdenstock?

Oh, my God. Molly fainted at her own party. What a loser!

"Molly? You awake?" My dad's voice filtered through my closed door. I debated for a second whether or not to answer him. He'd probably heard me stomping around and decided to check on me. After my run-in with Rath, I didn't really want to be alone. In fact, I had the insane urge to run into my dad's arms and cry.

He knocked lightly on the door. "Mol?"

"Yeah," I called out. I got up and walked to the door. When I opened it, I was shocked to see how haggard and upset my dad appeared. "Daddy? What's wrong?"

"I need you to come downstairs. You need to meet some folks."

"Now?" I was incredulous. It was mondo late and we had company? My gut curled. "Is it the police?"

"What?" He looked surprised for a second, and then comprehension dawned. "No, no. Nothing like that. The medics checked you and Rick out. You're fine. I'm sure his parents will want to talk to me tomorrow. Kid gets his head bashed at my place." He shook his head sorrowfully. "Accident or not, that's not a good thing."

"I'm sorry, Dad."

"Not your fault, baby." He looked me over. "Change your clothes and brush your hair before you come down."

It was a weird request. The curl in my gut tightened and tightened into a throbbing ball of nerves.

My dad smiled at me, but it didn't reach his eyes. No, in his eyes I saw worry and fear. Seeing my dad less than confident—worse, it was like he was ruled by dread—scared me.

What was going on?

"All right," I said. "Be down in a sec."

"'Atta girl." He hesitated a second more, looking as though he wanted to pull me into one of his bear hugs, and I wanted it. I waited for it. Instead he reached out a hand and awkwardly patted my shoulder. "You're a good girl, Molly. A real good girl."

"Um. Thanks."

He nodded, still looking sad, and turned away.

I shut the door and leaned against it, sucking in hot, stinging breaths. Not getting a hug left me feeling bereft. Since Dad hadn't given me a clue about who I was supposed to impress, I changed into a clean pair of jeans and an Aeropostale T-shirt. I brushed my hair until it crackled and then crept down the stairs.

As I entered the living room, I saw that all the decorations had been taken down. Everything was in its place, just as if I'd never even had a sixteenth birthday party. Wow. That sucked.

Two people sat on the couch, looking stiff and uncomfortable. I could tell right away by their clothes that these people were wealthy. Their hair was silvery gray, cut stylishly and they both seemed to wear their age well without relying too heavily on artifice. I was just guessing, of course. I dunno. There's just something about people who have a lot of money; I saw rich people all the time at the Zomporium. It was a vibe, an attitude. I guess knowing you could buy anything at any time made you feel superior. That was certainly the case with Mina and her friends.

Me? Not so much.

"Good evening," said the woman. Her tone was like glass, and when she took her measure of me, I knew instantly that I'd come up short.

The man nodded at me, giving me a small, tight smile.

"Hi," I said, feeling shy and intimidated. I glanced at my dad.

He cleared his throat, and gestured toward the couple. "Molly, meet your grandparents."

CHAPTER
6

"Some necromancers believe the original bloodlines can be traced. Even in these modern times, there are families who lay claim to being the Chosen of Anubis. Though some early texts indicate the original Gifts were granted to nobility, there is no evidence to support that this was, indeed, the case."

~THE BLOODLINE CONSPIRACY BY STEPHEN ROBERTS

DAD'S VOICE OFFERED POLITENESS, BUT I KNEW THAT UNDER-tone, one of controlled anger. Like he might pop any second if I said or did something wrong. But this time his fury was directed at the couple who sat primly on our living room couch.

Sweet Anubis.

My mother's parents.

Dread did a slow burn in my belly. Mom had told us that her parents had disowned her after she married my dad. I'd never met them before, and that was weird, right? Maybe they'd disowned us, too. Still, Dad had raised me with manners, so I crossed the living room and held out my hand to the woman. She took it, and I tried not to flinch at the cold, papery feel of her skin. Her handshake was firm, though.

The man's hand was warmer, and his handshake just as firm.

"I'm Derek Briarstock," he said. "Your grandmother's name is Sandra."

I nodded and slid my hand out of his grip. I wondered why my grandmother—*ugh*—hadn't introduced herself. Maybe her husband was used to doing it for her. I was getting the creeps, and bad. I went to stand next to my father. "Nice to meet you," I managed in a quiet voice.

"It seems you've had quite a night," said Sandra. I couldn't think of her as "Grandma." I couldn't believe my mother had been born to, and raised by, these chilly, distant people. Mom had been passionate and impulsive. She was all color where these two were all gray.

They seemed to be waiting for me to confirm whatever "quite a night" meant. Or something. I felt so uneasy, my stomach was roiling. I went for the simplest explanation.

"My bo—er, friend fell and hit his head."

"Ah. And you helped him?" Sandra asked. Her eyes reminded me of my mom's, except they were far colder. The blue of my mother's eyes had been warm—a summer sky— but *Grandma's* were like a glacier. She tilted her head, her gaze rife with disapproval, and I realized she was waiting for me to answer her question. I felt shaky all over again. What were they doing here?

"N-not really," I said. "Rick just got knocked out." The lie made my tongue feel thick, but I couldn't admit that I'd been able not only to see his soul, but also touch it.

My palms went clammy.

Sandra opened her mouth again, her eyes flashing with an anger that seemed, at least to me, old. Fury I hadn't caused but was directed at me anyway. She'd made it mine. My dad sent her a warning look. Her mouth drooped into a frown, but she pressed her lips together, obviously choking down the words she wanted to say.

"Molly, you need to sit." Dad patted the top of his favorite recliner.

I plopped down. My stomach worsened with the jitters. My mouth had gone dry and still tasted metallic, and I couldn't get words to form. The whole thing was seventh-vibe creepy, right?

I wasn't stupid. They knew—and I didn't know how or why—but they *knew* I'd given Rick his soul back. And that meant my dad had figured it out first. Or had he? Wait. Had *he* contacted my grandparents? Why? What did they have to do with anything? I looked at my dad, and he smiled, but his gaze was sad. He leaned down and patted my arm. "It's all right, Molly."

But it wasn't.

Somehow I knew it just wasn't all right.

My throat felt dust-coated. I swallowed painfully and licked my lips, which were cracked and sore.

"She needs to hydrate," said Sandra, her voice just short of imperious. She seemed to realize she sounded all queen of the manor, and I saw her cheeks go pink. She didn't apologize, though. I got the feeling that Sandra High-and-Mighty was never wrong enough to offer a sentiment as common as, "I'm sorry."

"Here, *bella*," said Nonna. She walked into the living room with a tray filled with lemonade and cookies. My father took it from her and put it on the coffee table. Nonna poured a glass and handed it to me. Then she leaned over and kissed my brow. "You gonna be okay," she said. Her brown eyes were kind, but behind that love, I saw her worry, too.

This whole situation was freaking me out. I drank the lemonade, but the sweet drink didn't quell my nerves. In fact, my stomach kinda rebelled. I held the chilled glass in my hands, staring at the ice cubes floating in the yellow liquid. After Nonna served Derek and Sandra, she nodded in that regal way of hers and turned to leave. She glanced at me as she headed back toward the kitchen, her gaze watery, and her smile flimsy.

"What's going on?" I blurted.

"You know when I went to Reno, honey?" said Dad. He knelt next to the recliner and put his hand on my knee. "It wasn't to scout a location for a new zomporium. I went to see your grandparents."

"Why?" I asked. I slid a look at Derek and Sandra. "No offense, but you haven't exactly been around much."

"As is tradition for necromancer families," said Sandra coolly, "we went to the Anubis Oracle."

I went cold all the way to my toes. "What?"

Sandra sipped her lemonade. "The sixteenth birthday for a necromancer is an important milestone. You come into your power fully. *Most*—" and here she gave my dad a wintry look "—parents go to the Oracle to find out their children's destinies." Her expression warmed up, in the same way a glacier might under anemic sunlight. "We went instead. You are especially gifted, Molly."

My heart felt as if it had dropped into my stomach. It lodged there, as heavy and rough as a brick. I thought about the Anubis dream, and then how I'd met Rath, and how I'd saved Rick. I wasn't a moron. It all fit together. Of course it did. All the same, I didn't want any of this to be real. I wanted it to be over. I wanted to wake up and just be plain ol' me. Going to school on Monday to face the stares and whispers about my party would seem like a cakewalk compared to what was going on now.

"Mol," said Dad, his tone heavy with sorrow. "You need to hear this. It's important."

"I don't want to hear it," I said. "I don't care about whatever the Oracle said. My life is mine. It's not fair to just…decide my fate for me." Tears gathered in my eyes.

"I know," he said. "But this isn't something you can walk away from, baby. You're special. Real special. You're gonna do some amazing things. Important things."

Panic welled. I had accepted Anubis's invitation to serve him. I guess I'd thought that there was some kind of waiting period. Or that I could at least finish high school before I went off and did whatever stuff the deity had in mind. I was only sixteen! What could I possibly do to help anyone? Right now, I couldn't even help myself.

"What did the Oracle say?" I asked. I couldn't stop my voice from cracking.

Dad glanced at my grandparents and nodded.

Sandra smiled, and it was almost sincere. "You're one of Anubis's chosen, Molly. *Within the girl dwells the warrior the world needs. She will serve the gods faithfully, and through her, Anubis will defeat evil.*"

"I don't know how to fight," I said. "I'm not a warrior."

"Your education has been somewhat lacking," said Sandra. "Not that we didn't try to help you, you understand." She looked at my father accusingly.

"She deserved a normal life," he said.

Sandra's silver eyebrows went up. Then she looked at me. "You're not a normal girl, my dear. Neither was your mother."

Her voice held a hint of sadness, but I didn't know whether it was from grief, or that she just was annoyed that Mom hadn't stuck around to live out a blueblood existence.

"I'm not my mother," I said. I looked at my dad. He nodded at me encouragingly.

"Your father agreed to meet with us in Reno, and when we gave him the news, he said no," offered Derek. His tone was kind. He briefly met my Dad's gaze. "He's a good man. He wants to protect you. But sometimes, Molly, no matter what you do, you can't protect your children." Derek's soft blue eyes met mine, and I saw steel there. Not in a mean way. It was more like strength. You know, I kinda liked this guy.

"Cynthia walked away from her destiny," said Sandra, her voice brittle. "Will you do the same, Molly?"

"Now, hold on," Dad roared, surging to his feet. Italian blood ran hot, and I'd seen him and Nonna in tempers that would make lesser people cower. "You won't push Molly around like that, y'hear me? I don't care what your fancy Oracle said."

Sandra's face mottled. "Anubis's will is absolute." She drew in a breath, and I noticed her hands were trembling. I realized my grandmother wasn't as much in control as she wanted us to believe. "We don't have much time, Alfonso. She needs training and education. If she does not go to her destiny, it will come for her."

Whoa. This was a whole 'nother level of WTH. I'd never known much about my mom's past. Her parents were never mentioned, and were never part of our lives. It seemed to me that Mom spent a lot of time walking away from the people she was supposed to love.

"You shouldn't have visited that damned Oracle!" said Dad.

"Al," said Derek in a placating tone. "This is about Molly." He smiled at me, but this time it wasn't exactly a comforting, grandpa-esque kind of smile. "You had the Anubis dream."

I glanced at my dad. Then I nodded.

"And you accepted." Derek seemed certain of this fact.

I nodded again. I wrapped my hands tightly around the glass of lemonade. Its chill did nothing to settle my nerves. My stomach was pitching around, and I thought I might vomit.

"Then you've chosen your path," said Derek. "Cynthia had the dream, too."

"She said no," said Sandra. Her voice held bitterness. "You've already shown wisdom, Molly. It is a great honor to be chosen by the god of death."

I didn't know what to say. My mom hadn't shared much about her life, and I would've remembered a conversation with her where she told me, "And yeah, I totally told Anubis to take a hike."

"Mol, you didn't tell me about the dream." Dad's anger gave way to a quiet angst. He rubbed at his temples. "Ah, baby girl." His sorrow seemed to deepen, to creep into the room like cloying smoke.

"I didn't know it was important," I said. "I mean, not like this."

"She accepted," said Sandra, her voice almost gleeful. "If Molly is truly the servant of Anubis, and the Oracle has confirmed her destiny, then you know what must be done, Alfonso."

I really wished she'd stop saying *destiny*. It made my skin crawl. I looked at my Dad's face and felt panic skitter over me like spiders.

"What?" I asked. "What has to be done?"

Dad took my lemonade and put it on the table. "I know you did something to Rick, to fix him. Right? I heard the kids saying how he was dead an' all until you touched him."

Was Rath right about me? No. Freaking. Way. I stared at my Dad. "I'm not a reaper. I'm not!" I waved my hands around. "For one thing, I'm not dead!"

"What are you talking about Molly?" Dad's brows drew together. "Who said you were going to be a reaper?"

I heaved a breath. "No one. I'm being stupid."

He looked at my grandparents, and they didn't look the least bit surprised that I'd blurted out something about reapers. They knew something about me, something about why I had abilities. I felt sick. Really sick. I clutched my belly.

My dad had gone pale. "You didn't say nothing about my Molly being a reaper."

"It isn't our choice, Al," said Derek.

"You are beyond special, Molly. Just like your mother. It's no wonder Anubis chose you." Pride had entered Sandra's tone, even though her expression was tainted by haughtiness.

I blinked. "You mean Mom was supposed to be a reaper?"

"You will go beyond being a mere reaper," said Sandra. "Your mother could have been Anubis's champion. Like you." Her eyes went distant for a moment, as though she were considering all the wonderfulness that would've been hers had Mom followed through with her fate. I felt a keen sympathy for the girl my mother had been—especially if she had to deal with this dragon lady every single day. I couldn't imagine how Mom had managed it. Maybe that's why she bailed.

Gah! Everything was so confusing. My mind spun with all the possibilities, all the freakiness. And I was really tired. If only I could go upstairs and sleep, then wake up and find out the only destiny I had was to date Rick and survive high school.

"The Briarstocks can trace their lineage all the way to ancient Egyptian nobility," said Sandra. "But your blood is even more—"

"Enough." My dad cut off Sandra coldly.

Derek cleared his throat. "You raised her, Al, and you did a fine job. But you know this is bigger than you, than any of us. The past is the past. This is about Molly, about what's right for her."

"What are you talking about?" I was so on edge, I was shaking.

Dad grabbed the lemonade and handed it to me. "Drink it all, Mol."

I gulped the liquid down, even though my stomach was still threatening to rebel. The nausea subsided, though. I sucked in a breath and tried to find some calm.

"There's a school," said my father slowly. "The Nekyia Academy of Necromancer Arts. Your mom and your aunt went to it."

"I have an *aunt?*" I asked.

"She died a long time ago," said Derek.

"Oh," I said. "Sorry."

Grandpa Derek acknowledged my sympathy with a short nod.

"You're a legacy," said Sandra, her voice eager. She'd completely ignored the mention of her daughters. "Generations of Briarstocks have attended Nekyia. In fact your grandfather's family helped found the school."

I'd seen commercials on television for Nekyia Academy, but never paid much attention. That school was for necros with lots of money, and it was in Reno, so… Oh, crap. As if everything that hadn't come before this moment, this terrible moment, hadn't been sucky enough. I looked at my father. "Dad?"

He looked tense. "It's the primo school, baby."

"How are we supposed to afford it?" I cried. We weren't poor or anything, but we weren't rich, either. We were normal. Just normal. At least, until the Anubis dream. And the incident with Rick. Rick! If I went to this stupid new school, I wouldn't see him anymore. I wouldn't see any of my friends. Becks. Gena. My whole life would be gone.

"We'll take care of all your expenses," said Derek. "We'll buy you a whole new wardrobe in addition to the uniforms."

"Uniforms!" I said, horrified. Well, this situation was just getting better and better.

"It's a boarding school," added Sandra. "So you'll be there full time except for holidays, of course. And we do hope you'll spend an occasional weekend with us. We would like to be part of your life, Molly."

"You mean you'd like to be part of my life now that I'm Anubis-certified, right?"

Her face drained of color and my grandfather placed his hand on his wife's shoulder. He looked at me with a frown, and I felt bad for being rude. But that didn't mean I hadn't hit on the truth.

"They stayed away because I asked them to, Molly," my dad said.

"Demanded is more like it," said Sandra softly.

"After what happened with—" Derek glanced at me and then turned his gaze on my father. "After what you had to go through," he said carefully, "we understood the decision."

"Your father sent us pictures over the years," said Sandra. She offered a brittle smile. "I don't suppose you remember seeing us when you were younger? You were two at the time. Ally had just been born. We went to the hospital. Your mother refused to see of us, of course, but we got to see you briefly. You said I had pretty hair."

"I'm sorry," I said. "I don't remember." I didn't want to connect with these people. It was easier to not like them 'cause then I didn't have to wonder about the family drama that had kept them out of our lives. Plus meeting them made me think about my mother, and I didn't want memories of her crowding my brain space.

"Your mother was...difficult. She excluded us from her life and trying to get to know our granddaughters wasn't possible. Then she left and I thought—"

"Darling." Derek tucked her against his shoulder, and she took the comfort, but she didn't let the tears glittering in her eyes fall. I could see the steel in her and I envied that strength. I wished I had that kind of resolve. Whatevs. I couldn't help but believe that she thought of me as redemption for the children she'd lost. I didn't care what she wanted. I wasn't gonna be Daughter 2.0 for her or anyone, not even Anubis.

"I had to protect them," said Dad. "I'm sorry that cost you, but Cynthia made her choice. And I made mine."

"What is going *on?*" I demanded.

"Tell her." The edict came from Sandra, of course. She straightened away from her husband and turned that chilly blue gaze toward us. "She needs to know."

I wasn't sure I could take another info bomb. I mean, I was a sort-of reaper, except for the dead part, my grandparents had been prevented from seeing me for some mysterious reason, I had to go to a boarding school because of my stupid specialness, and…now what? I turned toward my father.

That terrible sorrow in his eyes deepened until I saw nothing but grief. And tears. My father was gonna cry. My anger fled and anxiety filled up its empty place. "Daddy?"

"That's right," he said. "I'm your daddy. Always will be." He sucked in a breath. "But you're not my biological child, Mol."

CHAPTER
7

"Ancient references indicate that necromancy magic was bestowed among the five worthiest royal families in Egypt. No one knows much about these families, or why Anubis gifted certain humans with the ability to make zombies. These days, any child might display one of the Reaper gifts—but in Ancient Egypt, that was not the case."
~ANCIENT ZOMBIES BY ZACHARY MILLWOOD

Devastation rocked me to the core. It wasn't true. Dad was just saying mean things so I'd go to the stupid school. "Y–you're not my father?"

He flinched. "You were six months old when I met your mother. I loved you like you were my own, and you are. You hear me? You're mine."

I shook my head, staring at him, at the man who'd spent sixteen years lying to me. "No," I yelled. "I'm not! I hate you! I hate all of you!"

Dad—no, *Al*—reached out to grab me but I ducked away from his arms. I ran toward the stairs and paused. My heart was pounding so hard, I thought it might beat right out of my chest. "I'm not going to boarding school. I'm not gonna be a reaper. Or Anubis's bitch. You hear me? *I* choose my life. Not you!"

"Molly Inez Bartolucci!" said Dad sternly. "That's enough!"

"You're not my father," I yelled. Tears streamed down my cheeks. "Just leave me alone!"

I ran up the stairs, feeling like a spoiled brat, but I didn't care. My life was ruined. Rath had been right. Life wasn't just about boys and malls. But at least most people had a choice about what they wanted for themselves.

Why had I told Anubis yes?

Could I take it back?

No, probably not. That's why he'd made such a big deal about accepting the gifts.

I slammed my door and threw myself on the bed. I cried and cried until the tears ran out. I snuffled into my pillow, my face swollen from crying so much. My whole entire world had shifted. Had shattered. If I wasn't Molly Bartolucci...then who was I?

I should run away.

Yeah. Just pack my crap and go.

I tossed that idea around. Everyone would miss me, sure. But I wouldn't have to go to Nekyia. I could...well, do something. Get a job. Move to Mexico. Avoid Anubis until I died. Right?

"Molly?" Ally knocked on the door that led to the mutual bathroom. The one my sister would have to herself because hel-freaking-lo, I was going to boarding school.

"What?" I yelled.

Ally came in, and she looked stricken. She clutched a birthday present in her hand, and I recognized the wrapping paper. How the hell had she known that was Rick's gift to me?

"This one's from Rick, right?" It was as if she'd read my mind. She crawled onto the bed with me and gave the package. "Figured you'd want to open at least one before..." She stopped. "Well, you know."

"So you were listening on the stairs?" I asked.

She nodded. Her eyes were big as plates, and they glistened with tears. "You're really going away, aren't you?"

I picked at the corner of the package. "I don't know. I don't know anything apparently." I glanced at her. "Did you hear about...um, you know. Dad?"

"Yeah." She took a deep breath. "It doesn't matter. He raised you. You're still my sister. We are your family." She took on an exaggerated haughty expression and then spoke in a voice that suggested she had marbles in her mouth. "Not those people. You don't have the requisite stick up your butt."

She fluttered a hand near her face. "Pardon. I meant, stick up your *derriere*."

I laughed.

Ally reached out and patted my shoulder. "You gonna be okay?"

"No."

"If you need to talk or whatever..."

"Thanks, Ally."

She slid off the bed and padded to the door that led to our adjoining bathroom. "Are you really a reaper, Molly?"

"I have no idea."

She offered a small smile and left.

The small card attached to the gift said, "Happy Birthday," and inside, Rick had just scrawled his name.

I ripped off the wrapping paper and stared down at the brown leather journal. There was a note on the front:

It's a necro tradition to keep journals. At least, that's what Google said. I think you'll have lots of cool adventures, Molly. Maybe you can write them down.

He had gotten me a book. Not even one with pictures and writing. I opened it and flipped through all the blank pages. I'd never kept a diary. I had no idea that keeping a journal was a necro tradition.

I had to admit I was sorta disappointed. Still. He'd researched necros hoping to find me a special gift, so I had to give him props there.

The hairs on the back of my neck rose. I shut the book and put it on the bed. Chills raced up my spine. My breath lodged in my chest. *Someone was in the room with me.* I looked around. "Rath? I'm soooo not in the mood!"

I couldn't rid myself of the feeling that someone...or something…was in my room. But all I saw was darkness. "Who's there?"

I examined the wall near my dresser, alarm skittering through me. It seemed sorta wiggly over there, like the shadows were antsy. "I see you," I said. "Come out."

A dark shape detached from the wall, and—holy freaking Anubis!—the blob of black nothingness wavered in front of me until it shaped into a human form; the inkiness bled away into the dark, leaving the faded imprint of a woman. She was in a long purple dress, her skin as pale as cream. Her brunette hair was long and straight. She looked familiar. Kinda like Mom.

"Who are you?" I asked, my voice quivering.

"I'm your aunt Lelia."

Suspicion arrowed into my gut. Oh, sure. I'd just found out I had an aunt, who'd died, and boom, she shows up? Sorta. "What are you?"

"A sheut. Soul shadow."

I looked at her. "I've never seen a sheut before."

"Oh, there are more around than you think. But only necros can see us, and only when we want to be seen."

"I thought sheut hekas were extinct or something."

"Would you reveal yourself if you were a sheut heka?"

Point taken. I eyed her. "What do you want?"

"Now there's a question," she said with a small, sad smile. "You don't know much about our side of the family, certainly not all our dirty little secrets. You're one of them—an illegitimate Briarstock."

"Do you know who my real father is?"

"I don't have a lot of time, Molly. And that conversation… well, it's a really long one, believe me." Her lips pressed together, and her eyes filled with an emotion I couldn't decipher. I got the strangest feeling that she was trying not to scream. She grimaced and her body twitched. "I died when you were six months old. I tried to—" She twitched again, and took a shuddering breath. Her regret wafted like chilled lavender around us. "I came to warn you."

"Perfect," I said. "Because my life isn't awful enough right now. Gah! I just want everything to be the same! This sucks!"

Suddenly the idea of running away didn't seem as scary as going off with my wealthy, snooty grandparents to a boarding school. My dad wasn't even my dad! Why should I stick around?

Self-pity lodged in my belly like a pile of hot rocks. My mind reeled with the possibilities of ditching everything, everyone. If I could be some kind of reaper-warrior at sixteen, why couldn't I start over somewhere all by myself? I was old enough to kick butt for Anubis, so I was old enough to do everything else, too.

Okay, Molly. That's just stupid. Run away, really? And go where? And do what? I wanted to smack myself in the forehead. I didn't want to become some minor headline on Yahoo! News. I was pissed off—more than I'd ever been in my whole life. But it was moronic to take off into parts unknown.

"Why are you a sheut?" I asked.

She sighed. "I trusted the wrong person." She looked at me. "There are those who don't want you to go to Nekyia." Her eyes went wide and she shuddered like someone had just poked her with a cattle prod.

"Are you all right?" I asked.

"Not for a long time." She smiled, and I saw my mom's smile there, only better. "You fall under Anubis's direct protection. There are rules about the champion. They'll do everything to break your spirit, to kill you in other ways. They can't take your life, Molly. But believe me when I say they can take everything else. It's important that you go to Nekyia."

"And 'they' are...?"

"Those who serve Set. Those who wish for his return to this world."

I blinked at her.

"Another reaper war," she offered. "One humans will not survive." She sucked in a breath and closed her eyes. Her expression was pure pain for a moment.

"What's wrong with you?"

"Escaping the control of a sheut heka is not easily done," she said.

"You're a prisoner?"

"In a way, Molly, we are all prisoners."

Well, that was optimistic. I culled through what she'd told me because there was something...something she'd said that... oh. "What do you mean about the champion thing?"

"My true lord has chosen you as the warrior who will—" Pain laced her tone. She closed her eyes. When she opened them again, she had that indefinable look—one that gave me the shivers. "We all make our choices, Molly. I told you. There are rules. I can't reveal outcomes." She waved behind her, in the direction where my fake dad was probably working out my future with my grandparents. "What lies ahead will be difficult. You will train. You will learn. You will survive."

"Sounds fierce."

She chuckled. "Oh, yes. Fierce." She sobered. Her gaze pinned mine. She reached out, and I felt the cold fingers of her hand clutch my shoulder. Weird. Could sheuts actually touch people—or was that another perk of my so-called specialness? "I know this is difficult, Molly. You don't want to leave your friends, your life. But you'll like Nekyia. Trust me."

"Right. Because I know you so well."

"I wish we'd had time together, Molly. I really do." She squeezed my shoulder. "Go to Nekyia."

Zappy cold shot down my back, and I felt this *click* inside me. Oh, yeah. I needed to go to Nekyia. I felt that down to my soul. It was the only way.

"Okay," I said. My voice sounded soft, compliant.

Aunt Lelia smiled. "Very good, Molly."

She squeezed my shoulder again, and another electric chill zipped down my spine. "You're doing the right thing. The absolute right thing."

I was doing the right thing. Absolutely.

She let go, and I felt strange for a moment. Then everything seemed to snap back into place. I felt stronger, more resolved. It appeared that I had the Briarstock steel, too.

I looked at her. "You're really my aunt?"

"Really. If you want proof, look me up. Lelia Briarstock, Reno, Nevada. I existed," she said softly. She lifted her hands and stared at her palms. "I still do." She patted my face, and the cold of her non–flesh flowed into my skin. "Goodbye, Molly. And good luck."

"Thanks." I paused. "Will I see you again?"

"Not if I see you first." She faded into ink and then bled into the floor.

I stared at the spot where she'd disappeared. Urgency filled me. I felt so certain of what I had to do, I grabbed a duffel bag. I filled it with clothes, some of my makeup, my perfume and all the cash I had in my emergency shopping fund—$240. I also grabbed my netbook, an early b-day present from my Dad.

Well, my *not* dad.

Anger and sorrow threaded into my resolve. I didn't belong here anymore. I wasn't a Bartolucci at all. I'd been lied to. This wasn't my home. I looked around my room one more time, and my heart lurched. I felt separate from it all now. Different. I was living someone else's life, a stranger's. My chest hurt and tears crowded my eyes. *No.* I wouldn't cry anymore.

Besides…Ally and I didn't have the same dad, but at least

she was really my sister. Our mother was gone and our grand-parents had just... Well, I didn't know for sure. They hadn't mentioned Ally or said anything about connecting with her. Anger bubbled through me. I didn't have to like them, did I?

I grabbed my cell phone and checked for messages. Rick hadn't texted me back, and I was a little glad. I had another moment of regret, followed quickly by that sense of unease that I needed to go. If I didn't, I felt sure something awful would occur—and I couldn't bear another terrible thing.

As my gaze passed over the bed, I froze. A tiny, pink-wrapped gift box lay on my comforter. Had Ally somehow left another gift for me to open? I wondered why she hadn't just handed it to me with Rick's. Maybe she was being mysterious.

Anyway. I swallowed the knot in my throat. Ally. Not that I would ever, ever tell her, but I loved her. And I kinda—on some days—liked having her around. I felt bad for leaving her, but I had to go to Nekyia now. I didn't belong here anymore.

I'd never been so certain of a decision in my life.

Putting down my bag, I grabbed the present and ripped off the paper. When I flipped open the box, I gasped. The ring inside was silver and it gleamed like starlight. A falcon was etched in the middle. There was an inscription on the inside that I couldn't read. The band was wide and thin and gorgeous. I slipped it onto on to my right forefinger. It fit perfectly.

It felt warm, too, and seemed to take on extra sparkle. Well. That was the least weird part of my night. I liked the ring, and I was glad I'd opened the box. Since there wasn't a card, I didn't know who it was from...probably Becks or Gena. They both had great taste in jewelry. I'd ask them next time we talked. I grabbed my bag and opened my bedroom door... and hesitated. I couldn't help glancing back at the room that had been mine for sixteen years. Maybe I'd never come back. I didn't know, did I?

My heart raced as my sneakered feet hit the stairs.

I could hear the adults arguing in low, furious voices, but when I appeared in the living room, they all stopped and looked at me. Nonna was sitting in Dad's chair, taking in the drama while she knitted. Now she was looking at me with a mixture of grief and pride. "Yes, *bella?*" she asked.

That simple question seemed to encompass everything.

"I'm ready to go," I said.

"Hang on, baby. If you don't want to go to Nekyia, then that's that." He had a familiar stubborn gleam in his eyes. "You'll be just fine here with us."

"No," I said in a quiet voice. "I won't." I couldn't get myself to call her Grandma, so I said, "Mrs. Briarstock is right. Either I go to my destiny, or it comes for me."

"I'm your father." He looked at me, daring me to say different. But that was an argument for another time. I was still angry. It burned like a low flame in my belly. But I knew that going to Nekyia was the right thing to do. I would miss my friends. I wouldn't be able to tell Gena and Becks goodbye. Or Rick. My stomach clenched. Oh, man. That one kiss would be all that we had. What guy wanted to date long distance?

"Molly?"

Dad sounded stern, but I detected the desperation in his tone. I realized then that he was afraid he would lose me. He really did love me, and I knew that. I got that. But he'd lied to me.

"Who's my real dad?" I asked.

My dad looked stricken, as though I'd punctured him in the heart. I guess I had. But I had a right to know about my own life.

"We don't know," said my grandmother. "Cynthia wouldn't tell us."

"Did she tell you?" I asked my dad.

He swallowed heavily. "No. And I didn't care. You're my little girl."

"I'm not a little girl anymore."

Some guy I didn't know had created a baby—me—with my mother. It made me wonder if that was why Mom had bailed. Maybe my father had come back, and she'd skipped out on us to be with him.

That scenario was depressing.

"Alfonso," offered Nonna in a soothing voice. *"Bacio a tua figlia addio."*

Kiss your daughter goodbye.

He stared at me, and I saw the glitter of tears in his eyes. My dad never cried. Grief lodged in my belly like shards of ice. He opened his arms, and for a moment, all I could do was stand there and stare at him and just be angry. Finally I stepped into his embrace and gave him a stiff hug. It was the same kind of comfort he'd always offered me, but now I knew he wasn't my father. And it hurt. He kissed the top of my head. "Good luck, baby."

I was holding back tears, feeling choked by the tangle of emotions that knotted my insides. I scooted out of his arms, picked up my duffel bag, and looked at my grandparents. "I'm ready."

"Yes, Molly," said Derek, approval gleaming in his eyes. "I believe you are."

MOLLY'S REAPER DIARY

Second Lesson of Reaperhood

Your. Life. Will. Suck.

What's left of it.

Get over yourself already.

CHAPTER
8

*"Nekyia Academy is the premiere school for gifted
necromancers. We accept less than 2% of students who apply
for our program. Are you worthy of Nekyia?"*
~NEKYIA ACADEMY BROCHURE

My first glimpse of Nekyia Academy was through the tinted glass of a limousine window. The sleek black car drove down a twilight-lit road. On either side, tall trees stretched toward the dreary evening sky; wooden soldiers that stood in thick rows to guard the school.

As we rounded another bend, the gray mist parted to reveal what looked like the monster cousin of Notre Dame. *Hey, Dracula, I'm home.*

"Gothic much?" I muttered, staring at the gray stone building with its multiple towers, fancy spires, stained-glass windows and, oh look, rooftop gargoyles. Their vicious stone faces glared down at us. I didn't know what I'd expected, but they seemed kinda unwelcoming. I have to admit that I was nervous. My bravery and determination were still solid, but I was walking into an unknown situation. And after experiencing my grandparents' lifestyle for a mere weekend, I knew that I was way, *way* out of my league.

"Mind your manners," said my grandmother. Her voice sounded as steely as the crossed swords she kept above her fireplace mantel. That display was in the first living room. The other three living rooms featured various other ancient weapons above their fireplaces.

I glanced at her. She sat primly on the seat opposite mine, looking coldly fabulous in her designer pantsuit and high heels. Her silver hair was done in an updo with a few curls draping her cheeks to soften her features. Everything about her face was as sharp as a blade, especially her thin pink lips. Her eyes had crinkles, and lines bracketed her mouth, but even so, you wouldn't know she was fifty-six years old. Her hair really was silver, not that shiny sort of gray.

My grandparents bled money. As Sandra had explained three days ago when she'd swooped in and plucked me from Grimsby Avenue, she was sole heir to the generational wealth passed down since her family had migrated from their castles in Europe. Of course her reaper lineage was marital. I got the impression she'd gone after the Briarstock name. Poor Derek. He hadn't stood a chance. We hadn't spoken about Mom. I'd noticed that there were hardly any family photos displayed in their monstrously big house. There was one portrait of my grandparents, and one of Aunt Lelia in a super fancy gown. I'd asked about my aunt, but that conversational door was shut instantly. My grandmother hadn't even responded; she'd just looked at me until I'd decided I had something else to do.

Next painful subject. Finding out that Dad wasn't really my dad was such a huge, awful thing, I didn't know how to deal. And now all I could think about was…who was my real father? Was I some kind of one-night-stand baby? Or was she dating a jerk? Or…argh! Thinking about it made my head ache.

It had taken a couple hours to get to my grandparents' house, which was on the edge of a lake. Becks and Gena had stayed in touch the whole weekend, lamenting my sudden life drama. I could always count on them to be fiercely upset on my behalf while also sending out support vibes. Strangely, neither of them had given me the ring I now wore constantly, and Ally had denied putting the gift on my bed.

Rick never responded to my texts, and even though it made me heartsick, I understood why. He'd figured out I wasn't worth it. Getting your skull caved in probably changed your perspective. All that birthday drama, and I'd just...bailed. Yeah. I'd bailed on my family, my friends, my life.

I felt like I'd eaten a bunch of rocks, and they were piled up in my stomach. I hurt. I just...hurt.

Now the car slid smoothly to a stop in front of the castle. And yeah, it looked like a castle, not like a school at all. Narrow stone steps led to two ginormous wooden doors. My heart started to hammer in my chest. Now that we were here and this was real, I wanted to run back to Vegas.

"Remember," said my grandmother, her icy-blue gaze sweeping over me, "you represent the Briarstocks. You are a legacy and you will act appropriately."

I'd gotten at least six haughty different versions of the "you are a Briarstock so act like it" lecture. I don't know why my aunt Lelia wanted me here, but I'd been thinking it over. I figured Anubis wanted me to be here, too, and obviously I had a lot of work to do to get my reaper skills up to awesome. But after spending a couple days with Derek and Sandra and listening to all the rules and the expectations and the—ugh, Everything That Is Important—I didn't want to go to Nekyia Academy.

"Do you understand, Molly?" Her voice snapped like whip.

I turned my gaze to her, guessing I looked panicked. Even though I was pissed at her, I had the insane urge to throw myself on her mercy. For a quicksilver moment I saw her glacier gaze soften. Then she pressed her lips together. "Do not disappoint me."

Oh, yeah. I'd forgotten. Sandra Briarstock had no mercy. I grabbed my purse—my new Holy-Anubis expensive purse. My entire wardrobe, makeup, accessories and other stuff rich people apparently needed, had been purchased by Sandra's personal assistant and delivered to the school. Well, except for the clothes I was wearing. I didn't get to choose anything because I had "middle class" tastes. I didn't really argue much about the clothing situation because...well, what was the point?

I leaned forward and grabbed the door handle.

"A moment, Molly."

Surprised at the uncertainty that tinged my grandmother's voice, I paused. She opened her purse and pulled out a slim velvet box. "This was your aunt Lelia's."

"Oh." I took the box. "Um...did Mom have one of these?"

"No."

My grandmother probably hadn't kept anything of her youngest daughter's, aka Her Life's Disappointment. But the fact Sandra had offered me something of Aunt Lelia's meant... well, I wasn't sure. That maybe she missed my aunt, and my aunt's story, her death, had been important.

I took the box and opened it.

"It's a pen," I said.

It was silver, and for a pen, really nice. There was an engraving on it, a triangle, and inside the triangle, a spiral. "What does it mean?"

"Our family symbol," she said softly. "We had it engraved on the pen. Lelia was forever writing in her journal. Like you do."

I didn't know what to say. I hadn't realized my grandmother had noticed me writing in my reaper journal. Or that she would give me something so personal to commemorate it. I'd reminded her of my aunt, and that had made her do something kind. "What?" I asked, my voice cracking. "No skull and crossbones?"

Her eyes flashed with amusement, but she shook her head. "Your sense of humor leaves a lot to be desired, young lady."

There was no heat in her voice, and if I didn't know better, I'd think she was kinda joking. Suddenly there was a teeny tiny silver lining. Aunt Lelia and Mom had gone to this school, too. Maybe I could find out things about them while I was here.

I had so many questions. ·

"Thanks."

She looked as though she wanted to gripe at me for not being all la-de-da formal, but she gave a little sigh instead. Then she nodded toward the door. "Goodbye, Molly."

"'Bye." I gathered some courage, and I got out and stood on the bottom step. I watched the limo glide away, following the winding road as it disappeared into the gray mist.

"Miss Briarstock?"

"Crap!" I whirled around, slapping a hand to my chest. A thin, gaunt man stood behind me, his smooth skin an odd shade of gray. His eyes were really weird too—pinpoints of black in the whites. As if only his pupils were showing. He was very well dressed—in fact, he kinda looked like a butler.

"I apologize for startling you, Miss Briarstock. I am Henry. I serve you."

I vaguely recalled something about a Henry during Lecture 256 from my grandmother, but by the time we'd gotten to the Nekyia-etiquette portion of my torment, I'd started tuning her out. "You…uh, what?"

He blinked slowly as if processing my question. "I am your ghoul. Whatever you want, you need only to ask for it. Shall I show you to your rooms?"

"Ghoul?"

"There are not many of us," he said. "And none that are new. It is forbidden to make ghouls. Those who exist are bound into the service of their families. I am yours."

"Hoo-kay." I didn't know anything about ghouls. We'd never covered that in History of Necromancy…heck, not even Dem had said anything to me about ghouls. Aside from telling me that I would be attending Nekyia as a legacy and I should act like it, my grandmother hadn't answered a lot of questions. Although she had admitted that she and my grandfather had met at Nekyia...and then started another lecture about proper behavior of a legacy (yawn). *You'll be apprised of your classes and duties when you arrive, Molly. As a legacy, you receive certain privileges, and as a Briarstock, you are expected to meet the appropriate social obligations.*

"This way, miss." Henry extended his arm toward the big doors. He started up the stairs. With one last look toward the road that had taken me here, I turned and followed the ghoul.

"There's been a mistake."

I glanced around the room, which looked like something out of Sleeping Beauty's castle, and felt my heart drop to my toes. I clutched my purse. No way was this my room.

It was freaking huge. It had a king-size four-poster bed with red-and-gold curtains pulled back. The comforter was thick and silky red. And there were at least a dozen pillows in red and gold propped against the massive headboard. A big-screen television took up most of the opposite wall. In front of the TV were huge floor pillows and bean bags.

To the left of the bed was an old-fashioned dressing table with three mirrors. Three drawers offered space for makeup and hair accessories. Its chair matched the cherry wood of the desk and bed. There was a door on its left, which I assumed led to a closet.

Overwhelmed, I crossed to the bench seat at the foot of the bed and sat down.

"I've put away all your things," said Henry. He pointed at the furniture on the right wall. "You'll find your formalwear in the armoire. Your school uniforms are in your closet. Casual clothes and underclothing are in the dresser."

"Dude."

Henry looked at me. He did the slow blink thing. "Miss?"

I realized he'd been pointing at the right wall when he mentioned the closet. "Wait. If the closet is *that* door by the armoire, then what's the door by the dressing table?"

"Your bathroom, miss." He then pointed to yet another door—the one on the other side of the dresser. "Through there is your study. Your laptop is ready for use. I was unaware of your musical taste, so I was unable to load the song features."

"Um, thanks."

"You are most welcome, miss."

"This is mine?" I blurted out, hardly able to believe it. "All of this?"

"This room and all that is in it have belonged to the Briarstocks since the school was built. So long as you are a student at Nekyia, this room and its contents are, indeed, yours."

"Holy crap."

"If you say so, miss."

I thought over his words. "The legacies all have rooms like these?"

"Yes," said Henry. "The five necromancer families who settled this area of California built the school. As the founders, their heirs are entitled to certain privileges...and have certain obligations."

"Yeah, yeah. So I've heard." I moved off the bench and prowled around the room. I couldn't believe it. I'd had a good life with my dad, but we weren't rich. Not by a long shot. Maybe money couldn't buy happiness, but I'd bet it could come close.

"Where do you stay?" I asked.

"I have accommodations, miss. If you want me, simply call my name and I will appear."

Yeah, okay, because hey, what kind of rich girl would I

be if I didn't have a magic assistant ghoul who showed up on command? "You mean call you on my cell, right?"

"No," he said. "Simply call my name."

"Hoo-kay."

"Will you dine in your room this evening?" he asked.

"Is that an option?"

"Of course. You are required to take meals in the dining hall only during lunch. Breakfast and dinner are optional."

I thought about facing all those kids I didn't know. I had no friends, no allies. Being the new girl sucked. But it really sucked here at Nekyia, where everyone knew their pasts, their families, and what was expected of them. Me? Not so much.

"Yeah. Dinner in the room is cool."

I told Henry to get me whatever. I forgot I was dealing with a guy used to serving rich people. He ordered duck breast with apple-honey sauce, roasted saffron potatoes, mixed greens doused with raspberry vinaigrette and crème brûlée for dessert.

By the time I was finished stuffing myself, I was so sleepy, I could barely move from the private table Henry had set up for me. I grabbed some pajamas (silk, thank you) and went into the bathroom to change. When I opened the door, the lights came on automatically. The size of the bathroom was startling. It was freaking pink marble, too. A separate glass shower abutted a bathtub big enough for four people. There was also a double sink with shiny gold fixtures. I opened the two doors opposite the shower/bath and found a toilet in each one.

No way.

I changed into my pajamas. Between the sinks was a basket with a toothbrush and facial cleaning supplies. I brushed my teeth and scrubbed my face. I rubbed on some lotion. Yawning, I shuffled out and shut the door.

The first thing I noticed was that Henry had managed to

clean up the remnants of dinner and put away the table and its lone chair. He'd disappeared, too.

The second thing I noticed?

The woman standing oh-so-casually in the middle of my room.

CHAPTER
9

"When you think you've reached your darkest point and there is not even the slightest glimmer of hope...just wait, my sweet necros. Everything will always get a whole lot worse."
~MEDUSA CHILES, HEADMISTRESS OF NEKYIA ACADEMY

THE WOMAN WAS TALL AND SLENDER. HER WHITE BLOUSE WAS tucked into a black pencil skirt. She wore sensible but expensive black heels. Her red hair was tucked into schoolmarm's bun. She wore no makeup, but she didn't need to, not with that killa complexion. Her green eyes were curious and friendly. She held out a hand.

"Hello, Molly. I'm Medusa Chiles, the headmistress of Nekyia Academy. I instruct some of the advanced necro courses, too. I wanted to welcome you personally."

Her grasp was firm and cool. I pulled my hand from her grip. "Thanks...Ms. Chiles."

Her eyebrows rose. What? I knew how to be polite. Okay. I wasn't going to pretend to be all hoity-toity no matter what my grandmother said. Also wasn't it weird that Medusa Chiles hadn't bothered to, you know, knock?

Stifling another yawn, I looked longingly toward the bed. Ms. Chiles saw the direction of my gaze and smiled. "I promise I won't take too long. Since you're starting classes tomorrow, I wanted to talk to you about our expectations."

Oh, joy. If my lack of enthusiasm showed on my face, she didn't mention it.

Instead she gestured toward the bench in front of the four-poster bed, and we both sat.

"You've settled in?"

"Yeah. Henry's been a big help."

She seemed to find that funny. "I expect so. He's served your family for a rather long time."

Maybe that explained why he looked so old.

I drew my knees to my chin and wrapped my arms around my legs. Silence stretched between us, but it wasn't uncomfortable. I got the impression she was giving me a minute to get myself together.

"As a legacy, you have many responsibilities to Nekyia and its students."

I had a lot more to worry about than Nekyia's blue-blood policies. "Why?" I asked.

"When Nekyia Academy was built, the founders made certain provisions for their progeny—which gives you certain perks not necessarily available to other students." She looked around the room. "Such as your quarters. But you are also expected to fulfill more duties and responsibilities." She studied me. Then she laid a hand briefly on my shoulder. "You're different, Molly, and that's good. Most legacies are…well, they feel entitled, and act as such."

She was saying my middle-class background might work out for me because…um, why? I had no idea what the social strata was like at Nekyia Academy, but I had a feeling it was much more complicated than my previous high school. No doubt being illegitimate would knock me down a few pegs on the cool scale.

"You'll be expected to join the Nekros Society." She offered a thin smile. "Another so-called perk. Legacies do not have to apply, unlike the rest of the student body. Getting into the Society isn't particularly easy. But then again, not much at Nekyia is considered easy. You will be challenged here, Molly. In many ways."

I wasn't sure how to take that. I'd already been challenged— in the way I viewed myself, in the new destiny I was determined to embrace, and in the way I perceived my life. Not to mention I'd had a big reality check.

"I can see you're tired," said Ms. Chiles. She gave me another quick pat. "I'll let you rest." She stood and crossed to the door. "I'll see you tomorrow, Molly. We'll talk some more."

"About what?"

"Tomorrow," she said. Then she gave me a little wave and left.

Exhaustion poured through me. I headed toward the massive bed, ready to crawl into the comfy-looking covers and pass out.

Then I heard a knock.

Had Ms. Chiles returned?

I switched directions and opened the door.

Rick Widdenstock stood on the other side.

CHAPTER
10

"Death is only the end for the corporeal form, not for the soul. No, the soul moves on to the next world, and it is there you will be rewarded…or penalized…for the acts you do on the Earth."

~ANPUT

"RICK!" MY HEART, WHICH HAD FELT SO HEAVY, AND MY thoughts, which I'd kept away from him—the boy I wanted to fall in love with—exploded with sudden joy. I moved toward him, and then freaked, because, hello, I was without decent clothes or makeup.

Now I felt self-conscious.

Rick grinned at me, and his eyes drank me in like I was somehow water in the desert he'd been crawling around in.

"Hi, Molly."

"What are you doing here?" I asked. I let him come to me because my knees were shaking so bad, I couldn't move. "Are you okay?"

"Me?" He knuckled his skull and grinned. "Fine. It's you I'm worried about. I missed you." He reached me and grabbed my hand.

His skin felt cold and he seemed…well, I didn't know. Maybe I was looking at him with reaper eyes, (if that's possible). I could see he was fully alive, and I'd made sure his soul was sorta intact. I wasn't sorry that I'd saved him. But there was a doubt or two that I might have done something irreparable to him.

"Mr. Bartolucci told me you were going to Nekyia, so I came to see you."

"By yourself? You're kidding!" My happiness zoomed upward like a shooting star. "That's so awesome!"

He stared at me and nodded. "I couldn't stop thinking

about you, Molly. I'm glad you're okay. And that we're here together." He took my hand and pressed my palm against his chest where his heart beat. "I need to be near you."

I'd never heard such romantic words before. My heart trilled in my chest. OMG. Rick Widdenstock totally wanted me. We were *this close* to being boyfriend/girlfriend. "How long can you stay? Don't you have school back in Vegas to worry about?"

He shrugged. "It's no big deal." He leaned forward and kissed me briefly.

I hadn't realized he'd been so affected by me. I mean, we'd kinda planned to start dating, but we hadn't even gone on one date. "I'm not going anywhere," I promised. "Where are you staying?"

"I have a place." He stared at me for a really long moment, and then slowly blinked. His grin appeared, and the tension strumming my belly disappeared. "Look, I know it's late. Probably not cool for me to be in your room." He waggled his eyebrows, and made me laugh. "I'll see you tomorrow. Lunch?"

"In the cafeteria?" I asked. "Do you have a room in the school? It's just...I don't know how things work around here. I didn't know we were allowed visitors."

"I'm here, aren't I?"

"Yeah. And I'm glad."

Still, it was kinda weird that he'd showed up on the same day I had. I mean, it was also romantic. Like Romeo and Juliet, only with a better ending.

He kissed me again and turned. He paused by the door. "Good night, Molly."

"Good night, Rick."

He shut the door quietly behind him, and I locked it. Then I crawled into the comfortable bed, feeling a little less like my life sucked. Rick was here at Nekyia! And I hadn't seen him at all since my birthday fail. I wondered why he hadn't answered my texts. That reminded me… I checked my cell and saw that the phone had digitally imploded with text messages from Gena and Becks. I was too tired to read them all and respond, so I shut it off and plugged it in to charge.

I went to turn off the bedside lamp, but then I felt the cold swish, saw the flash of black.

Rath appeared.

Damn it. Really? *Really?*

I sat up. "What do *you* want?"

"Nice to see you, too, brown eyes."

"Shut up."

Rath stared at me, one eyebrow quirked. "Aw. Does someone have a crush on me?"

"Not even."

He grinned. And my stomach did that tingly squeezy thing. *Rick,* I thought, feeling weirdly desperate. *Rick is my almost-boyfriend.*

Rath was…annoying.

"It's cute when you scrunch your nose like that."

I looked up at Rath. "You think I'm cute?"

"Not really," he said. "I think you're immature, irresponsible and ditzy. But the nose thing, that's okay."

I wanted to lash out, to tell him that he wasn't exactly a prize human being—or reaper, whatever—himself. But I was tired. I didn't want to fight. So I shut it all down and stared at him mutely. Actually I was stealing this technique from Ally. It was effective because it made people uncomfortable and they usually walked away. My problem was that I'd much rather spout off. Cold anger was harder to express.

"No searing comeback?" he asked. He pressed a knee on the bed and leaned down. "What? You're not even gonna stick out your tongue?"

My stomach squeezed and my breath caught. I was unnerved by him being on my bed, and he knew it, too. He was

trying to make me uncomfortable. "If you're through insulting me," I said, trying to keep the tremble out of my voice,
"you can leave."

"Oh, I'm not through, brown eyes." He offered another
wicked grin that made my insides squirm again. Yikes. "Not
by a long shot."

These inappropriate feelings for Rath were really gigging
up my ju-ju. I didn't even like him. Okay, he had the hotness
factor, but he was also a jerk.

"Seriously, Rath, what do you want?"

"I'll let you know." He pulled back from the bed, crossed
his arms and looked at me with an expression I couldn't quite
figure out. "See you tomorrow."

"What? Why?"

The grinned turned evil. "Oh, we're going to see a lot of
each other, brown eyes." He leaned down, way down, until he
was mere inches away. "I know Rick is here. He shouldn't be."

"None of your business," I said.

"And by here, I mean on the earthly plane." His expression
turned serious. "You get that, right?"

"Whatevs."

He had the nerve to flash me a look of disappointment,
and then he shook his head. "You have a lot to learn, Molly.
I just hope you're up to it."

Then he disappeared.

I slammed back into the bed and muffled my scream of
frustration. *What* was that guy's problem? And what did he
mean about seeing me tomorrow? And seeing me *a lot?* As if!

I was exhausted. Despite all the nightly visitors, and the
strangeness of my first evening at Nekyia, I was too brain-
dead to think about much.

I quickly fell asleep.

I was in a very large stone hallway. *Nekyia entrance hall,* I
thought dazedly. I had no form. I merely floated around, feel-

ing wispy and vague. On the left wall was a portrait of Anubis, his silver scythe held high above his canine head, his human legs crushing skulls beneath his feet.

He was the father of death.

And he had called me daughter.

Daughter of death.

To the right was a huge, impossibly wide staircase with a polished wood railing and big stone steps.

In the middle of the hallway was an overweight, blond-haired girl whose pale face was riddled with acne. She was dressed in a dark blue nightgown covered with a matching robe that wasn't belted. Her feet were bare, and her toenails painted metallic purple. "Hello?" she called out in a timid voice. "I'm here. You said to meet by the Anubis portrait, right?"

She turned, as though she'd heard a response, but I couldn't hear anyone. Or see anyone.

But the girl apparently could. She put a hand to her chest and whispered, "What is that? What are you doing?"

I watched as she was somehow driven to her knees, her mouth opened in a soundless scream, and then her soul—that wondrous blue orb pulsing with terrible beauty—was ripped out of her chest.

She turned gray, as gray as stone, her features frozen in horror, her arms forever outstretched in supplication. Then she fell forward, and her body clunked against the floor...

...and shattered.

I looked around, everywhere, to see who had done such an awful thing. But the hallway was empty.

Except for me.

I hovered above the dead girl, as helpless as a ghost, and I wept.

CHAPTER
11

*"And Set turned Anubis's most loyal reaper against him,
and together, they recruited other reapers to their cause. Set
believed Death was a commodity, one to be traded or bought.
Humans were cattle, built to serve the whims of the gods.
Death ravaged the human population as Set's fallen
and Anubis's warriors fought and shook the foundations
of the earth."*

~THE SECRET HISTORY OF REAPERS, AUTHOR UNKNOWN

I AWOKE TO BRIGHT SUNSHINE SLANTING ACROSS MY FACE. I threw my arm over my eyes. "Gah!" I said. "The light! It burns!"

"I'm quite sure you are not on fire, Miss Briarstock," Henry's rasping voice assured me. "Come now, miss. You must prepare for classes."

"Whaaa?" I muttered as I rolled across the bed to get away from the relentless sunshine. It was everywhere, though, so I was forced to sit up and swing my legs off the bed. "What time is it?"

"It's 6:00 a.m."

"Ugh. What time do classes start?"

"Nine-fifteen," he said.

"Are you kidding me?" I asked, horrified at losing so much sleep time.

Henry did his slow blink. "I'm afraid I do not have a sense of humor, miss."

I looked at him and laughed. "Seriously?"

"Quite."

He did look serious, but maybe, just maybe, there was a twinkle in his odd gaze. "Hoo-kay." I rubbed my eyes and yawned. "Why do I need three hours to prepare for classes?"

"I estimated three hours for you to eat breakfast, take a shower, do your hair and makeup, get dressed—with time for you to change your mind on at least two shirts, present yourself to the registrar to receive your schedule, meet with

Headmistress Chiles and arrive at your first class five minutes before the bell rings."

I stared at him. "Wow. You are an organizational genius."

He inclined his head. Then he gestured toward the private table he'd set up once again. "Breakfast is served, miss. Please enjoy scones with jam and clotted cream, chamomile tea, orange juice and fresh fruit."

"Cool." I got up, rounded the bed and patted Henry's shoulder. "Thanks. You're awesome."

His odd eyes widened a fraction. Then his lips seemed to almost smile. "Thank you, miss."

Ol' Henry had been right about the amount of time I needed to get all my crap together. Uniforms were black pants and girls had the additional option of black skirts, with a choice of white, light blue or pearl-gray shirts. Same color choices for socks, and though there weren't massive restrictions on types of shoes, the only acceptable color was black. So, I wore a gray Oxford shirt, a black pleated skirt, and a pair of knee-high socks with Converse Hi-Tops I'd managed to pack from my own wardrobe despite all the black Mary Jane loafers my grandmother had bought for me to wear. I'd curled my hair and done light makeup knowing that, at some point, I'd see Rick again.

My heart skipped a beat.

With everything going down with Anubis, my grandparents, Nekyia and my necro magic, contemplating having a boyfriend seemed almost normal in a wonderful way. Having a little bit of wonderful wasn't a bad thing, right?

I'd forgotten my cell phone in my room, and I felt a little bereft without it, as if I was missing an arm. Oh, well. I'd survive the disconnection until I could retrieve it.

Henry had given me a map of the school, which was freaking huge—the school, not the map. I got to the registrar's just fine, and the little old blue-haired lady behind the counter gave me a printed schedule and the advice to "smile more."

Even with Henry's neatly penned directions, I got lost trying to find Medusa Chiles's private office. I had to maneuver through all the kids clustered in the hallways gabbing and the waves of students hurrying down the stairs. I caught a few curious looks as I wove my way through. On the second floor there were fewer kids to battle. By the time I reached the third floor, I didn't see anyone, which was okay by me. The third floor landing was huge, and it bridged the main entrance hall. I'd never thought I was afraid of heights, but looking over the edge of the wall sent my stomach into the spins.

I turned and looked around. Stone, stone, and more stone... and more portraits of Anubis, various other gods and people I didn't recognize. There were no signs in this place, which I thought was soooo not right, especially in the supposed administration part of this monstrosity.

I debated which direction to try first, as I couldn't figure out the map (was I holding it upside down?). I chewed on my bottom lip and finally decided to go left. I wandered into a narrow passage that was lit by—get this—torches. I realized after a couple of minutes they were really electric lights designed to look like torch flames.

Maybe this really was Dracula's castle. It kinda had that vibe.

I rounded a corner and *wham!* I smacked into someone.

"Watch it, bitch!" The redheaded girl reared back, nearly colliding into the three girls who followed her. She made a big show of dusting off her light blue short-sleeved shirt while shooting me a look of evilly hate.

I rolled my eyes. Wow. Really? Wiping off invisible new-girl cooties? *And* a death stare? This was the Mina Hamilton of Nekyia Academy, no doubt. Mean girls all had the same look, the same vibe and the same minions. Well, I wasn't gonna be intimidated by this latest entrant into the Asshole Olympics. If I'd stood up to Mina, maybe she wouldn't have thrown punch on me at my own birthday party. I was New Molly, or at least I was trying to be. And New Molly refused to be pushed around. I figured I'd just ignore her stupidness and move on with my day.

I made a move to go around her, but I'd made her look foolish—probably by forgetting to cower before her awesomeness, and she stepped in front of me. "Where do you think you're going? These are the senior dorms." She gave me a scathing look. "You're not a senior."

I looked her over, wondering who she was trying to fool. "Are you?"

Her lips mashed shut. "Why do you care?"

"Good point. I don't." I turned around and started walking away. Then I heard a swishing sound, and something hot and sharp wrapped around my ankles. I went down on my knees, banging them hard on the flat stones, but rolled over before I went face first into the floor. I saw black ropes of magic dissipating. What the—? How was it possible to use magic like that? What kind of necro was she?

Miss Thang and her Posse of Evil sauntered by.

"Walk much?" she asked, smirking. She laughed. "Wow, Molly. You're such a klutz. Better watch those monster feet of yours."

She and her friends giggled and swished off across the bridge, looking back at me then returning to whisper to each other.

I stared at the redhead, but not because I was trying to make her skull explode or anything. I didn't know her. Had never seen her before today, either.

But *she'd* known *my* name.

Why did a complete stranger know who I was? And why was she so pissed at me?

"Oh, my great gracious! Are you all right?" A girl with big green eyes and two blond ponytails knelt next to me. Her accent was as thick as maple syrup. "That Clarissa Jacobs is so impolite."

"Not the word I would use," I said as she helped me to stand.

I got a good look at her. She wasn't wearing makeup, but she had one of those enviable complexions that were all creamy and smooth, with just a hint of blushing red in her cheeks. She wore black pants with a white shirt and black high heels.

"How do you climb stairs in those?" I asked in awe.

"Pshaw! I'm used to it." She waved a hand in dismissal. Then she offered me the same hand. "I'm Autumn Star Lebowski."

I stared at her for too long. A grin split her face. "I know. My mother's a Southern Belle turned vegan hippie—my grandmother's definition, I'm afraid—and my daddy immigrated from Poland."

"Um, wow." I took her hand and shook. "I'm Molly Bartolucci."

"*De*-lighted," said Autumn. "What are you doing up here?"

"Looking for Ms. Chiles's office."

"Oh, sure!" She turned around and pointed across the bridge. "You go down there and follow the hallway around a little ways. Just past the portrait of Eudora Helmnot..." She paused and looked at me. "Is something wrong?"

Not wrong per se. There was a line of ghosts behind Autumn. Six or seven, maybe more, because a few were flickering and it was difficult to actually count. I'd seen ghosts before, because SEERs were popular and lots of places had them—restaurants, clothing stores, ice cream shops. But it kinda creeped me out to see ghosts all loose and floating around, mostly because I shouldn't be able to see earthbound spirits that weren't attached to SEERs. This was a totally different heka power, one I'd never had.

"You have…er, company," I said.

"Oh, them." She sighed. "I'm ren heka. The thing is, most of the spirits I meet want to stick around. It's not like I'm a reaper and can escort their poor souls to the afterlife. And they won't listen to me about moving on." She smiled. "It's like having cats, really. So, you're a ren heka, too?"

"No. Ka heka," I said.

"And you see the spirits? *Ah*-mazing." She did look amazed, but not suspicious. I mean, not in a why-she-must-be-a-super-reaper-weirdo kind of way. She waved to the spirits behind her. "I'd introduce you, but it'd take too long. Also, I can't keep 'em all straight."

"Are there any SEERs at the Academy?" I asked.

Autumn made a face. "No. Zombies and ghouls are one thing, but trapping a poor spirit to do your laundry? It's against Nekyia's policy to have any SEERs on campus." She offered me a wide smile. "How about I show you where Ms. Chiles's office is?"

"That'd be awesome. Thanks!"

She turned and walked across the bridge, her cadre of ghost buddies trailing after her. I didn't fail to notice that most of them were of the teen boy variety. I think Autumn had a bunch of admirers who were not pets at all.

One of them disengaged from the line and hovered near my shoulder. He didn't say anything, but I could tell he was looking at me. I didn't really want to look back. I couldn't help but glance, though, and got the general impression of someone gaunt and unwashed, wearing an orange shirt, torn jeans, and biker boots.

"Any deets on Clarissa?" I asked, as I caught up with her.

"Legacy." Autumn sniffed. "Thinks she owns the academy, just like the rest of 'em. Probably best to avoid her when possible. Legacies have a sorta *carte blanche* around here, if you know what I mean."

"Um, no," I said, my heart dropping to my toes. Autumn had friend potential, and I didn't want to lose the only contact I'd made so far. I was kinda only half-legacy anyway, because I had the taint of being illegitimate. I guess. I didn't feel all woe-is-me about it, but it wasn't something I wanted to advertise.

"Legacies are *pri*-vileged out the wazoo," said Autumn. She held up five fingers. "You have the Jacobses, the Mooreheads, the Callihans, the Freemans and the Briarstocks. Although, you don't have to worry about the Briarstocks—they don't have any legacies here now."

I offered a weak smile, but she didn't seem to notice my discomfort.

Autumn wiggled her fingers. "Goodness gracious. You should see their rooms. Not that I have, mind you, but I know people who've been at legacy dorm parties and such, and supposedly, those places are *ah*-mazing." She shook her head and then looked at me. "It's probably best to stay out of that stratosphere. Rarified air, not meant for regular folks like us."

"Right," I said. We were traipsing down a hallway. Then we came across a huge portrait of a woman dressed in black robes, a gold book held aloft in one hand and a mace in the other. She looked fierce. "Eudora Helmnot," said Autumn. "One of Nekyia's first instructors. I heard she was a bitch on wheels."

I snorted a laugh and Autumn grinned. Then she started walking again and I followed. She stopped when we reached a narrow twisty white-stone staircase that wrapped around a turret. "Up there. Only the one door."

I glanced up the stairs and felt my stomach squeeze with anxiety. "Okay. Thanks."

Autumn held out her hand and I shook it.

"It was nice to meet you, Molly. Maybe we'll have a class together, but even if we don't, I'll see you at lunch."

"Sounds great," I said. "I appreciate your help."

"No problem." She gave a little wave, and then she and her ghosts marched away.

I looked up the staircase and sighed. Why would the headmistress's office be in such a strange location? And how did anyone find anything around this place?

I went up, up and up, twisting and twisting until I was dizzy and feeling out of breath. Finally I saw an elaborately carved wooden door. It had symbols on it, but no name.

I knocked.

"Come in."

I squeezed the wrought-iron handle and pushed open the heavy door.

Ms. Chiles was in the middle of her office standing next to a tall person draped in a black robe, hood up. Um. Did instructors dress like that? Or what?

This was the weirdest office I'd ever seen—filled with big, dark furniture, intricately patterned rugs, and shelves that sported books, skulls (OMG, were those real?), mini cauldrons, sparkly items and million other odd things.

"Welcome, Molly." She pointed to a circle of red leather chairs positioned near a narrow, stained-glass window. "Shall we sit?"

"Okay," I said. I felt nervous, but I didn't know why. Maybe it was the mysterious robed figure, or the headmistress's solemn manner. Because I was raised by my dad and Nonna to respect my elders, I waited for the adults to sit down before I took the last chair.

"How are you settling in?" asked Ms. Chiles.

"Fine," I said.

"Excellent." She gestured toward the hooded person. "This is Macintosh Jacobs."

He threw back his hood and eyed me with a less-than-friendly look. He had thinning red hair spiked with gray and a pair of piercing blue eyes. His face and expression reminded me of a bulldog's.

"So you're the great progeny of the Briarstocks," he said. "How nice."

"Mac," said Ms. Chiles in a warning tone.

His lips thinned. "I'm the representative of the Nekros Society, here to judge your worthiness."

Ms. Chiles sighed, and I felt as though she just stopped short of rolling her eyes. "He's here to induct you into the Society."

"Um...that honors society thing?" I asked.

"Ah," said Ms. Chiles. "This is different, Molly. This society was created after the reaper wars. They train the Chosen, Molly, like you, to prepare for the day when Anubis names his champion."

I said nothing. Ice coated my spine. Um, wasn't I the champion? At least, that's what Aunt Lelia seemed to think. Then again, she was just a sheut and no one I really *knew* knew. Still, Anubis had hinted my destiny was special-esque, and what about that Oracle prophecy? And PS, how come my grandparents had never mentioned the Nekros Society? Or that there were other Chosen? Sheesh. All the people who were oh-so-conveniently planning out my existence for me really should have a meeting and get an actual game plan going.

Well, did it matter? I'd accepted the gifts. I'd chosen Nekyia. I was in. All the way.

"What am I supposed to do?" I asked. "Anubis didn't really go over this part."

Both adults turned sharp glances at me. The silence grew as thick as syrup and as sour as spoiled milk.

"You spoke to Anubis?" asked Mr. Jacobs. He eyed me with suspicion. "What does that mean?"

"She had the dream," said Ms. Chiles. She, too, was studying me with an odd expression. "She means that she accepted Anubis's offer to be Chosen. That's why we're here."

"I know," snapped Mr. Jacobs. "How do we know she had the dream?"

"Her gifts," said Ms. Chiles in a we're-done-discussing-this-topic tone.

I expected Mr. Jacobs to ignore the warning in her voice, but he pressed his lips together and sent me a narrow-eyed glare. I suddenly had the impression that they'd argued about me, maybe even more than once, prior to this little meeting.

I also got the feeling that Ms. Chiles didn't want me to pursue the conversation. Maybe she was worried I'd say, "Oh, yeah. Anubis and I are total buds. And hey, the Oracle said I was the warrior who would save the world. Boo-yah!"

"Where did you get that ring?" asked Mr. Jacobs. His annoyed gaze had zeroed in on the silver band. "It's unusual."

"Birthday present," I said.

"Is that a falcon etched on the top?" He scooted to the end of his chair and leaned over to peer at my hand.

I resisted the urge to hide my hand behind my back. I didn't like Mr. Jacobs. I didn't know what his problem was with me, but it sucked to get all this Judgy McJudgy stuff from people I didn't even know.

And that's when I realized his last name was the same as Clarissa's. Father and daughter…and both had it in for me. *Sheesh.*

"Headmistress!" The breathy voice trilled into the room and scared me. I jumped and caught a smirk from Mr. Jacobs.

"What is it, Norma?" asked Ms. Chiles

A woman flickered into the room, and I realized she was a ghoul. She was pretty—or as pretty as a ghoul could be, with that odd gray skin and those pinpoint eyes. She had blond hair pulled into a ponytail, and she wore a pink dress that flared at the knees with matching heels.

"I'm sorry, Headmistress. One of the students is…" She paused, her gaze turning to us and then back to Ms. Chiles. "Indisposed."

Ms. Chiles's face drained of color, and she gripped the arms on the chair so tightly, her nails dug into the leather. "Dear Anubis," she muttered.

CHAPTER
12

"The soul is fickle. Don't mess with it."
~*REINCARNATION AIN'T FOR SISSIES* BY ZERINDA JEFFRIES

"WHAT IS SHE TALKING ABOUT?" DEMANDED MR. JACOBS. He stood up, and so did Ms. Chiles. I felt awkward sitting there alone, so I got to my feet, too.

This was a crazy first day of school.

"This is a Nekyia matter, Mac," responded Ms. Chiles coolly. "I'll handle it. Please induct Molly into the Society."

Mr. Jacobs put a hand on my shoulder. "Welcome to Nekros. Be true to our goals, honor our wisdom and serve Anubis faithfully."

"Um…okay?"

He followed Ms. Chiles to the oversize desk that had been carved to look like a crocodile. "What's going on?" he demanded.

"You may be in charge of the Nekros Society, but Nekyia Academy is my domain."

"I am also a teacher at this facility," he said. "And that means I have the right to know what's going on. Are students in danger?"

Ms. Chiles stared at him, her expression cold. "Go to class, Mac. If I require your assistance, I shall let you know."

Oh, *snap.*

Mr. Jacobs obviously didn't like her tone or being dismissed, but again, he didn't argue. "As a concerned parent and legacy, as well as an instructor of advanced studies, I expect a report about this incident."

"Expect all you want," said Ms. Chiles. "Welcome to Nekyia, Molly. I hope you enjoy your classes."

"Thank you," I said. I lit out of there like my shoes were on fire.

I shut the door behind me and went down the steps as fast as I dared. I stopped on the last one and put my hand on my chest where my heart was beating like a frightened bird.

A student was indisposed?

Did that mean...dead?

My dream. No. My nightmare.

What did it mean? Had I somehow witnessed a soul being taken? Was that even possible? Or had Anubis given me a vision? And if so, what the hell was I supposed to do about it?

"Hey."

I yelped and nearly jumped out of my freaking skin.

The ghost gave me an "oops" kind of shrug.

"Um...who are you?" I asked.

But I recognized him as the ghost who'd been hovering near me earlier. One of Autumn's so-called pets. I took a good look at him now, especially since he was lounging right in front of me. He was thin, his long hair greasy, his eyes a faded blue. He wore torn black jeans, biker boots with big silver buckles and a grubby orange shirt touting Jailbait: We will rock your ass off. He had some acne, too. I didn't understand why spirits couldn't get rid of the stuff that had plagued them as humans. I mean, ghost acne? Really?

"You scared me."

"Well, that's just sad," he said. "I'm nothing compared to some of the things hiding around this place." He stared at me, his eyes so strange that I got the shivers. "My name's Rennie. Autumn asked me to rescue you from the administration wing."

"Oh. That was nice. Thanks."

He eyed me. "Well? You gonna get moving, or what? You're missing your first class."

"Crap!"

My morning classes were a lot more interesting than anything I'd taken at Green Valley High School. Except for my killa room, the most surprising thing about Nekyia was that I liked what I was learning. I'd even taken notes. Looked like I really was New Molly. I was also grateful that I didn't have Mr. Jacobs for any of my classes. That guy was a douche.

By the time lunch came around, the school was buzzing with the news that a girl had been found dead somewhere on school grounds. The rumors I'd heard so far were:

She'd been found naked, lashed to a tree, with obvious signs of torture.

She'd committed suicide in one of the empty turrets, leaving a note about lost love.

She'd been wandering around late at night, fell down the stairs and broke her neck.

No one seemed to be discussing the soulless issue, which meant my dream was just a dream or the administration was keeping that info on the down-low.

Still. I'd been chewing on the idea of soul stealing all morning. If the girl really was dead—and the school rumor mill didn't mean she was—had her soul been taken? How? A soul being released from a dying person was way different than one being yanked from a live person. And why bother? A soul couldn't be nearly as useful as a zombie or even a spirit. What was the point?

I thought about my dream, and I wondered about the girl turning into stone and shattering. No one did that, right? I'd seen plenty of kas taken and never once witnessed a body turning into stone.

So, it was just a dream.

Like the dream of Anubis had been?

Okay, had I been sent a vision? Or was I just having night-mares? I wondered if I should try to find out what the girl looked like. Maybe…but, nah. It would look weird if I had asked questions about a dead student. Why didn't Anubis just send me a message? One that made sense?

My brain was starting to cramp.

Anyway, as stories about the dead girl went flying around, the school vibe became part excitement, part fear. Nobody had a name, either, so that made it hard to believe anything had happened.

"Yoo-hoo!" Autumn waved to me as I maneuvered through tables and crowds of chattering students. I held a tray full of food. I'd totally gone for the full-on nachos instead of the wholesome salad. What? I was stressed, and cheese made me happy.

I saw Clarissa sitting at the table I was about to pass, noted the smirk sitting like poison on her lips, and saw her lean forward and whisper to the group of girls sitting with her. What-ever Clarissa whispered to them garnered multiple gasps, and several narrow-eyed looks in my direction.

I went another way and tried to puzzle out the unwarranted hatred Clarissa seemed to harbor for me. I mean, really? *Really?*

"Molly, I'm so happy to see you!" Rick appeared in front of me, beaming as if he had just won the lottery.

"Hey," I said, startled by his sudden appearance.

He gave me a wicked grin. "Can I carry your tray?" He took the tray and then leaned down, his eyes sparkling in that way that made my stomach squeeze in jittery expectation. "Maybe we could spend some time alone later?"

I nodded, anticipation wrecking my concentration. Still,

there was something kinda weird here. "Look, I'm happy to see you. But...what about you going back to Vegas?"

"Soon," he said. "Everything's cool, Mol. Promise."

Autumn popped up next to us. "Hi!" She stuck out her hand. "I'm Autumn. And you're..." She stared at him for a minute. "Are you necro?"

"Just here to see Molly." Rick took her hand and shook. "I'm Rick."

"Nice to meet you. C'mon, y'all. I'll introduce to you to the gang."

"There's a gang?" asked Rick. He winked at me.

Butterflies swirled in my stomach. And even though there was a...well, a taint somehow to my feelings, like something wasn't quite right, I dismissed it. He was okay. Granted, he didn't have a complete soul—but, see? He was perfectly fine.

We followed Autumn to a back table occupied by four living people. This section of the cafeteria wasn't as crowded— I wasn't counting Autumn's spirits, which lay on the floor or leaned against walls. A couple of them floated above the table as though they were lounging in a pool.

Rennie detached himself and wandered over to me, studying Rick with a narrowed gaze. "Who's the stiff?" he asked.

"Shut up," I muttered.

"You say something, Molly?" asked Rick.

I smiled brightly at him. "Nope."

Rennie refused to go away. He floated right above Rick, his ghostly boots tapping the top of Rick's head. He looked down at me and grinned.

Even dead, boys could be idiots.

Rick set my tray down in an empty spot and waited for me to slip onto the bench seat. Autumn sat across from me, her smile welcoming.

"I'm so glad you joined us for lunch," she said. She beamed at the other kids at the table.

I noticed that no one really beamed back.

"Hey," I said.

"Oh, now. C'mon y'all. We need some new blood around here! This is Molly...er?"

"Bartolucci," I said. "And this is Rick Widdenstock. He's visiting."

Everyone looked at Rick and nodded, and I noticed that no one seemed to question that he was a visitor.

Autumn poked the tall, thin boy next to her. He seemed extraordinarily interested in his mashed potatoes. "This here is Daniel Moorehead. And he's a legacy, except his older brother gets the cool room."

"He also gets all the crap, so shut up." He wore mirrored sunglasses, and when he looked up to greet me, I saw my own mini-reflections. "I've heard all the jokes about my last name," he said without any real heat. "So don't bother."

Rick and I exchanged a glance. Rick shrugged and put his arm around my shoulder. It felt good, like a real boyfriend thing to do, and I scooted closer. I ignored the little voice in the back of my mind whispering, *Wrong, wrong, wrong.*

Autumn pointed to the girl next to Daniel. "That's Barbie Madison."

Barbie was as far from her namesake as anyone could be. She was short and on the anorexic side of thin. She wore her hair short and dyed a shade of red that looked like congealed blood. Her nose, eyebrows and lower lip were pierced, and she wore a lacey black dress with the words *Reap This!* scrawled on the front in white. Her pale arms were scarred with thin, puckered lines.

"Welcome to the freak zone," she offered. "I'm rich, depressed and just another ka heka. Smiley over there is rich, depressed and an ib heka."

"Whoa." I looked at Daniel with a whole new level of respect and awe.

"Yeah," said Daniel. He tapped the side of the sunglasses. "My grandfather had these made. It protects our eyes, keeps us from going all judgerson on people."

"So you really can see into the heart of someone?"

"Sure. When I want," he said. "Which is never, by the way. People suck."

"He's really fun, isn't he?" asked Barbie. "Autumn's a scholarship student, a ren heka and she's also addicted to caffeine and positive attitudes. Trina over there is nouveau riche, so she doesn't much impress the legacies."

"As if I wanted to," she grumbled. "My daddy owns Ghoul Aid. And like almost everybody else, I'm a ka heka."

Barbie pointed her fork at me. "What's your baggage?"

"I'm not rich or depressed, and I'm a ka heka."

She nodded. "That's reap."

Reap? Huh. Also they were really open about their powers, as if it was such an everyday thing. It was weird to be among kids who could do what I could—well, sorta—and have it be normal. Nekyia was a lot cooler than Green Valley High School. I just wished Gena and Becks could be here, too.

Autumn rolled her eyes in a way that suggested she did that often when Barbie spoke. "Like Barbie said, pretty in pink girl is Trina Molina."

"Yeah, Trina Molina. My dad has this thing about rhymes." Her skin was the color of mocha, and she wore a pair of pink chinos, a pink blouse and pink lace-up boots. Her hair was a gorgeous waterfall of black braids, interspersed with pink ones. She looked kinda like a walking ad for Pepto-Bismol, though in an actually good kind of way.

"Nice to meet all of you," I said.

"So why doesn't Clarissa like you?" asked Trina.

"No clue."

"Anyone she doesn't like," said Barbie, "*we* like."

"True," said Trina. She scooped a chip from my plate and licked off the cheese. "She's a bitch."

"I got that impression." I ate one of the nachos. It looked like Clarissa was responsible for getting me some friends here at Nekyia. I wasn't surprised that people didn't like her. Well, other than her minions, of course.

"Okay." Barbie heaved a sigh. "We must convo. What's up with all the rumors about the dead girl?"

Autumn shook her head. "It's so strange! I heard that they found her stuffed in a janitorial closet. One of the ghouls opened it to get a mop or something, and she fell right on him."

"What's a ghoul?" asked Rick.

"You're dating a necro and you don't know about ghouls?" asked Trina.

"A lot of people don't know about ghouls," said Autumn. "It's not like they're talked about...except in history books, maybe."

"A ghoul is a zombie with a soul," said Barbie. "Sorta. They don't rot like zombies. Anyway. No one makes them anymore. Even though the process is voluntary. Too much like slavery. Like a SEER, you know?"

I glanced at Rick, who was gazing at me with a dreamy kind of adoration. I smiled, but I have to admit I was getting more weirded out. Eh. What did I know about having a boyfriend? Maybe his behavior was normal. I turned to Barbie. "Soooo...ghouls are like zombies?"

Rick straightened suddenly, and took his arm off my shoulder, and I looked at him, startled.

"Sorry," he said. He looked at me regretfully. "I gotta go, Mol."

"Already?" I asked.

"Oh, just for a while. I'll see you later." He gave me a quick kiss on the cheek, and then he bailed. I watched him hurry through the cafeteria, exiting through the doors that led to the dorm rooms.

"He seems nice," said Autumn.

"He is," I said. "He's from my old high school. I used to live in Vegas."

"Oh," said Autumn. "Well, it's awful sweet of him to visit you. Have you been dating long?"

"Not really."

"Weird," said Barbie. Her expression was odd, as though she were putting together some kind of mental puzzle that was taking too much effort. Then she looked down at her plate and sighed. "I hate mushrooms."

"You shouldn't keep getting the Stroganoff," said Daniel.

"Suggestion noted," said Barbie sarcastically. She flipped him the bird. Daniel sighed and went back to picking at the food on his plate.

"What's your schedule like for the afternoon?" asked Autumn.

I shoved my plate of nachos closer to Trina, who grinned at me and dove in. "Shoulda gotten these instead of the salad," she said as she picked up a cheese-covered chip. "Thanks."

"No prob."

I grabbed my book bag and dug through it until I found my crumpled schedule. Organized, I'm not. I smoothed it out on the table. "Independent study," I said, frowning.

Trina leaned over and looked at the paper. "For two periods? Lucky. It's really hard to get independent study, especially if you're not a senior."

"Independent study is a big deal? Why?"

"It's for hardcore students," said Barbie. "Necros who're gonna specialize in some archaic shit."

"Barbie's got independent study, too," said Trina. "But she won't tell anybody why."

"Don't have to," said Barbie. "So shut up."

Trina and Autumn shared a look, and they both rolled their eyes. Autumn turned her gaze toward me. "What's your independent study for?"

"I have no idea," I said. "I didn't pick my classes or anything."

"Oh, sure," said Trina with a dramatic sigh. "The new girl gets everything handed to her on a plate."

Autumn giggled. Then she looked over my shoulder, and stilled. "Hey, it's a ghoul."

Barbie stopped drawing shapes in her Stroganoff and looked up. "That's the Briarstock ghoul. Henry. He hasn't seen the light of day in forever."

I looked over my shoulder and saw Henry headed toward us in a slow, serious, determined way. I didn't want Henry to get to the table and bust me. I had a feeling the minute my new peeps found out I was a legacy, it would be the end times.

"Lelia Briarstock is a legend," said Autumn in a reverent voice.

"Um…really?" I asked. I wanted to know more about my family. It was hard to keep my excitement from showing. I looked back and was suddenly glad at how slow ghouls moved. Still, Henry was getting closer. Ack!

"Lelia Briarstock holds the records here for almost everything," said Autumn. "Nobody's beaten 'em, and it's been like, twenty years."

Barbie leaned in. "Check it. Her younger sister went here, too. Word is, Cynthia Briarstock banged an instructor…and got pregnant."

CHAPTER
13

*"The first ghoul was made because a common house slave fell
in love with his mistress. Still in his prime, he contracted a
deadly disease. As he lay dying, he begged a priest of Anubis
to grant him the ability to serve his mistress forever, but in
a way that he would still know his own heart. The priest
created the first spells that enabled a dead man to carry his
soul around and to remember his humanity. Becoming a ghoul
is a cruelty only the brave—or the foolish—seek."*
~THE HISTORY OF NECROMANCY, VOLUME 6

"She was sent away," continued Barbie. "The Briar-stocks almost imploded from the shame."

My entire insides went cold. My mom'd had sex with a teacher? Was some dude here my dad? "How old was she?"

Barbie shrugged. "She was a senior, I think. She didn't graduate."

"Henry's headed right for us," said Autumn. "That's weird. You guys know any Briarstocks?"

"Aren't any here," said Daniel.

"Except maybe the illegitimate one," said Trina with a smirk. "You know, if Cynthia really did have a baby...it'd be old enough to go to Nekyia."

"And he, or she, would be the sole heir," added Barbie.

"What?" I asked.

"Cynthia's kid would be the heir apparent. There're all these rules about how necro families handle their estates—especially for the Briarstocks, who claim to have blood ties to an original reaper family. Anyway, their wealth and possessions can only pass to someone in a direct line of descent."

"Then Cynthia would get everything," I pointed out.

"Oh, they had her excised from the bloodline. I don't know what she did to deserve that," said Barbie, "but it's a big deal. No one has been removed from their family rosters and stripped of bloodline privileges since the Salem witch trials."

"That Briarstock bastard will get everything eventually," said Trina. "Lucky."

"You already own half the world," said Barbie.

"But I want the other half, too."

"Oh, y'all!" said Autumn. "Money doesn't buy happiness."

They continued good-natured bickering, but I stopped listening.

Holy freaking Anubis.

I was an heir? Derek and Sandra hadn't told me that. I wondered why. Were they afraid I was like my mother?

I glanced over my shoulder and saw that Henry was nearly at the table, his pinpoint gaze on me.

"I have to go!" I stuffed my schedule into my bag and disentangled myself from the bench.

"But lunch isn't over," protested Autumn. "We haven't exchanged cell phone numbers yet."

"I'll meet you here tomorrow," I said. I gave everyone a huge smile, a way too enthusiastic wave, and then I booked it.

I still had half an hour before I had to attend my mysterious independent study. I figured I'd chill in the room, call for Henry to figure out what he wanted and maybe see if there was some snackage.

Trina had eaten all my nachos.

Finding my room wasn't particularly difficult since it took up practically a whole floor. I felt kinda guilty about that, which was weird, because it wasn't like I'd chosen to be a Briarstock.

When I got to the door, I took out the old-fashioned brass key from a side pocket on my book bag. Henry had given it to me this morning.

I went inside and dumped everything onto my bed, then said, "Hey...um, Henry?"

"Yes, miss?"

I screamed, whirled and did a really lame hi-ya kinda of kick.

Henry lifted one gray brow at me.

"Holy crap!" I slapped my hand against my chest, my heart doing the cha-cha, as I stared at him. "How did you do that?"

"I am connected to the Briarstocks by magic. If you call me, I am immediately taken to your location."

"Oh." I sucked in a breath. "What if you need me?"

Henry did one long, slow blink, as if he were a computer trying to process the information and getting an error. "If it is necessary for me to give you a message, or find you for another reason, I simply track you down."

I held up a hand. "Wait. I need you, you're zapped here by magic. You need me, you gotta hoof it?"

"Yes, miss."

"Sorry, dude."

He cocked his head, and his odd gaze flickered. "May I say, miss, that you are delightfully unusual?" He paused. Then he offered, "You remind me a great deal of your aunt Lelia."

I grinned. "Thanks." Then I realized the biggest source of information about my aunt and my mom was standing a foot away. "Hey, Henry. Do you know if Cynthia Briarstock really had some Nekyia professor's baby?"

He stilled, and then looked down at the floor. "I am sorry, miss. I have taken an oath to never reveal information about Cynthia Briarstock's time here at the academy." He lifted his gaze. "If you are interested in learning more about the school's history, may I suggest the Nekyia special archives? As a legacy, you have access to many wonderful rare and archaic texts."

Okay. Was he saying there was something about my mom there? Or was he suggesting I really needed to do some extra studying? "Any suggestions?"

"*Anubis and the Seventh Warrior* is an excellent read. You may find it very illuminating."

"Thank you, Henry." I crossed the small space between us

and gave him a hug. He stiffly put his arms around me and offered a single pat on the back. I withdrew. "Sorry I ditched you in the cafeteria. But my new friends are anti-legacy, you know? They'll freak if they find out I'm a Briarstock."

"The truth arrives," said Henry. "Not always sweetly, either."

Huh. Henry was kinda poet-y. "I get it," I said. "But maybe we could keep our relationship on the down-low till I figure out how to tell 'em. Cool?"

"You wish for us to deny knowing each other publicly?" He sounded disappointed, but his voice wasn't like that of humans, and I couldn't really tell. His expression was stoic, so no clue there, either.

"Not forever," I said. "Just for a while."

"I will do as you ask."

Because he didn't have a choice, I realized. Why would anyone ever decide to be a ghoul? I mean, zombies didn't know they were being bossed around. I felt bad for Henry. Did he hang out with other ghouls? Did he have friends? Did ghouls date?

"I needed to convey a message," said Henry. "That is why I was in the cafeteria."

"I really am sorry I ditched you, Henry."

He acknowledged my apology with a regal nod. "You've been invited to attend the Nekros Society Social, which will take place on Friday at 7:00 p.m."

"Ugh. Is this a regular thing?"

"The Society hosts a social gathering every month."

"Sounds fun," I said. "Except not. Is this thing a have-to?"

"Yes, miss."

I sighed. "Fine."

"If you leave now," said Henry, "you won't be late for your next class."

"What?" I grabbed my cell phone from the nightstand where it was still attached to the charger. I couldn't believe I'd forgotten it. It was almost like leaving my arm behind. I had ten minutes. Damn. No time for Cheetos and a Coke. I snatched up the phone and my bag. "See you, Henry."

"Until next we meet." He offered a half bow, and I offered one back. When I looked up, Henry was actually smiling.

"You're late."

Rath stood in the middle of the workout room, arms crossed. He was dressed in a T-shirt and a pair of black sweats. His feet were bare. He pointed to a door across the room. "You can change in there."

I stared at him. "Change into what?"

"Appropriate clothing," said Rath. "For getting your butt kicked, brown eyes."

Two hours with Rath while he humiliated me with his warrior moves? *Uh...time to change classes.* "This is my independent study?" I said.

"Yeah, and I'm your instructor." He spread his arms wide. "Welcome to reaper warrior training."

So much for getting my schedule changed.

He smirked at me. "If you're wondering, no one but Ms. Chiles knows about your independent study. And it's Anubis-approved, brown eyes, so no getting out of it."

Great. I was stuck here. With Rath. I resisted the urge to flip him off.

I trudged to the door and went inside. It was a large room, with lockers, showers and toilet stalls. I put my bag on a long wooden bench that stretched out between locker rows, and realized I didn't have anything to change into.

Wait. Henry had packed my bag, and he was Mr. Efficiency. I opened it, and underneath the books and papers I had crammed into it during my morning classes was some clothing. I pulled out a workout bra with a matching set of yoga pants.

I didn't suffer from low self-esteem, and I guess I was a normal-sized girl. I wasn't model-thin, because I was raised in an Italian family whose motto was If You're Not Eating, You're Dead. But I wasn't overweight, either. I guess. Still. The idea of wearing tight, show-it-all workout clothes intimidated me.

I put them on and looked down. A wide strip of skin was visible between the sports bra and the pants. I studied my belly. Okay, it wasn't concave, but it wasn't rolling out over the band of the pants, either. I poked my stomach. A little doughy.

I could live with that.

I pulled my hair into a ponytail and went back into the workout room. At the edge of the mat, which was huge, black and at least ten inches thick, I stopped and waited for Mr. I'm-a-bad-ass to start his instruction.

It didn't look like Rath had moved an inch. He eyed me for a moment, but his expression didn't change.

"First you learn defense," he said. "Then offense."

"I can be pretty offensive already..." I joked.

He crooked a finger at me and wiggled it in a "come here" gesture.

I sighed and walked across the mat until I was less than a foot away. "Okay, what do I—"

He swept out his leg and the next thing I knew, I landed hard on my backside. Pain shot up my spine. I glared up at him. "What are you doing?"

"Lesson one, Molly. Always be prepared."

"You're a jerk."

"You're disrespectful."

"Respect has to be earned," I said.

"True. Get up."

I rolled onto my hands and knees and got back onto my

feet. Wary now, I walked back to Rath. I watched his feet, trying to ready myself to jump out of the way.

He shoved me.

I flew backward and landed on my ass. Fury boiled through me. I stood up, marched over to him and…he lifted a leg, fast as a whip, and connected with my knee.

It buckled.

And so did I.

Tears gathered in my eyes. Pain throbbed in my knee, my ass, my spine. He really was beating the crap outta me. I sat on the mat and had a little pity party. Reaper warrior training sucked.

"Get up."

Argh! I shot to my feet and dove for him. I didn't have a real plan. I just wanted him to go down. He blocked me, swept a leg out again and then punched my shoulder with his palm.

I found myself airborne.

Again.

When I landed, the air left my lungs, and my back seemed to explode. I didn't get up. I lay there, trying to catch my breath, and tried not to cry.

Rath padded over to me, and squatted down, assessing my face. "Had enough?"

"You're supposed to be teaching me!"

"I am," he said. "You learn a lot from failure." He offered a grin. "What did you think? You were just gonna be given all that you needed?"

"That'd be nice."

"You said respect had to be earned, Molly. So does everything else. When you work for it, when you sweat and you bleed to get it, then it's worth more."

I sniffled. "I suppose."

His expression softened, just a teeny tiny bit.

That's when I rolled, fast and hard, and banged into his legs. He was knocked onto *his* ass. I popped up and jumped on him.

I landed on his stomach, and he managed a surprised, "Oof!"

I tried to pin him, but I didn't know what I was doing. I grabbed at his arms, and tried to wind my legs around his to make sure he didn't move.

Mistake.

He grabbed my arms, clamped my legs and rolled us over.

We were thigh to thigh, chest to chest, and breathing hard.

"Pretty good, Molly," he said. His breath ghosted over my cheek. "But not good enough."

"Just you wait," I said. I struggled, trying to wiggle out of his grip, but he was strong and in a primo position.

"Stop," he said softly.

I did.

Something in his eyes had changed— going from glittering fury to…well, I wasn't sure. It was still a dark emotion, tormented almost. The tension thrumming between us shifted. It was still physical, just more intense. And confusing.

"You really are beautiful," he murmured.

I gulped.

My heart, already pounding from the butt-kicking, went into overdrive.

Rath leaned forward, his gaze on mine, his lips dipping close to my ear. "But you're still a brat."

Rath rolled off me and popped to his feet.

"C'mon. I'll teach you how to throw a punch."

He wrapped my hands with really long cloth strips, then put boxing gloves on them. The gloves felt weird and smelled awful. For the next hour, I was told over and over and *over* to hold my arms up, protect my face, and stop hitting like a girl.

"Make your jabs count," said Rath. "You want your op-ponent off-guard when you come in with the right cross."

The heavy punching bag we were using was six feet long, so you could punch, kick and knee it. I had gotten past the punching stage. I was exhausted and sweaty, and my muscles were starting to ache.

"Again, Molly."

Jab. Jab. Punch.

"No! Not like that!" His eyes flashed with irritation. "Quit doing chicken wings with your arms. Keep them tucked in and your hands up! Are you sure Anubis chose you?"

OMG. He was mean. And had no—and I mean *no*—mercy.

I suspected he was sorry he'd called me beautiful. And there was that moment…that awesome, strange moment where we were breathing together, looking at each other, and…he'd called me a brat.

Whatevs.

"Quit sleeping and punch!"

I snapped back into focus.

Sweat soaked my sports top and shorts. My muscles pro-tested movement. I kept my arms in, my gloves up.

Jab. Jab. Punch.

"Better," said Rath gruffly. "Do body blows, like I showed you."

Right. Left. Right.

I smashed the middle of the bag with my boxing gloves. I was breathing hard, and my arms felt like noodles.

"You're weak," said Rath. "Soft. You wanna get your ass kicked?"

I was beginning to understand that Rath's insults were another training exercise. At least I hoped so. Every time he pissed me off by saying something rotten, I lost focus and got my ass handed to me.

Rath pushed his face into mine. "You getting bent out of shape?"

I didn't respond. I'd like to say it was because I was being a bad-ass, but I was really just too tired.

"Good," said Rath. "If you let someone rile you into acting rashly, then you give him the upper hand. You need to be rational and calm, even if someone is trying to push your buttons." He touched the top of my head. Ow. Even my hair hurt. "You fight with this first, Molly. Use your mind, your wits. And if you can't get out of trouble—then kick the living shit out of your enemy."

I managed a tired laugh. "Got it."

"You're done, brown eyes. See you tomorrow."

I lifted my hands up. "Woo."

"'Atta girl." He unstrapped my gloves and pulled them off. "Get going."

I leaned over to pick up my towel, and wiped my neck as I walked off the mat.

"Molly."

I stopped and turned to look over my shoulder.

"You did good. For a rewbie."

"Thanks," I said, trying not to show how much his approval meant. Pride shuffled through my exhaustion.

I wanted a shower and some food. And to lie down and pass out for about two years. I went into the changing room and looked at my cell phone display. I had about forty-five minutes until my next class, plenty of time to shower and catch a power nap.

Despite the cool things I was experiencing here at Nekyia— killer room, awesome friends, decent classes—I really missed my family. I'd spoken to Ally a few times since I had left home, but she was irritated about me ignoring Dad's phone calls.

Nonna didn't like cell phones or computers. I'd already received one letter from her with a, "PS, Call your father, bella."

I missed my not-dad. And yeah, I'd have to talk to him one day.

I was still mad that *Al* had lied about being my real father. I knew he'd raised me. I knew he loved me. He'd stuck around even when Mom hadn't. And yet...I felt betrayed. I should get over myself. Forgive him. Move on. But I couldn't. Alfonso Bartolucci hadn't contributed any DNA to me. There was something about knowing your genetics. Your truths were formed by family connections. Suddenly none of those people, their stories, their physical characteristics, their quirks, were mine. I mean, there was Ally, of course. We were sisters. But we had whole other histories, now—only I didn't know mine.

I didn't belong.

And it hurt.

I hadn't heard from Anubis at all. I guessed the Chosen got the one dream, and then we had to stumble around trying to figure out his will. Sooooo not fair.

When I got to my room, the bed looked so inviting, I fell face-first onto it. I managed to set the alarm on my cell phone before I closed my eyes and instantly fell into dreamland.

I was floating through the woods. Late-afternoon sunlight sparkled in the leaves. A boy with shaggy blond hair sat against a tree. He wore the Nekyia uniform—black pants, shoes and dull gray button-up shirt. It was hanging open, revealing a Metallica T-shirt. He held an iPod in one hand—one earbud lodged and the other hanging loose—and a cigarette in the other. When he went to take a puff, I realized whatever he was holding was too thin to be cigarette, and it was also dark purple. What on earth was he smoking?

A twig snapped behind him and he jolted.

Then he smiled, shaking his head as though mentally deriding himself for being a weenie.

"Geez, man," he said, getting to his feet. "Thought I was going to smoke this Wizard's Choke all by myself."

He turned and faced whoever was just on the other side of the tree. His grin faded.

"Who the hell are you? Hey!"

He was driven to his knees, the same as the girl in the hallway, and his mouth opened in a soundless scream.

I saw his soul…that blue, pulsing orb…being wrenched out of his body.

I didn't want to look.

I didn't want to know.

Then he turned to stone, his expression of shock forever etched on his young face. He fell onto his side, and…then imploded.

I woke up totally freaked.

These were not dreams. Nobody had dreams like these. So…visions? I put my hand on my chest, as though that might calm my raging heartbeat.

My cell phone display showed I'd only napped for ten minutes.

I was still tired, but I wasn't going back to sleep.

I needed to tell someone about these dreams. These visions. I needed help. What should I do? How did I stop what was going on?

How did I save the students of Nekyia?

MOLLY'S REAPER DIARY

Top Five Reasons to Pay Attention During Butt-kicking Class

When you don't hold up your arms to protect your face, your instructor might box your ears so that you get the point. Or tweak your nose, which is more annoying, especially since he's laughing at you.

If you punch like a sissy, your opponent won't be impressed, and may proceed to show you a real punch, in which case, you'll go down like you turned into a bowl of spaghetti noodles.

Learning to be a warrior is about mind and soul and magic. The Chosen can access their necro abilities and use magic for multiple purposes (like when Clarissa used hers to trip me). Most necros can only use their one ability for its singular purpose.

You won't be taught how to use magic until you learn physical skills and strengthen your mind...no matter how many times you ask your instructor to please, pretty please, show you magic, too.

You will sweat. You will bleed. You will ask for mercy and not get it. Get stronger. Get meaner. Get reaper.

CHAPTER
14

"The dead don't love."
~*LIES MY ZOMBIE TOLD ME* BY WENDY BOCOCK

I knocked on Ms. Chiles's office door. Henry had delivered her summons along with another fancy breakfast. I was stuffed to the gills with scones, and I was tired. After all the drama yesterday, and that weird vision during my nap, I hadn't slept well. And when I had slept, I'd had nightmares. The images were murky and faded, but the feelings of dread were still pretty strong.

"Come in."

I opened the door and saw Ms. Chiles at her desk. She was rifling through papers and looked somewhat harried. She looked up and offered me a smile.

"Oh. Good. I just wanted to let you know that Rath has been called away on business. You'll have a new instructor for a while. Her name is Irina." She paused. "You understand, don't you, that students with independent study keep what they learn private. You're very lucky to be in advanced studies—especially when such classes are usually reserved for seniors."

Okay. *Don't talk about independent study.* Not that I would, because I wasn't sure how to explain the whole reaper-training thing.

"You know who Rath is, right?" I asked, because it had been bugging me that no one else seemed to know his deal. And since he was dead and only other reapers could see him… how had he become an instructor?

"More important, Molly, I know who you are." She folded her hands on top of the papers she'd been looking at. "Irina will be focusing on helping you learn to use your magic. Most of the Chosen have been training a lot longer than you... You have some catching up to do."

"Okay," I said. "When will Rath be back?"

"After his business is concluded." She offered a thin smile. "Well, you should get going, Molly. Class starts soon."

"Okay. Um, thanks." I left Ms. Chiles's office feeling unsettled.

Where had Rath gone?

"No! Not like that. Dolt!" Irina Derinski's ice-blue eyes flashed with irritation. "You must think about the magic. You must envision it in your mind before you wield it."

OMG. For three days, I had been under the tutelage of Irina. She was mean. And had no—and I mean *no*—mercy. She was teaching me to use my necro magic, mainly for defense, but it was way harder than learning how to kick ass.

So, here it was Thursday, and I faced another two hours of independent study with a cranky Russian reaper.

"Dolt!"

I snapped back into focus.

Irina's Russian accent always thickened when she was annoyed—and with me, she was always annoyed. I knew better than to move out of my current position, which was supposed to give me optimum energy flow. The last time I'd moved, Irina had whacked me with her scythe. Luckily with the staff part and not the blade. Sweat soaked my shirt and shorts. My muscles ached. But I was learning.

She went at me with her scythe, and I sent out ropes of black magic to ward of the blow, and then attempted my own attack. She easily countered it with a shot from one palm, and then dropped the scythe. "Ach. Enough," said Irina. "I'm tired of teaching one so dumb and useless."

The insults didn't bother me much, mostly because I'd been insulted enough by Rath. Irina was a big fan of that teaching technique. Only she was super lecture-y about it. Still, it was Rath's voice that echoed in my head. *If you let someone rile you into acting rashly, then you give him the upper hand.*

"You're dismissed," Irina said. "Go to your room and rest."

I couldn't wait to go back to my room and chill. Sessions with Irina always wore me out. I leaned over to pick up my towel, and wiped off my neck as I walked off the mat.

"Molly."

I stopped and looked over my shoulder.

"You don't suck as much."

"Thanks," I said.

The rest of the day passed quickly, and I was glad. My first week of school felt as if it had been a year long, and I was tired in mind, body and soul.

Autumn had invited everyone to watch a *Dark Shadows* marathon in her room. I texted Rick about joining us, and he texted back that he was at a friend's for a while and would meet up with me in time for the fun. Honestly? I wanted to crash and not wake up for a week.

Still, I was excited about seeing Rick again and spending time with my new friends. I decided I needed to suck it up. And by suck it up, I meant down a Red Bull.

After I was appropriately caffeinated, I picked out a short-sleeved green shirt and faded jeans. Then I took my clothes into the bathroom and got ready.

When I came out of my bathroom, I yelped.

Rennie sat on the edge of the bed, staring at me. He wore the same thing he always did: torn black jeans, biker boots with big silver buckles and a grubby orange shirt touting the band Jailbait.

He saw me looking at his shirt. "My girlfriend was the lead

singer. I used to be the guitarist. Our sound was sorta between Marilyn Manson and Paramore. We weren't the kind of band invited to play the prom."

"What happened to you?"

He gave me a small, sad smile. Then he held out his arms and I saw the track marks. "I was seventeen. Hooked on smack. I died because my girlfriend wouldn't call 911."

"Why not?"

"Because she didn't want to go to jail. Because she's a bitch. Because she didn't love me enough to save me."

"I'm sorry."

He shrugged. "I'm dead, so who cares." He eyed me. "You going somewhere?"

"To Autumn's."

"Aw, shit. *Dark Shadows?*" He groaned. "She's obsessed with that show."

"Well, it'll be fun. Besides, I like popcorn."

"Your stiff going with you?"

"Yes," I said primly. "My *boyfriend* is going, too."

"I don't think he's your type."

"What do you know?" I asked, even though I thought it was dumb to get into an argument with a ghost. And what did Rennie care anyway? I didn't even know why he was hanging around me.

"She killed me."

"I know. You told me."

Rennie hadn't moved from the edge of the bed, and his stare was somber.

"Your boyfriend's hiding out in the basement," he said.

"What?"

"The. Baaaaaasement. He's been lying to you about where he's staying. He's been lying to you about a lot of things."

My belly filled with a cold ache. "Rick wouldn't lie to me. That's not like him."

"Right. 'Cause you know him so well."

"Better than you do."

Rennie rolled his eyes. "Why do you pretend not to know what I mean?"

"Because, hel-lo, I don't know what you mean."

"Everyone's trapped," Rennie said softly. "My girlfriend, Jennette, and I used to sing duos, and we sounded awesome. I loved doing that with her. Then I got so bad into drugs that I stopped singing. Shit, I could barely play the guitar."

I stepped back just a little, because the vibe had changed. Rennie's form was flickering, and his eyes were dilating, his body twitching.

"The dream, man," said Rennie. "The band was the last thing I held on to from my old life, the one thing I claimed as mine. Stupid. 'Cause I had to let it go, just like everything else."

"I'm sorry," I said.

Rennie grinned maniacally and showed yellowed, rotted teeth. What the—

I grimaced and moved away from him. The reminder of his drug habit made me a little sick. Rennie started pacing and muttering to himself.

"Rennie?"

"I need a fix," he said. "Just one." He looked at me, his eyes red-rimmed. His lips were blue, and flecked with white. "C'mon, Molly. C'mon!"

I wasn't sure what to do, but I heard Rath's instructor voice echo in my head. *Stay calm. Use your mind first.*

"You know you can't have a fix," I said calmly. "You can't ever do it again."

"You bitch!" he railed. His fists rammed against the bed, and it shook like it was resisting hurricane winds.

"Enough, Rennie! Go cool off!"

"If you didn't want me to stay around," he whispered, his lip curling into a sneer, "then you shouldn't have let her kill me."

"I didn't," I said. "That was a long time ago, Rennie. You don't have to do this. Be like this."

Rennie flipped me the bird before he walked through the back wall of the room. Awesome. I really did feel sorry for him. I wished I could reap him, but…ghosts were a different kind of reap.

Maybe I could talk to Rath about it. If Rennie was even interested. Spirits who chose to stay earthbound had issues.

I went into my massive closet, trying to find a pair of shoes that looked good with my jeans. Rick would be here any moment, and then we'd head over to Autumn's room for junk food and horror movies.

"You are useless."

Hearing Irina's acerbic Russian voice behind me nearly scared me outta my denims. I whirled around, slapping a hand against my chest. She eyed me from the closet doorway, and then sighed deeply.

"You learn nothing." She tapped her lower lip, her gaze assessing. Then she offered a small shrug. "Anubis insists. So, you go."

"Go where?"

Irina gave me another measuring look, and then she snorted. "Ah! You are still too soft. So, soft, dumb girl, you must complete a task. I do not have high hopes you will." She reached out and awkwardly patted my shoulder. "Work on your ruthlessness."

"Yes, Irina."

She turned to go. "Come."

"Now?"

"*Da.*"

"Um...no *da*," I said. "I have plans."

She turned back toward me, one blond brow raised. "You must learn sacrifice, Molly. Being the champion of Anubis does not mean you fit your duties in between your *plans*."

"But why now?" My voice verged on whiny. "How about later?"

Irina covered her ears. "Oh, your screeching enters my brain like acidic worms." She removed her hands from her head. "Do you really choose to ignore the will of Anubis?"

I wanted to, but I suspected this was part of the challenges that everyone was always going on about.

"It's a test," I said.

"Yes," said Irina. She gave me a long look, the kind that made my stomach squeeze. "I suggest you pass."

I dressed in dark clothes as Irina directed. It seemed silly to go CIA-ish, but what did I know? I had no idea what Irina had in store for me.

It was disappointing not to see my friends, but I was sucking it up. Mostly. Also, it was a little exciting to go out on some kind of secret mission. I wondered what Anubis expected of me.

Irina looked at my outfit then nodded in approval. "Let's go."

I texted Rick and Autumn that I had puked up my guts and was totally staying in bed until I no longer felt like dying. Ironic, right? Autumn texted back immediately with directions about some kind of vegan stomach cure, and Rick... well, Rick didn't text back at all.

CHAPTER
15

"Rumors abound that some of the very wealthy collect famous spirits. In fact, a certain computer genius is said to have a special museum that displays his collection of spirits along with some of the items they owned in life. Of course, we'll never really know—such accumulation of ghosts is an illegal act."
~HEDDY DALMAR, GOSSIP COLUMNIST

"Irina said you were...discreet." Mitzy Neuberg sat on the velvet sofa opposite the one that Irina and I occupied. The couches faced an antique coffee table where a tea service had been set up. She'd been taking my measure since inviting me inside, and I let her. Irina had told me it was better if I said nothing, if I waited for Mitzy to make her judgment and move on to the problem. *In the end, Molly, no matter what people think of you, your clothes, your demeanor, your hair, they will dismiss their concerns in favor of utilizing your gifts.*

Mrs. Neuberg was obviously waiting for someone to speak. Irina slanted me a look with one quirked eyebrow.

"Yes, Mrs. Neuberg," I said, glancing at the portly woman. "I'm discreet."

"Ah. Good. Very good. So, the problem..." She offered a quick, tight smile. "My husband's great aunt passed last October. They were not...close. I'm afraid he found a vast amount of pleasure in raising her spirit to work in the kitchen. You see, she was never fond of cooking and, in fact, made her own kitchen staff's life a living hell. I must admit to enjoying the delightful irony in Aunt Myra doing dishes and serving food." Mitzy paused and cleared her throat, maybe trying to clear her conscience, too. "You are aware that some of the recently raised spirits are not as...bound to their haunting. There's been some speculation that the new batch of Ruddard's SEER machines are experiencing...issues."

Mitzy's way of speaking quickly and then pausing was getting on my nerves. Seriously. I tried to focus on the problem, which was apparently to get back Great Aunt Myra.

"Irina said your abilities were quite strong. I'm curious how you manage to reattach the spirits to the SEER."

My mouth dropped open. She thought I could attach spirits to SEERs? Crap. I pressed my lips together. I was a zombie maker. A soul wrangler. A freaking reaper. But a ghost slaver? No way.

"She's persuasive," said Irina. She'd gone tense, and it was probably from the effort not to slap the back of my head. "The spirits listen to her."

"I see." Mitzy didn't see at all (and neither did I). She stood up, giving us one of those polite stick-up-your-ass smiles. She wore a white dress that did not suit her doughy form, and a lot of fancy gold jewelry. Everything about her screamed, *I have money!*

"You're rather young, aren't you?" asked Mitzy as we followed her out of the formal living room, down a wide hallway and through a set of double wood doors. "I mean for your line of work. Most girls your age are worried about college entrance exams and parties and driving."

I resisted the urge to roll my eyes. Mrs. Neuberg reminded me a lot of Mrs. Woodbine, the zombie abuser.

"I'm not most girls."

She glanced over her shoulder, her brown eyes questioning. I merely smiled and shrugged.

We passed through a dining room and then another door. Mitzy paused. "Here we are. The kitchen." She looked around the space as if she hadn't seen it before. Like the other rooms in the house, it was huge. Above the center island hung a pot rack dripping with copper pans. The gleaming appliances included two refrigerators, a double oven, a stove with eight burners, and black marble counters free of unsightly cooking debris.

"How long has Aunt Myra been gone?" asked Irina. She studied the kitchen as though she were planning a military siege on the appliances.

"Since this morning." Mrs. Neuberg glanced at me. "You were not my first choice to handle this situation."

What did that mean? I glanced at Irina, but her expression was like glass.

"My husband remains...unaware of the situation. You understand it would be best if things were resolved before he arrives home this evening." She smiled and her eyes went cold. "Ten o'clock, every weekday night. Never late, my Harold."

So it wasn't marital bliss in the Neuberg household. Big surprise. I glanced at the wall clock in the kitchen. It was almost 8:30 p.m., which gave me about an hour and a half to find the ghost and get it back to its SEER tether. And, oh yeah, figure out how to do that. Maybe finishing my SEER paper for Mrs. Dawson would have helped....

"Rush jobs cost more," said Irina. "Double the fee."

"That's outrageous!"

"So you will tell your husband that you have lost his great aunt Myra?" Irina's voice was as cold and smooth as ice.

Mitzy sucked in a breath. She vibrated with outrage, but her desperation won out. "Fine," she said in a hissing voice. "Fifty-thousand dollars."

I looked at the floor to keep from giving away my shock. That was double the fee? Holy crap. Then I hesitated. Why would Anubis charge for anything? Did gods need money?

I was getting a bad feeling about this whole thing.

Irina was a reaper. She was my instructor. And it seemed like she was using her powers for things outside of the reaper realm. Had this operation really been authorized by Anubis?

I didn't know. But I was stuck here with Irina. If I just did what was asked of me, she'd take me back to Nekyia. And maybe Anubis could contact me when he actually wanted me to do something.

Mitzy looked around the huge kitchen as if she might see Aunt Myra floating around. Regular people couldn't see ghosts, not without the SEER. "I'll leave you to your work. I expect Aunt Myra to resume her duties within the next hour."

She strode out, obviously still angry that Irina had blackmailed her into a higher rate. Irina walked around the massive island, staring at its shiny marble surface. "So rich. So stupid."

"Irina, we're charging her?"

"I have expenses. Do not worry. Anubis does not mind that I charge for our services."

"I didn't think reaping was a money-making business."

Irina snorted. "You have much to learn."

No doubt. "What am I supposed to do?"

"Catch the ghost. Put her on the machine."

"I've never done that before."

"So?"

"Isn't this psychic work?" In this day and age, saying you were psychic was like saying the sky was blue. People went to school to open their chakras and third eyes and stuff.

"Most psychics are frauds," said Irina. "And they are liars."

It sounded like Irina might've had a run in or two with some psychics. I wondered if she'd whacked them with her scythe.

"We will check the kitchen to make sure we are alone," she said.

The place was cavernous, but obviously empty. Still, I went around with Irina to make sure no one was lurking. When we were sure nobody living—aside from us—wasn't hanging around, Irina pulled me into the center of the room. "Open your senses. Like I showed you. She is hiding, Molly. And she's close."

"If you know where she—"

"Shh!" She snapped her fingers in front of my face. "You must learn what I'm teaching you. Open your senses. Figure out what is different. Feel where she might be."

I inhaled, closed my eyes and opened up my senses the way Irina had taught me. I didn't know what I was looking for, and I have to admit that I was freaked. I was a reaper, not some sort of ghost buster. I didn't like the SEER machines in the same way I thought black market zombification sucked.

People should be allowed to choose what they wanted for their lives—and their deaths.

"Concentrate!" The directive was punctuated by a sharp slap to the back of my skull.

Ow! I bit my lip to stop the complaint from rolling out of my mouth. You know that saying...you get two for flinching? Well, Irina was more of the opinion that you get three for flinching, bitching or not doing it right the first time.

Her way of teaching made me miss Rath.

I wished he'd come back.

I kept my eyes closed, deepened my breath and concentrated. I focused on the kitchen, moving from point to point until...*huh.* "I feel a sorta blank spot." I opened my eyes and then looked behind me at Irina.

She gave a sharp nod, approval in her gaze. "Good."

The blank spot seem to hover in the pantry. With Irina following behind me, I grabbed the handle and yanked open the pantry door. We stepped inside the massive supply closet.

Aunt Myra, dressed in furs and dripping in diamonds, cowered in the back next to a shelf of canned goods.

"Wow," I muttered. "They really like green beans."

Irina snorted. "Look at her. Most raised spirits come back

in the clothes they died in or their funeral clothes. Stronger ghosts figure out how to manipulate their own energy and create whatever clothing they want." She slanted me a look. "Or not. Trust me, Molly. Naked ghosts are not delightful to view."

"I would never be naked!" trilled Aunt Myra. "I've been in here all day. I can't go any farther. Stupid machine. I wished I'd written my great nephew out of my will!"

It seemed like the SEER had weakened just enough to let Myra go invisible, but not completely out of range. Most SEERs emanated a magnetic "net" that prevented ghosts from leaving the vicinity, even if they did manage to wrest their energy from the attachment device. I was surprised other psychics hadn't been able to find Aunt Myra.

Unease crawled through me. Something was wiggy with the situation, but I couldn't bail. Irina would kick my ass. And I would disappoint Anubis.

Maybe.

"Grab them," said Irina. She pointed to the ethereal chains snapped around Myra's substantial ankles.

"Don't you dare!" Aunt Myra attempted to scramble up the wall, but the chains groaned in protests. "I demand a lawyer."

"Shut up," snapped Irina. She looked at me sternly. "A reaper controls all aspects of the dead. You will grab the chains, and we will take her back to the SEER and reattach her to it."

I didn't want to do that. Not only because I sooooo didn't want to touch Aunt Myra, but also because SEER machines were cruel devices. Still. I could guess what would happen if I didn't.

"Okay," I said, as though I'd had some kind of choice. I reached down and slowly I wrapped my hands around the ghost chains.

Myra stared at me. "You can let me go," she said. "Don't send me back to that dreadful machine!"

"Sorry," I said. "But you'll have to work that out with your great nephew." Who sounded like a real prize—but then again Aunt Myra didn't sound like a spiffy human being herself. At least, when she'd been one.

"No!" cried Myra. "I demand that you reap my soul!" Then she looked down at my hands, which gripped the chains. Man, it felt really weird.

"Ew! You can touch it." Myra sounded horrified. Then she grabbed on to one of the top shelves, digging her well-heeled feet into a long row of canned creamed corn. Had she forgotten she was a ghost? There was no hanging on, for Anubis's sake!

"Oh, I can do more than just touch these tethers," I said, my voice hardening.

I pulled, and she held on for dear life, her manicured fingers digging into the wood. "My dear girl, I will give you anything, anything in the world, if you will free me."

I was having a difficult time finding any sympathy for Myra. I kinda understood why her family had stolen her spirit to humiliate her. "I suggest you let go or this whole thing's gonna get a lot worse."

"We've heard such things before," said Irina. "All spirits offer the promise of buried treasure or a forgotten lockbox or hidden jewelry." She wagged her finger at Myra. "Ghosts will do anything, including lie, to get away from the SEERs."

I didn't blame spirits for not wanting to spend their after-lives working, especially for crappy family members. It was worse than zombie enslavement—that was just reanimating somebody's abandoned corpse. The soul didn't reside there anymore. A SEER machine trapped the entire soul—from sheut to ka, and the people knew what they were suffering.

"I'll tell you where the diamonds are," screeched Myra. "I hid them!"

"Why should we care about diamonds?" asked Irina in a bored voice.

Ectoplasm felt kinda squishy and sticky. Like old chewing gum. I tightened my grip and yanked. Myra was ripped away from the shelf. She floated above me, arms crossed, her expression angry.

"What did they promise you?"

Irina shrugged. "A hundred thousand dollars," she lied. She offered a small, mean smile. "They must like you very much."

"Ha!" Myra tapped her bottom lip. "That's a lot of hatred money. And it doesn't seem like my idiot nephew's style." She studied Irina, obviously suspicious. Then she pursed her lips. "Fine. The diamonds are worth more than half a million."

Irina rolled her eyes. "So you say. We let you go, you lead us to some grave or dark woods, and then nothing. You are free, but we are still poor." She shook her head, her blond ponytail bouncing. "No. We won't take such risks. Molly, escort her to the SEER."

Reluctantly, I took Aunt Myra out of the pantry and into the kitchen, holding on to her SEER chain. Crud. I had no idea where the SEER machine was located. I glanced up at Myra questioningly, and she snorted.

"I'm not going to tell you," she said. "Let me go, and I'll give you the diamonds."

"Do I look like a diamond merchant?" I asked. "I'm a kid, not a cat burglar."

"You're a reaper! And you're supposed to reap souls, not make them suffer."

"Don't tell me how to do my job," I said, offended even though I was a reaper-in-training. I had no practical soul escorting experience. Rath had basically abandoned me, too, so everything I'd learned so far was from Irina—and her motives weren't exactly on the side of good.

"Mitzy and Harold are terrible people," said Aunt Myra, trying another useless tactic. She should've gone for the sympathy first, and then bribery.

"Most people are," I said.

Irina had stayed in the pantry, but I heard her voice drift out of the opened door. She was speaking in Russian.

I started opening cabinets; most were filled with dishes or foodstuffs. I'd assumed that the Neubergs would buy a top-of-the-line SEER, maybe one of the new ones that... Oh.

I walked to the refrigerators that were side by side.

"No!" Myra sucked in a breath, realizing too late she'd confirmed my suspicions.

The first one I checked was an actual fridge, which meant that the other was the SEER.

"Please," wailed Myra. "I'll do anything. Anything!"

"Sorry," I said. And I was. A little.

CHAPTER
16

"A ghost cannot inhabit a zombie. Many spirits have tried, but nearly all have failed. Oh, sure. There are a very few instances of ghosts squeezing into the walking dead, but they never last for long. Part of zombification includes protections against spirit invaders, though it was likely the Egyptians were trying to keep demons from having corporeal forms."
~*WHAT YOU KNOW ABOUT ZOMBIES IS WRONG*
BY VINCENT STEVENSON

THE MACHINERY LOOKED COMPLICATED, BUT IT WAS OBVIOUS where the chains were latched. The mechanism that kept the tethers in place was bent. I glanced up at Aunt Myra. "Did you do that?"

"It took me a while," she said proudly. Then she deflated. "But apparently it wasn't enough."

I had never really thought about the kind of energy ghosts have. Obviously dear Great Aunt Myra had enough determination to physically manipulate a machine that had been designed against that kind of resistance. I peered closely at the bent part. I wasn't sure how to fix it. Maybe there was some way to shorten the chains. Sheesh. I really had no idea how a SEER worked.

"Wait, Molly."

I stood up and looked at Irina, keeping my grip tight on the chains. "What?"

Irina studied Aunt Myra. "I've checked with my sources. It appears that your family is missing some diamonds. That's why Harold has you trapped here, yes?"

Myra nodded. "The hell I'll tell him or that moronic wife of his."

"If you will take us to the diamonds, we will free you."

My mouth dropped open. "We will?"

"She makes the better deal," said Irina simply. "And *you* should be happy not to put her back on the machine, with all your puny whining."

"And she will reap my soul?" asked Myra. "She must promise. Because no reaper can break a promise."

I blinked. Well, I hadn't heard that one before. I glanced at Irina, who was frowning. The whole promise thing must be true if she was getting grumpy about it. I wasn't sure about reaping when I knew so little, but...well, it was better than reattaching Myra to the SEER.

Aunt Myra had figured that out, too. Her expression turned triumphant. "Well?"

"In exchange for showing us where the diamonds are—and we are able to procure all of them—Molly will release you from the SEER."

Myra's gaze narrowed. "She will reap me."

Irina huffed out an irritated breath. *"Da."*

"She must agree first," said Myra.

"Okay by me," I said. I held up my free hand as if I was taking an oath in court. "Promise." *Ugh.* I was zapped out from training, not getting enough junk-food fuel and now tracking down a SEER ghost. I wanted to be normal again. You know, maybe just a ka heka working for Big Al's Zomporium and nothing else. Just that. I yearned for the Molly I'd been before my birthday.

"Let's go," said Irina. She pointed imperiously at Myra. "Show us. Quickly."

"Take me to the third floor," said Myra. "There are stairs in the back of the kitchen for household staff."

We followed Myra's directions and found ourselves squeezing up a narrow, winding staircase. When we got to the third floor, Irina quietly opened the door and peered into a wide hallway.

"Clear," she said.

"All the way down," said Myra. "The last bedroom on the left."

It was creepy quiet. All I could hear was the rapid beat of my heart, which seemed to have lodged in my ears. The hand gripping Myra's chains was getting sweaty—at least I hoped it was sweat. Maybe it was ectoplasm. Blech.

Irina got to the door first, and opened it slowly, peering into the room. Then she reached inside and flipped on a light. We all went through, and Irina closed the door behind us.

The room was full of boxes and tarp-wrapped paintings. There was a hearth on the far wall that looked as though it had never been used. And there wasn't any furniture, either. Some bedroom.

"Where?" demanded Irina.

"The large painting over there," said Myra, pointing to a huge rectangle that had been loosely covered with a white drop cloth.

I was feeling creeped out. I didn't like being in someone's house, sneaking around and stealing. And I was bummed that I had to lie to my friends, and to Rick. A girl could do only so much wrong during one day. My conscience was being stabbed by too many guilt-knives.

Irina ripped off the cloth, and we both stared at the painting.

"My babies," said Myra. "I love them so."

The portrait was of Myrna and at least a dozen shih tzu dogs of varying sizes and colors. Every single one had pink-ribboned ponytails.

"What happened to them?" I asked.

"They live at my mansion, of course. They are cared for by my household staff."

"Your dogs inherited your money?" asked Irina. Her tone held bewilderment.

"So long as Harold makes sure they're cared for, he gets a generous stipend. When they all die of natural causes, he'll get everything. Bastard." She looked around. "These are things from my house. He's been taking them without permission and selling them."

I opened my mouth to ask why he'd take a portrait of her and her dogs, but Irina sent me a "zip-it-or-die" glare so I pressed my lips together and shut up.

"The diamonds are sealed into the back of the canvas," said Myra. "Bottom righthand corner."

Irina flipped over the portrait and tugged at the corner of the canvas. It released from the frame and a small pink bag fell out onto the floor. She picked it up and opened it. Then she grinned. "Good." She looked at me, jerked her head toward Myra, and then went to the door. She opened it, obviously planning on keeping watch while I reaped a soul.

Which I'd never actually done. Um...on purpose.

"You really are a reaper," said Myra. "You took me away from the SEER without even trying."

Whoa. She was right. I'd carried her around like my very own Thanksgiving Day parade balloon without even thinking about her SEER tethers.

I wasn't sure how to release her permanently. Some of my lessons with Dem about soul work combo-ed with Irina's information about reaping, and none of it was particularly helpful. It seemed to me that what had worked before should work again, right? I get into the Shallows and send Myra on her way to the blue light.

"Um...Irina? Do I need a scythe?"

Irina scowled at me. "Do not be stupid." She returned to the doorway, her blond ponytail shaking in indignation.

"So helpful," I muttered.

She turned back. "Use the ring. Hurry."

I looked down at the silver band on my finger. "What?"

"It is your scythe, Molly. You carry it around all the time and do not know this?"

"Obviously not," I said. "Nobody tells me anything."

"Because you must figure things out for yourself. It is how you learn!"

She turned away again, and I could hear her muttering in irritated Russian. Well, fine!

"Well?" Myra was looking irritated, and you know what? I was getting tired of all the pressure coming at me. *Do this, do that, Molly.*

Argh!

"To the Light," I said as I let go of Myra's ethereal form. I sorta pointed my ring finger at her.

She floated above me and looked around. "Light? What light?"

"Crap." I glanced at Irina, but her back remained turned. What was up with that? She'd spent the past three days riding my butt about reaping, magic, fighting, everything reaper, but when it came to me actually doing a reap, she was out.

Nervous now, I twisted the silver ring on my finger. Dem had told me that it was the power behind the words that mattered most. I drew in a big breath, looked at Myra and said, "I hereby reap you!"

"That's the silliest—"

My ring went icy cold. And then the room did. Even Aunt Myra sensed the change because she didn't finish her sentence. She stared at me with wide eyes.

Then the falcon symbol on the top of my ring detached itself.

That's right. It came *off the band.*

I gulped.

I stared as the bird grew bigger and bigger and bigger, until it was such a huge, black shadow, it darkened half of the large

UNDEADLY   185

room. It looked at me with obsidian eyes then it reached out
a claw.

In it was a silver scythe.

"Um…thanks." I gingerly reached out and took the scythe.
It pulsed with power, with warmth. I swear it was kinda
purring. Like it was alive. It felt right in my hands. Perfect.
"Goodbye, Myra."

Then I twirled the scythe and on the second turn, I sliced
the blade into her ghostly middle. Her spirit disappeared. And
in its place was a grayish orb.

The falcon cawed. His shadow fell over me, and all the
color in the room bled out. All but the pulsing glow of Myra's soul. *The Shallows.*

The blue light and its odd chanting music appeared. I
watched Myra's soul wiggle up toward the glittering beam.
I kept vigil until it was gone, joined with the mysteriousness
of the beyond.

Then the Shallows faded, giving way to the real world.

Holy Anubis.

The falcon cawed again then flapped its massive, shadowy
wings. It reached out a claw toward the scythe, but I hesitated. It didn't seem right to give up the scythe, but the bird
cawed impatiently and seemed to point with one claw toe toward the reaper tool.

"Fine." I placed the silver staff back into its claws. I'd swear
that the scythe was less than thrilled by this—and so was I. It
felt like mine, like I should keep it.

The scythe disappeared into the dark that was the falcon,
and then it folded into itself until it was miniaturized once
more. It settled like an etched shadow onto the ring.

I stood there for a moment, shaking, amazed and overwhelmed. The ring wasn't some plain ol' birthday present.
Wherever it had come from…how it came to be at my house…

I didn't know. But it was obviously a reaper ring. And I hadn't known that reapers had jewelry.

I joined Irina at the door, excitement bubbling through me. "Did you see that? The ring—"

"Pah!" She held up a hand as though to stall my words. "I saw nothing. I heard nothing." She glanced at the silver band. "It is just a ring, Molly." Her gaze seared mine. "Is it not?"

"No, it's not," I said. I swallowed the knot in my throat, my excitement giving way to frustration. For some reason, Irina didn't want to admit that she knew about the ring and its powers.

"You must learn to keep secrets," she said. "A reaper's scythe is a most vital tool. We do not share our tokens with anyone. It is unspoken rule."

"Why?"

"So that history does not repeat itself. The ring will not leave its current owner. No one can take it from you. Ah. Well, that is not exactly true. The point is to protect yourself."

"Okay," I said, unsure what she was trying to say. I mean, yeah, shut up about the ring, and keep its powers a secret. No problem.

She looked at me, her blue eyes suddenly filled with an ancient sort of weariness. "The world is not always as it seems, Molly," said Irina quietly. "You must work on your ruthlessness."

"Yes, Irina."

We walked out of the bedroom and almost knocked over a very shocked Mitzy. "What are you doing up here? Where's Aunt Myra? Oh! How dare you! I'll call the—"

Irina punched Mitzy hard and fast with a powerful uppercut. The woman's eyes rolled back in her head, and she dropped like a sack of rocks to the floor. In that terrible white dress of hers, she looked like a messy pile of marshmallows.

"See?" said Irina. "Ruthless. Easy." Then she marched ahead, the pink bag of diamonds clutched in her hand.

When we returned to school, Irina dropped me off by the side entrance. It had felt sneaky leaving that way, which I guess was the point. The door led to the basement storage area. I would have to climb a narrow set of stairs into a hallway that led to the kitchen area and find my way to my room from there.

I reached for the door handle. "Thanks, Irina." I wasn't sure what I was thanking her for. Um, an adventure? Thievery? Lessons in being ruthless?

"Wait."

I kept my fingers around the handle, but I paused, and I looked over at her. She gripped the steering wheel, staring straight ahead. Then she started cursing in Russian.

"Irina?"

She heaved a sigh. Then she pulled out the pink bag, opened it, and extracted a pea-sized diamond. "You must learn, Molly, to take care of yourself. Rely on no one. Think of people as alliances, not as friends. Everyone has the potential to be your enemy, even those you love."

"Does it work the other way?" I asked. "Enemies who become friends?"

She smiled faintly. "Rarely. But yes." She handed me the diamond. "Payment for this night's work."

"Does Anubis really know about this kind of stuff, Irina?"

She shrugged. Then she closed my hand over the diamond. "Think of this as your emergency fund." She looked at me, and I couldn't figure out what emotion lurked in her gaze. "He will come for you, Molly. You will have to fight. Perhaps you'll have to run."

"Who will come for me?"

Irina rolled her eyes. "The enemy of Anubis, girl. The one who will soon slip his bonds and reenter this world."

"Set?" I swallowed. Hard. "Isn't he in a cage or something?" My heart skipped a beat. "Why does he want me?"

"It makes no difference." Her expression shuttered. "Pay attention. Be ready." She paused. "I will not be your teacher anymore."

"Okay," I said. I wasn't exactly sad about that, but as hard as she'd pushed me, as mean as she'd been, I'd walked away with a lot more knowledge and skill. "Thanks, Irina. Really."

"Yes, yes. Go." She returned to staring straight ahead, her jaw tense.

I hopped out of the car and headed toward the door. Irina turned the car around and slowly drove away. She didn't turn on her headlights.

I had the feeling that we had done something really bad. I didn't understand why she'd needed me. She was a reaper, too. She could've easily done that creepy job with Aunt Myra and not given me anything.

I wondered if Anubis would be pissed at me when he'd found out what we'd done. I mean, maybe he knew about Irina's little side activities and just ignored them. I decided I'd say an extra prayer tonight to Anubis, offering both an apology and a question. I hoped he answered.

I hurried to the side door and grabbed the handle.

Locked.

Oh, man! I jiggled it, as if that would help, and then let go. I checked my cell phone, saw that it was after ten o'clock, and realized the whole school was locked down. Curfew was at 10:00 p.m.

I looked down the road. Irina's car had already disappeared. Where had she gone? And why hadn't she at least opened the door for me?

Crap.

I stared at the door, trying to figure out what to do. If I texted Autumn or any of my friends, they'd know I'd lied to them. Then I'd have to explain why I wasn't really sick, and how I'd ended up outside, shut out from the school. And that certainly wouldn't be using the discretion Irina had asked—and technically paid—for.

I tapped my lower lip, considering the possibilities.

Then I heard a noise. I stilled, my heart turning over my chest. Slowly, I turned. A stretch of gravel road went around the school. It was mostly for delivery trucks and for the staff to reach the back parking lot. On the other side of the road was the dense forest filled with darkness and creepiness.

Snap.

Adrenaline spiked. I put myself into a stance, wondering if I could really use the moves I'd been taught. I wondered if I could even remember what to do.

Snap...snap...snap.

I could see the figure now. Whoever it was trudged up the incline, wending through trees in a careful, if not silent, way.

I went into the first offensive stance that Rath had taught me, and I readied my magic.

And waited.

CHAPTER
17

"Sometimes, in life, you're just screwed."
~*ADVICE TO YOUNG NECROMANCERS*, EUDORA HELMNOT

CLARISSA JACOBS EMERGED.

She looked terrible. Her hair was pulled back into a pony-tail, and she wore dark clothing that was torn in several places. Her neck was scratched up, and her knuckles were bloody.

Well, well, well. What was Clarissa doing out in the woods after curfew?

She saw me standing there, staring at her, and she paused at the edge of the road. "What the hell are you doing out here?"

"I'll answer that question if you do," I said.

She eyed me. Her mouth looked swollen, and I saw twigs in her hair. "What I'm doing is none of your damned business."

"Well, then, ditto."

"Whatever." She walked forward and stumbled. She paused, taking a deep breath, and then moved again. She grimaced. That's when I realized she'd been walking slowly because something was wrong with her left leg.

She limped some more and then paused, drawing in another shuddering breath.

I sighed. Then I crossed to the middle of the road. "I'll help you."

"No, thanks."

"Okay, then I'll call Ms. Chiles. Then we can both explain what we're doing out of school." I smiled. "I have permission." I took refuge in the truth. "I went on a field trip with my independent studies instructor."

She looked at me, probably trying to see if I was bluffing.

"Yeah, then why aren't you at the front door ringing the bell to get in?"

"Because I'm *very* polite and don't want to disturb anyone."

She snorted in disbelief. Then she offered a shrug. "Fine. But don't think this makes us friends."

"Uh, no," I said. "That's never gonna happen."

She nodded, and with our mutual hatred established, she slipped an arm around my shoulders. I grabbed her waist, and with her leaning on me, we made our way to the locked door.

"I know," I said. "I can call Henry."

"Your ghoul?" she asked. "Don't be an idiot. Ghouls are bound by the school's code of conduct. They can't lie if asked a direct question by any school administrator."

"Can they lie at all?"

"Not really." She reached into her right pocket and pulled out a big black key with a skull and crossbones at the top. It looked too big to fit into the lock, but when she pushed it into the keyhole, it went in perfectly.

"Skeleton key," she said. "It'll open anything."

She turned the key, and there was a click. I pulled on the handle, and the door opened.

"Cool," I said.

"Yeah," she said in a sarcasm-laden voice, "super cool. Just like the 1970s."

I ignored her snark and helped her through the door. It shut behind us, and we headed across the dark room to the staircase.

"Not enough room for the both of us," she said.

"You go first. I'll prop you up if you fall or something."

Gratitude flashed in her eyes—at least, I thought it did. Then her expression went all snooty, and she started up the stairs. I followed one step behind.

She used the skeleton key again and opened the door at the top. She stepped through it and turned, holding the edge of the door and effectively blocking my exit.

"What are you doing?" I asked.

"Tell me why you were outside the school."

"No," I said.

"Tell me why, Molly."

"Why were *you* out there?"

Her lips thinned. "You're a joke. I've been training my whole life to be one of the Chosen, even before I had the Anubis dream. You're nothing. No one. You think Anubis will choose you because you're half Briarstock?"

"He's already chosen me," I said. "Live with it." I tried to push through, but she held firm. She was strong, and her face held a mixture of fury and determination. I had a bad feeling she planned to lock me in the basement. Or maybe push me down the stairs.

"You're not going to be the champion," she said through bared teeth. "I am."

I wasn't going to argue with her. Maybe Anubis had more than one champion. Maybe the Chosen would be a whole new reaper army. I didn't know. Only Anubis did. And PS? It would be awesome if he would actually convey some decent info. Wandering around here trying to figure things out on my own wasn't exactly working out.

"Fine," I said. "You'll be champion."

Her eyes narrowed. "You're not my competition."

Actually, I was. And I really wanted to kick her butt. "Let me through, Clarissa."

"No."

She shut the door in my face and locked it.

Even though I'd been sorta expecting her to do that, I still felt some shock. Wow. What. A. Bitch.

It was pitch-black down here, except for the pale line of light that shone underneath the heavy wooden door. I was back to the same choices as before: text my friends for help or call for Henry.

Awesome.

I leaned my head against the door and tried to think about the best option. If I called for Henry, he could potentially rat me out. If I called on my friends…well, that would be way too much explaining. They didn't know I was a reaper. Or at least one in training. Or a Briarstock. Or a big, fat liar.

I heard a noise, and before I could decide if I should shoot down the stairs and hide, or risk that some staff member was about to discover me…the door swung open.

I looked at the person staring at me, and launched myself forward.

"Rick!" I wrapped my arms around his neck. "How'd you know where to find me?"

"I saw that girl lock you in. Why'd she do that?"

"She's a jerk," I said. I pulled back, and the smile on my face faded. "What happened to you?"

He looked exhausted. And pale. And his eyes were red, as if he'd been crying. His clothing was messed up, and he had a scratch on his cheek.

"Are you okay?"

"Fine," he said. "Just got into a fight with a tree. Had to park down this hill and walk up." He smiled wearily. "I'm kinda tired, Mol."

"Let's go to my room. I'll fix up that scratch, and you can tell me what happened."

Rick put his arm around me and leaned on me. I forgot about everything, even stupid Clarissa. Being with Rick made me so happy. And he was always showing up at the right time. Sorta. "Did you go to Autumn's get-together anyway?" I asked.

"Nah. I was already on the way when I got your text, so I just waited for you."

"How'd you get into the school?" We reached my room and I pulled the key out of my back pocket.

"I've got my ways," he said, offering me one of those awesome twisty grins. Then he leaned forward to kiss me. My heart skipped a beat, and I met his lips.

He opened his mouth, and...ohmygod.

His breath was rank. Not I-just-ate-an-onion-sandwich... more like I-ate-roadkill stank.

I drew back.

His gaze was all dreamy, and I appreciated him looking at me like that, I really did. But I couldn't force myself to kiss him unless he brushed his teeth. And maybe flossed.

"Let's go inside," I said.

"What's wrong?" He tucked a loose strand of hair behind my ear. "You seem upset."

"Not at all," I said. Worried that he might try to kiss me again, I pushed open the door, and he followed me inside.

"Sit on the bench," I directed. "I'll get medicine for that scratch."

He did as I said, and I went into the bathroom and started searching the cabinets for antibiotic.

So, how could I suggest that Rick might benefit from a good tooth scrubbing? I didn't want to hurt his feelings, but there was no way I could kiss him again. Maybe I could offer to brush my teeth, and then say, "Hey, I've got an extra toothbrush, if you want brush yours, too." Then it wasn't so insulting. Probably.

Except I didn't have an extra toothbrush.

I opened a drawer and looked down. It was full of toothbrushes. Okay, delete previous thought. I had enough toothbrushes to last me for the next five years.

I found a tube of antibiotic and a box of bandages. They were sparkly pink, though, so I wasn't sure if Rick would be down with wearing one.

He sat on the bench, staring straight ahead. I sat next to him, and he slowly turned his head, as though it were too heavy to move. His eyes were even redder, and the wound on his cheek seemed worse.

"Man," I said. "Are you feeling all right?"

"Little dizzy," he said. "I…I didn't eat."

"Oh. Well, I've got snacks here. Even got a little fridge with Cokes and stuff."

"Not what I need, Mol. Thanks."

His hands were shaking, and his behavior was starting to scare me.

"Stay still." I swiped some gel on the wound, and when I pulled my finger away, I could see flakes of his skin stuck to my fingertip. Ew. What was going on with him? "Do you mind?" I held up the glittery bandage.

"Nah."

I put it over the wound lengthwise. It didn't really cover it, and it didn't seem to help much in staunching the ooze factor.

"Hey, Molly?"

"Yeah?"

"I don't feel—"

Rick slumped over, his weight bearing him to the floor.

Holy Anubis! My boyfriend had fainted.

Panic welled. I squatted next to him and patted his non-injured cheek. Then I leaned close. He was still breathing, but in a shallow, pant-y way. I didn't know what to do. Call Henry, risk exposure among the administration. Call my friends, risk their ire about my lying. Maybe even lose them.

Rick moaned, a sound full of pain, and I made my decision.

I flipped open the phone and texted the crew: 911. Briarstock dorm.

CHAPTER
18

"You used me, abused me,
Made me want, made me cry,
And now, you arrogant prick,
I want you to die."
~KAMINA SINGING, "DIE, BOYFRIEND, DIE"

AUTUMN SHOWED UP FIRST. WITH ALL HER GHOSTS, OF COURSE. They floated into the room and dispersed, apparently fascinated with my dorm. Rennie wasn't among them, and I wondered if he was still in druggie land. I didn't want to admit I was worried about a dead guy, but…well, I guess I was.

But right now I had the living to worry about.

Autumn wore a long purple nightgown and purple bunny slippers. "Oh, my," she said as she came inside and spied Rick. "What happened?"

As she got a look at my room, her eyes popped. "Sweet tea and Anubis!"

"So reap," said Barbie from the doorway. Behind her were Daniel and Trina. Daniel was wearing his trademark mirrored sunglasses, and Trina was in pink silk pajamas. Barbie was wearing something that looked like a black sack cloth.

They entered, and behind them, a zombie dressed in jeans, a T-shirt that said Have You Seen My Zombie? and sneakers. His hair was combed, and he had a beard. And glasses.

"'Bout time you invited us to the pad," said Barbie. Her gaze dropped to Rick. "Different circumstances would've been appreciated." She saw the direction of my gaze. "Oh. This is my zombie, Jon Lemons."

"Call him Jon," said Trina with an ornery grin. "Or Jonny."

The zombie opened his mouth and offered an irritated, "Uuuuuh."

"He hates that," admitted Barbie. "You have to call him Jon Lemons."

Everyone was silent for a moment as they took in the room, the prone boyfriend, and me.

"I guess I should admit that I'm Cynthia Briarstock's daughter," I said lamely.

"Oh, we knew that," said Trina. "We were waitin' for you to tell us."

"You *knew?*"

"Yeah. After Henry made a beeline to our lunch table and you seemed to absorb all that info about Cynthia...I had the school system hacked ten seconds after lunch," said Barbie. "We were waiting for you to decide to tell us. Sorry we bashed your mom."

"And I do apologize for being such a Negative Nelly about legacies," said Autumn.

"Thanks," said Daniel in a dry tone. "We appreciate it."

Autumn rolled her eyes. "You know we don't think about you being a legacy. You don't act like one."

"Neither does Molly," said Barbie.

I noticed that her arms were bandaged, thin red lines of blood marring the white.

"Don't ask," said Autumn in a low voice. She was standing on my left. "It's a touchy subject for all of us."

"What happened to boyfriend?" asked Trina.

Everyone gathered around Rick. I was still reeling from the info that my new friends knew about my so-called secret and had just been waiting for me to admit that I was a Briarstock. They didn't seem to care that I was a legacy after all.

"He passed out," I said. "He said that he was hungry. He looks like someone beat him up, but he said he ran into a tree." I was babbling, letting my fear override me now that I had backup.

"Tree, my ass," said Barbie. She looked at me. "What's the plan?"

"I have no plan," I said. My knees were starting to give out. Autumn grasped my arm and led me to the bench seat.

"Stick your head between your knees and breathe," she directed. "Where's your boyfriend from? Vegas, right?"

"Yeah," I managed. I did as Autumn directed and sucked in some steadying breaths. Some freaking reaper I was turning out to be. I was feeling strange with my semi-Yoga pose, so I sat up. Blood rushed to my head, and I got dizzy. Ugh. Perfect.

"Trina," said Autumn as she held on to my shoulder. "I think we should take him to Vegas."

"White girl say what?" said Trina.

"You have a plane," she pointed out. "And a very cooperative pilot."

"And a father who doesn't pay attention to anything you do," added Barbie.

Trina put her hands on her hips. "All true," she said. "But we have to get him to the private airport. How are we gonna do that?"

They all looked at me, and I said, "I don't even have my license yet. And I don't have transpo."

"You'll have to use Henry," said Daniel.

"But what if he gets caught?" I asked. "Will he get in trouble?"

"No," said Barbie. "*You'll* get in trouble."

"He can't lie," I said, repeating what Clarissa told me.

"Not if he's asked questions by Nekyia staff," confirmed Autumn. "So we just make sure he doesn't get caught."

"If I ask him to do this," I said, "then I'll do it alone. I don't want you guys here, in case he's forced to confess."

They all looked at each other, and I detected their relief. I figured they were glad they didn't have to explain why they wanted to bail. I guess we hadn't quite reached the "one for all, and all for one" mentality as friends quite yet. I was a little disappointed, but I totally got it. I didn't exactly want to get in trouble, either. But this was Rick, and he was worth it.

"What about you, Trina?" I asked. "It's your plane."

"No big," she said. "I'll just say you asked to use it, and I didn't know why."

"They are sooooo used to that excuse," said Barbie. "They'll buy it, too. Trina M.O. Plausible deniability, it's what all the politicians use."

"Don't worry," said Trina. "I'll make sure a limo is there to get him all the way home."

"That's awesome, Trina. Thanks," I said. "Thanks, everyone."

"No prob," said Barbie. "And next time we do movie night, you don't lie to spend time with boyfriend in your rad room."

I didn't correct her notion because I couldn't begin to explain the bizarre night I'd had with Ms. Chiles. "Next twenty movie nights are here," I said. "If this all works out and no one finds out about Operation Rick and I don't get kicked out of school."

"It'll be fine," said Autumn. She was being nice, but I heard the doubt in her voice.

"Yeah," I said.

"Let's roll," said Trina. "I need something cheesy and laden in fat to sooth my nerves."

Everyone waved goodbye, even the zombie, and left. I gave them a few extra minutes to get as far away from the dorm as possible. Then I said, "Henry."

He appeared in the blink of an eye. Just one minute not there, and the next...totally there.

"Okay. Weirdness," I said.

"If you say so, miss." His gaze took in Rick. "Is your young man all right?"

"Not really. I have to ask you for a mondo favor, Henry. Like big time."

"I serve the Briarstocks."

"Trina Molina is authorizing her plane to take Rick to Vegas. And a limo to get him home. I need you to take him to the airport."

"As you wish."

"Wait. Just that easy?"

Henry nodded. "It is my duty to serve you, Miss Briarstock. If taking this young man to the airport is what you need, then I shall do so."

"Thank you, Henry!" I enveloped him in a hug. He stiffly offered one back. When I pulled away, he looked at me and I saw him smile slightly.

"You really do remind me of Miss Lelia," he said. "I very much liked her."

"I think I would have, too," I said.

He nodded. "It's best that you get ready for bed now, Miss Briarstock. I will take care of everything."

"You're the best, Henry." I went into the bathroom and shut the door. I felt like a coward for letting my ghoul handle the situation, but I didn't know what else to do.

Later, when I came out of the bathroom from taking a shower and brushing my teeth, the room was empty.

I crawled into bed, but I didn't fall asleep for a long time.

The next morning, Henry confirmed that Rick had been delivered to his home. Rick didn't respond to any of my texts, and when I called his parents' house to check on him, nobody answered.

I almost called Ally to see if she'd walk to his house and

see what was up, but I decided to chill. Plus, the last time I'd talked to Ally, she sounded super distracted and still annoyed that I was avoiding Dad. Dad kept leaving me voice mails that were supportive and nice, which just made me feel worse about not talking to him. Almost as bad as I felt not hearing from Rick.

Rick would text me when he was feeling better.

But I had a terrible feeling in the pit of my stomach. I just wanted to hear that he was okay. Maybe then, I could breathe again.

I texted Gena and Becks to see how they were doing, and then, because I couldn't help myself, I asked if they'd seen Rick.

Not at school. Heard he had flu, texted Becks. Think he's grounded for eternity re: Reno?

Broken heart is more like it, responded Gena. He likes you. Went. To. Reno. 'Nuff said.

Wasn't feeling well when he left here, I texted back. Probably the start of the flu. Thanks, peeps. TTFN.

It seemed all was as well as could be hoped. So why did I feel like I'd missed something of major importance? I wouldn't feel better until I heard from Rick directly.

It was agreed, via a round of texting with my Nekyia friends, that I should keep myself busy and not think about Rick. I went to my classes, kept my head down and waited for someone to discover that I'd spirited away a non-student and totally used my ghoul and my friends to do it.

I felt awful for most of the day.

When I went to independent study, no one was there. Not a soul. I waited ten minutes for Rath to show up. At that point I wouldn't have minded if he gave me crap about how much of a brat I was. Maybe even kicked my butt a little. I even missed Irina.

I waited another five minutes. No one ever showed, so I headed to Ms. Chiles's office. She didn't answer my knock on the door, and I really didn't know who else to talk to about independent study, especially since Ms. Chiles had made it clear it wasn't supposed to be discussed with anyone. So, I bailed.

I figured the best way to spend my unexpected free time was to seek out the special archives in the library. I'd been once or twice to the main floor to look up stuff for my classes. Necro profs loved to give homework. I was kinda glad it was Friday, so I could get some breathing space.

Getting to the special archives meant going two floors down into the dark, small part of the library. The librarian, an older lady with *Miss Neff* emblazoned on her gold name badge, didn't question my entry into the gated area. She merely opened it up and gestured for me to go inside.

"Um, do you come back?" I didn't really want to be locked inside the tiny space with its overcrowded shelves and moldy smells.

"I stay here," she said. "I have the only key." She offered a frosty smile. "No one comes down here. *Most* aren't allowed."

"Oh." I walked inside, because dealing with Miss Neff was the opposite of fun. I wandered around the shelves. There didn't seem to be a system in place, certainly not the Dewey decimal, not that I'd ever understood it. I was more a Google kind of girl.

I don't know how long I poked around the shelves, but when I heard Miss Neff's long-suffering sigh, I went back to the opened gate. "Have you heard of a book called *Anubis and the Seventh Warrior?*"

"Yes," she said. She got a strange look on her face. "It went missing a couple days ago."

"What?"

"What interest do you have in that book?" she asked. "It's not typical fare for legacies."

"Homework project," I said. I shrugged as if the book wasn't a big deal. "But I'll just figure out something else."

Miss Neff nodded, though her gaze took on a suspicious gleam. Did she think I'd stolen the book and then returned to act as though I was looking for it? That would be a double-trick criminal genius type of move. Okay, maybe I shouldn't sell myself short—that *would* be pretty clever of me, had I done it. Huh. Well, at least someone would think I was a superspy bad ass.

"Well, thanks again." I waved at her and hurried off, taking the stairs two at a time while she locked up the section.

I headed toward my room, thinking about the missing book. Who would take it? Why? And did whoever snatched it know that the book might have something to do with my mother, and maybe even my own legacy at Nekyia?

I didn't know.

But I intended to find out.

CHAPTER
19

*"And Set was banished into the darkest part of the Shallows,
tossed into the deepest pit where no reaper dared to tread,
and bound into a magical prison created by the bones
of the old gods."*
~THE SECRET HISTORY OF THE REAPERS, AUTHOR UNKNOWN

No word from Rick. The school was on super lockdown, too, because a student had gone missing in the woods. I was trying to keep chill, but I knew that my vision about the necro boy who'd been doing drugs and then got attacked had come true. I really wanted to talk to someone about it—but who? I thought about finding Clarissa in the woods all banged up and wondered if she had something to do with the missing kid. Maybe she'd also had something to do with the dead girl. I had no idea why Clarissa would murder students—or how— but the whole situation creeped my out.

No one was allowed outside of the grounds, so everyone was looking for stuff to do inside the school. The population was getting restless, though, so hopefully the authorities would figure out what was going on and fix it.

I hadn't told anyone about my dreams.

I didn't know who to tell. Who could help me.

I'd debated seeking the counsel of Ms. Chiles, but I hadn't seen her. She was around, taking care of school stuff. But every time I stopped by her office, she didn't answer the door. I started lurking by the administrative office, but I was always told by blue-hair that Ms. Chiles had "just stepped out" or was "busy." Maybe she was avoiding me.

Rath would know what to do about the dreams. Probably. But he hadn't returned from his business trip, whatever that meant for a reaper.

I found it really strange that no one seemed to care what

I was doing during independent study. I had no instructor. I couldn't talk to Ms. Chiles—who wasn't returning voice mail messages, either. I supposed I could've told the office about it and gotten a new schedule, but I didn't want to do that. So I spent those hours working on the moves Rath and Irina had taught me.

Unfortunately, despite the school being shut down and all outdoor activities cancelled, anything scheduled for inside the school was still a go. Including the Nekros Society soiree. What a way to spend Friday night.

I looked at myself in the full-length mirror that was situated in my massive closet. The dress was simple but lovely, and a beautiful silver color. Henry had some stylist skills—my hair had been French-braided and intertwined with tiny white flowers. I even had on a pair of matching high heels. Well, not high by Autumn's standards, but plenty enough for me.

"So, how long do I have to stay?"

"An hour would be acceptable, so long as you are seen mingling."

"Henry, I don't think I'll like any of these people."

"That is not a requirement of being a Nekros Society member, miss."

"Okay. I am officially sucking it up." I patted my dress and took one last look at my hair. "Thanks, Henry."

"You are most welcome, miss."

The party wasn't actually too far from the legacy wing. I had to manage one flight of stairs and go down a narrow hallway to a banquet hall. I handed over my invitation, and the person basically standing guard at the door waved me inside.

The room had been decorated with skulls and black crepe paper. Nah. I'm totally kidding. It was all normal stuff—low lighting, soft music, low-key deco. People walked around carrying glasses and small plates of food.

My phone beeped, and I reached into my wristlet and pulled it out. The text was from Autumn: How goes the party?

I texted back: So far so boring. Will text if anything exciting happens.

Autumn sent me back a smiley face.

I walked toward the buffet table. I didn't see anyone I knew, and why would I? I hadn't really hung out with the legacies, and ever since Clarissa had locked me in the basement, she'd made herself scarce.

Until now.

There she was in the corner with her two idiot friends, looking fabulous. I caught her glance and turned away.

I picked up a plate and piled on some quiches, a bacon-wrapped thing and a pinwheel.

My phone beeped.

I balanced the plate and checked the text.

It was from Barbie: Lame, or what?

Extra crispy lame, I texted.

Knew it. Keep me apprised of any awfulness.

Will do.

I wandered around with my plate, nibbling the food, but my stomach was in knots. I didn't know how to talk to these people. I'd bet my grandparents would. Oh, yeah. Sandra Briarstock would be holding court right now.

"Good evening, Molly."

I froze. It was as if my very thought had conjured her. I turned and saw my grandmother and grandfather standing there, looking at me with slight smiles. Sandra wore a dress that seemed overkill for this party—it was silvery gray, a little prom-looking, actually. And Derek was in a tuxedo.

"We're only dropping by," said Derek. "We have a gala to attend in Reno. How has your first week been at Nekyia?"

"It's been interesting," I said. Then, to shock them, I offered, "Two kids have died."

"Yes," said Sandra and her lips thinned. "I've been in touch with Ms. Chiles about that dreadful situation. She assured me all precautions were being taken regarding student safety and investigations are ongoing. But if you don't feel safe, Molly, you can come home with us."

I blinked. It never occurred to me that my grandparents would be paying attention. I guess I should've suspected, given all the lectures about legacy. But this seemed more along the lines of caring about me.

"Thanks, but I'm good. Really."

Sandra nodded. "Very well. We thought…perhaps, you would like to come over this weekend."

Surprise #2. And she almost looked hopeful, too. But I couldn't quite bring myself to accept her offer. "I'm kinda buried in homework…maybe we could do it another weekend?"

She smiled. "Yes, of course." She leaned forward and gave me a peck on the check. Derek folded me into a quick hug. "Call your dad," he said into my ear. "He's worried about you."

"Good night, Molly," Derek said as he pulled back. "Sweet dreams."

Then they turned and left.

Relief flowed through me. Whew. Any more unexpected encounters and I might faint.

My phone beeped.

Okay, deets. Who is there? texted Trina.

Johnny Depp, I texted. Kidding! Clarissa's here.

She's nobody. Text me when you see someone awesome.

K.

I finished off the food, put the plate on a tray with a few dirty dishes on it, and went toward the bubbling fountain. Whatever was flowing down the three-tiered waterfall was pink and frothy. I held a cup under the flowing liquid, and then took a sip. Not bad for fruit punch, I guess.

My phone beeped.

What kind of food? texted Daniel.

Tiny.

Too bad. Look for cake. If it's chocolate, steal me a slice.

Sure.

I put down the glass, my stomach not really appreciating the syrupy drink. I looked at the phone's display and realized I'd been here for only fifteen minutes. Ugh. I wandered around some more, trying to look as if I was mingling. I made another circuit around the buffet table. Clarissa and her minions had vacated the corner. I didn't really feel like eating anything else, so I headed across the room.

The music went up a few notches, and I realized people were going onto the dance floor. I stopped at the edge, watching the elegant, staid dances of the couples. The music was…I don't know, classical or something. It wasn't the kind of dance music I was used to.

"Hello, brown eyes."

Startled, I turned and spied Rath standing next to me. He was dressed in a tuxedo, and oh-my-gods he looked hot, hot, hot.

"Where have you *been?*" I hissed.

He grinned. "Aw. Somebody miss me?"

"No," I said.

His grin widened. Then he cupped my hand in his and led me onto the dance floor.

I almost had a heart attack. "I can't dance to this stuff," I protested.

"Yes, you can. Hang on to me and follow my feet." He wrapped an arm around my waist, and I placed a hand on his chest. He took my other hand into his free one and lifted it.

We began to dance.

At first all I could do was think about following his feet and not stepping on them, but soon, I caught the rhythm, and I relaxed. For a dead guy, Rath felt solid enough. And warm. And he smelled really nice, too.

"Why did you leave? And why didn't you tell me?" I asked.

"Anubis called me into service."

"And you couldn't take two seconds to let me know?"

He studied my expression. "You really did miss me." He brought me a little closer, and I got those dang tingles. "Usually getting called in by the boss isn't something I can control. But I promise, Molly, if I have to leave again...I'll tell you."

"Good." I sniffed. "Because I really want to learn how to kick your butt."

He laughed.

Then we danced, and he said nothing else.

My stomach felt tight and jumbled. I couldn't stand it, so I finally asked, "Are you coming back to independent study?"

He looked down at me, his gaze glittering with that odd, dark emotion. It set my heart to tripping. "Do you want me to?" he asked in a soft voice.

I could've been a smart ass. I could've been a liar. But instead, I said, "Yes, Rath. I want you to."

The arm around my waist pulled me in tighter, and I was pressed more firmly against him. Vaguely, I thought about Rick. But my mind had gone foggy, and I was looking at Rath, at his expression, at his mouth.

"Molly," he whispered.

My breath hitched.

He leaned down, his gaze intent, and—

"Excuse me." Clarissa grabbed our arms and stalled us. "I need to talk to Molly."

"Uh, no, you don't." I jerked my arm out of her grip. "Go away."

"'Fraid not." Her gaze pinned mine. "It's important."

"The lady has made her wishes clear," said Rath.

Clarissa's gaze was drawn up to Rath's, and I saw her expression change. She offered a coy smile. "I'm sorry, but I really need to talk to her, Mr...."

Rath offered one lifted an eyebrow and silence.

Her mouth turned down. Her eyes flashed fire at me, as though she blamed me for Rath's response. "When I say important, I mean *important*."

"Fine," I said, sighing. I looked up Rath. "I'll be right back."

"That's okay, brown eyes. Song's over. I'll see you." He brushed his thumb across my chin then turned and sauntered away.

I sooooo wanted to kill Clarissa. Again.

"What is it?" I said between clenched teeth.

"Nekros work," she said. "Apparently, you're on the team now."

"The team for what?"

"We're hunting the soul stealer," she said.

"The soul stealer?"

"Yeah. That night you saw me coming out of the woods—"

"Oh, you mean the night you locked me the basement?"

"Ugh! Get over yourself. I was doing a routine patrol and I found a boy in the woods."

"Don't you mean found something that used to be a boy?"

Her gaze sharpened. "What do you know about it?"

I didn't think I'd be confiding to Clarissa Jacobs about the visions I'd had, but…she'd seen the boy, and she could confirm he'd been turned to stone and shattered.

I quickly explained my visions to her.

Clarissa was a Class A bitch, but she was also, unfortunately, intelligent.

"This started when you got here," she said. She grabbed my arm. "Are you the one doing it?"

"Right. Because I was standing on the road without a scratch on me and you came limping toward me… How did I manage that if you battled me and I ran off?"

"In the other direction," she admitted. "Damn. I was really hoping you were the problem."

"You're super sweet," I said. "In a bitchy way."

She let go of me. "We don't have time for this crap. C'mon."

I followed her. We left the banquet hall and headed toward the legacy dorms. We passed mine, and one more, and finally reached another.

"We're here, Dad," she said as we entered the luxurious suite.

"Miss Briarstock," said Mr. Jacobs. "Glad you could join us." He didn't sound glad at all, but I knew the reason I was standing here was because of Ms. Chiles. She was next to Mr. Jacobs, dressing in a black outfit.

"My name's Bartolucci," I said. "Not Briarstock."

Mr. Jacobs sneered at me.

What a jerk.

"Here," said Ms. Chiles tossing me some clothes. "Get dressed. Shoes are over there. We have to be on the roof in five."

"The roof?" I asked as I toed off my shoes.

"Helicopter," said Clarissa. "We're going to Vegas."

★ ★ ★

We'd been told to fan out over Fremont Street and look for anything unusual. Considering we were smack in the middle of downtown Las Vegas, that description wasn't much help.

It was Friday night, so the street was crowded. The blast of music from the Fremont Street Experience was tremendous. I'd done a report about it once. I knew that the canopy stretched for four blocks over the area once known as Glitter Gulch, that more than twelve million LED lamps lit it up, that two hundred and twenty speakers emitted 550,000 watts of sound.

No matter how pretty the tourism honchos tried to make downtown, the glam veneer was thin and the real Vegas dirt was thick. Especially in the nooks and crannies surrounding the shiny pedestrian mall with cheap gambling, cheaper buffets and "free" entertainment.

I'd been given an earpiece, like some CIA spy, and I could hear other people from the team checking in. I could not believe I was suddenly some reaper teen super ninja freak.

Nobody bothered me. Most people intently ignored me, as if they wanted me to be invisible. It was a vibe, I think. I didn't control it, and I didn't know how to turn it off. Maybe Rath could show me.

This reaper stuff was like opening a beautifully wrapped present on my sixteenth birthday and getting a box full of scorpions.

The dead looked almost alive, so much so that it was hard to tell everyone apart. Well, unless a ghost was attached to a SEER. Then the spirits looked as thin and see-through as paper-dolls. Ghosts were energy, and the SEER sucked just enough out of them so that they couldn't escape its tethers.

The closer I got to Fremont Street, the more crowded the sidewalk became. At one particular point, people were giving wide berth to something. When I caught up, I saw what—or rather who—they were avoiding. A woman in a multicolored dress and flip-flops stood there, holding a cardboard sign. The big, block letters stated: FREE THE SPIRITS!

"Natural law has been violated!" she wailed. "We have taken from heaven! We have opened the doors to hell!"

She wore a headdress that dripped with silver beads. Every time she made a proclamation, the beads rattled. Her makeup was garish and theatrical, and strands of gray hair escaped from the odd headgear.

I stopped next to three or four people who were actually listening to her. Propped against the brick wall behind her was another hand-lettered sign that declared her president of the Society Against Spirit Enslavement. I thought about how much Ally would enjoy this woman's spiel. My sister loved a good protest.

"We must free the spirits!" she cried. Her gaze swept through her few listeners, and then rested on me. Her eyes widened. "You." She took a step back. "I'm not ready," she yelled. "I have more to do. Away from me, Death!"

CHAPTER
20

"Zombie hunting is a sport in most countries except the United States, where it is illegal. However, that hasn't stopped zombie hunts on private lands. The English have done zombie hunts longer than fox hunts. France's annual La Chase de Morts has been around since the French Revolution in 1793, when King Louis XVI was turned into a zombie, chased by citizens and then beheaded."

~THE UNOFFICIAL GUIDE TO ZOMBIE HUNTING
BY DILLARD MAHONEY

I STARED AT HER. WOW. SHE WAS LEVEL TEN CRAY-CRAY. AND that was a whole lot of crazy. Plus she was outing my reaper abilities, which was so not cool.

"Do you not see?" she screeched as she pointed to me, her be-ringed finger quivering. "The reapers are without jobs, and they will take any souls they please. We must give them back the ghosts!"

"Sylvie." A uniformed police officer stopped his downtown stroll to take in the scene. "I've told you before. You can't panhandle here."

"I'm *preaching*," she said, affronted. She scooped up the plastic bowl at her feet, which had some change and a few bills in it. She clutched the sign in one hand and the bowl in the other.

He rolled his eyes. "Move it along," he said, pointing down the street. "I don't want to arrest you."

"I shall take my message elsewhere!" she declared.

"Take yourself home," he insisted. "Or you're going to jail."

I felt sorry for Sylvie. I agreed with her message, although she hardly seemed serious about it. The spirit harangue was just another entertainment to procure some coin and she was just another Vegas character, a story for the tourists to take home.

I turned…and felt as though I'd fallen into a snowdrift.

What the—

To my left, I saw a flicker of black. I felt something. Someone. This felt familiar. If I tried to focus on the flicker, it slipped away. Frowning, I reached out with my power and pushed aside the odd energy blocking my view.

Rath appeared in front of me.

He was back in his regular wardrobe. Both the T-shirt tucked into his jeans and his sneakers were black. He crossed his arms, which showed off the muscles. Did he do that on purpose?

"What are you doing here?" I asked.

One chocolate eyebrow rose. "I don't think *you* should be here, Molly."

"Well, I am," I said. "Apparently, part of being a Nekros Society member is chasing after soul stealers."

"This won't end well, brown eyes."

"Thanks for the vote of confidence."

Fury flashed. "You are so stubborn! You're vulnerable out here. You're not ready, damn it." He snaked out a hand and grabbed my elbow. "You gotta come with—" He glanced over my shoulder, and his eyes widened. "Molly!"

I turned to see what he was freaking out over, and saw Clarissa a couple feet behind me. She aimed a big, black ball of pulsing energy. It hit Rath full force and he disappeared.

"What the hell are you doing?" I yelled at her.

"We don't have time for your love life," she said, fury boiling. "Do your job." She gave me one last evil look, then slipped away into the milling tourists. Okay. Dude. I had a healthy respect for Clarissa now, because I didn't think anyone, other than Anubis, could kick Rath's ass. And she'd done it with necro magic. I'd kinda expected Rath to pop back in and punch Clarissa, but he hadn't. Was he okay?

I didn't have any way to find out.

Well, my job was to find a soul eater and…call in the cavalry. Rath was right. I shouldn't be out here. I wasn't prepared.

And why they'd want me on the team when they hated the idea of me being in the Society... It made no sense.

I strode forward and noticed the hapless Sylvie ducking into an alleyway, her arms full of signs and the plastic bowl.

I wandered through the mass of people in the brightly lit mall area, occasionally stopping at kiosks to view the wares. I watched one of the canopy light shows. Like most native Las Vegans, I tended to ignore the flash. I wasn't old enough to gamble, and I wasn't stupid enough to try.

On the concert stage at the opposite end of the mall, a ghost of an Elvis impersonator offered a fifteen-minute show. He was good, right down to the "Thank ya, thank ya very much." Vegas had a lot of impersonators, alive and dead. Nobody had been able to call forth the actual ghost of the King, not even the company that had bought the rights to his spirit. It had led to speculation that Elvis wasn't actually dead.

Many celebrities sold the rights to their spirits for limited engagements to various venues. They often had the same managers in death that they'd had in life. Not every "callback" was successful, though. Spirit energy was fickle. As for regular folks, well, they were just screwed. The process for getting a spirit waiver was complicated and expensive. If you weren't a millionaire, then spirit-you was pretty much up for grabs.

According to the check-ins I was hearing in the earpiece, nobody was having luck finding the "unusual." Surely they had some sort of clue about the soul stealer. They hadn't said what had led them to downtown Vegas, or what the soul stealer looked like. Someone had mentioned energy surges, or something. Gah! I really didn't know what I was doing. Still. The directions had been clear: when you find the thing sucking out people's souls, call for backup immediately. Ms. Chiles and Mr. Jacobs would then subdue the whatever-it-was.

I decided to head back. I was unnerved by the lack of a sign, maybe a freaking clue, about my so-called job as part of this team. I didn't have a good feeling about any of this.

"Excuse me, miss?"

I turned and found myself facing the same cop who'd busted Sylvie the Preacher earlier. Crap. I was underage and it was after midnight. I couldn't believe I had gotten caught. I couldn't exactly send out a code to the other necros without making the cop suspicious. You'd think the Nekros Society would've clued in the local PD about our mission. Or maybe not. We didn't want to panic tourists.

"Miss?"

I affected an innocent expression. *"Da?"*

He frowned. "You speak English?"

I shook my head, trying to act as if I couldn't understand him.

"There's a curfew," he said slowly and loudly, as if I were stupid and deaf. I took offense on behalf on foreigners. "Are your parents here?"

I brightened. *"Da!"* I made excited gestures, pointing at a group of people down the street.

"I'll escort you," he said, gesturing for me to walk ahead of him. "You're too young to be out here alone."

I had an idea that he didn't quite believe my Russian act. I turned and walked determinedly toward the people I'd pointed to, wondering how long I could push the charade until I had to make a break for it.

A woman's piercing scream stalled us.

"Wait here," the cop said sternly, pointing to the ground and making a gesture that I assumed meant "stay." He unsnapped the holster of his gun and headed toward the commotion. Three drunken women were leaning against each other as they peered into the darkness of alleyway. The middle chick was the one making all the fuss.

"Oh, my God!" she screamed. "That crazy bitch is dead!"

"Um, guys?" I said into my mic. "I might've found that unusual thing we're looking for." I told them where I was.

"On my way," said Clarissa in my ear. Man, I did not like having her voice in my head.

I didn't want to find out if there really was a dead body or just a passed-out homeless person. Nor did I want to wait for the cop to come back. But I didn't have a choice.

Clarissa loomed ahead of me and grabbed my elbow. "Come on."

I allowed her to haul me the short distance to the edge of the alleyway. The cop had drawn off the hysterical women, who were now hugging each other and babbling. He was trying to calm them down, and he didn't notice us slip past him.

Clarissa let go of my elbow, and I followed her deeper into the narrow alley, resigned and fearful. She took out a flashlight from the band around her waist, and the wide beam cut through the dark and soon revealed the prone form of the female preacher.

Sylvie lay in a pool of blood. Her eyes were wide, but not empty.

"She's alive," I said.

"Barely," said Clarissa. She knelt down and studied the poor woman. "Her soul is still—"

She was knocked to the side, the flashlight slipping from her hand and rolling until its beam shone beyond Sylvia. Clarissa flew across the alley, into the deeper dark. I heard a thud and a wounded moan.

Rick stumbled into the light, landing hard on his knees. His eyes were completely red, and the wound on his face had enlarged. Skin was flaking off.

"Molly," he said. "You're here."

His voice was raspy, as though his throat had been rubbed with sandpaper. "So…hungry."

I was horrified. I couldn't move, I could only watch as Rick cupped his hands and leaned over Sylvie.

"Stop!" I cried. "What are you doing?"

"I have to," he said. "It's the only way."

"Did you do this, Rick? Did you hurt her?"

He blinked up at me, and I didn't recognize the look in his eyes at all. He put his hands over her heart, and to my shock, I saw Sylvia's soul begin to stream upward into his palms. He leaned over as if he was going to drink it.

"No!" *Rick* was the soul stealer? Oh, Anubis! I jerked into motion, and jumped over Sylvie, knocking Rick away from her. "Stop it, Rick!"

"Don't want to hurt you," he said. "Please, Molly."

The pleading in his tone nearly killed me. What had I done to him? I stayed between him and Sylvie. "You can't do this. It's wrong."

"Have to." He reared up and hit me across the face, hard. "Move!"

I staggered away, but I righted myself. Tears fell, but Rath's voice was in my head, an echo of training, telling me to go low and hit hard. I used a low kick to knock Rick off balance, and followed with a punch to the chest. He fell, and I jumped on top of him.

He struggled, and he was supernaturally strong.

But so was I.

I couldn't let him go down as the soul stealer. I couldn't let him be taken by Nekros. I owed him that much.

"Henry!"

He appeared instantly. "Miss?"

"Take him," I said, my tears clogging my throat. "Keep him safe."

"Yes, miss." The ghoul lifted me off with one hand, and then leaned down and punched Rick hard in the face.

He went limp.

Henry scooped him up, and said, "I will take care of him."

"You have to get Rath," I said. I swallowed the knot in my throat. "Do you know him? He's a reaper. Clarissa…did something to make him disappear. I don't know what."

"I know how to contact reapers, miss. I will find him."

I nodded and watched him carry away the boy I should've let die.

I went to check on Clarissa. She was out cold. I tried to call for the others, but my earpiece was gone. It must've been knocked out when Rick hit me. My face throbbed, and my lip was swollen.

I returned to Sylvie and stopped cold.

Irina was kneeling next to the woman. She looked up at me. "Are you here to reap her?"

"*Nyet,* stupid girl. She's almost gone. And when she goes— you grab her soul and you come with me."

"What?" I backed up a couple of steps. Irina and I had practiced soul-binding magic in independent study. But never with an actual soul. What the hell was I supposed to do with a loose soul? Carry it around in my hands? "How do you expect me to cart her soul away?"

Her answer was a steely stare.

"Why?" I asked. "And don't tell me Anubis said so!"

"She's dead."

I looked down at Sylvie. Irina had picked up the flashlight and aimed it at Sylvie's face. She hadn't made a sound at all or tried to utter any last words. She'd just…died. And now she was in danger of being a spirit. But before someone could be a ghost, their soul had to reject the Light.

When I looked back up, Irina was pointing a big, nasty-looking black gun at me. "She's dead," she repeated. "And you will be, too, if you don't take her soul."

I swallowed as new fear gouged at my insides. "Hoo-kay," I said.

The world around me went gray. Just like with Rick, I was somehow blending into the Shallows. It was like the presence of a soul drew me in—it was easy, like moving from one room to the next. Not even Irina had offered an explanation about why I could go into the Shallows.

I saw Sylvie's soul pop free, just like Rick's had when he'd almost died, except the orb hovering above Sylvie was teardrop-shaped and purple. Once again, I heard the strange music, saw how Sylvie's soul danced upward. She wasn't going to stick around. For a moment I was glad she wanted to leave the earthly plane.

Irina was watching me. Waiting.

I lifted my hand, cupped my palm a little, and as Irina had taught me, said, *"Adstringo."*

The soul floated toward me, completely intact. That single word had bound it—not only so that it couldn't separate, but so that it would come to me. The soul settled like a tamed bird into my hand. It had worked.

"You got it?"

I nodded, staring at the pulsing orb. I didn't know what to do with it. It wasn't like I had a sandwich baggie handy. I carefully put Sylvie into one of the bomber jacket's pocket and zipped it up.

The Shallows faded away, and then I was standing in the dark alleyway with a reaper and a corpse.

Nausea roiled.

"Why didn't you do it?" I asked dully.

"Because it is not a reaper gift, foolish one. You think we can handle the souls as you do? We must wait, untether, guide. You can control them. Touch them."

I didn't have much to say about that. Since I was only just

learning about my reaper gifts, I didn't know if Irina was telling the truth or not.

"What now?" I asked.

"We walk." She waved the gun at me. "Not far. Stay a little ahead of me. Don't run. I will shoot you, Molly. And not even Anubis will be able to save you."

CHAPTER
21

"Destiny sucks."
~Molly Bartolucci

WE DIDN'T TALK. AND I DIDN'T TRY TO RUN. TEN MINUTES passed before we were turning into a parking lot for a place called Casa Villa. People spilled out from opened doorways, smoking and drinking and laughing. Music boomed from both sides of the U-shaped building.

"Every weekend," said Irina in disgust. "Fights. Idiots over-dosing. Police. All the time, police!" She sighed. "Go to the middle unit."

I hunched into my jacket and walked through the parking lot. I got shouted offers of cigarettes, beers, joints and one joker promised to give me "the night of my life."

I ignored everyone. Except the woman with the gun.

But I couldn't ignore the car that screeched into the parking lot and stopped about two inches from my thigh. The high-beams of the Jaguar pierced me, and I shielded my eyes as I stumbled back, my heart hammering.

Four doors opened and four men exited. They were dressed in dark, expensive clothes and wore menacing expressions. Three of the men passed by, unconcerned they'd almost mowed me over, but the fourth stopped and looked down at me. He was built like a linebacker. His head was shaved, and his eyes looked like chips of Arctic ice. His face was scarred on one side, a web of damaged skin that went from his tem-ple to his neck.

"You are very pretty, *little rabbit*," he said in a thick Russian accent. His gaze devoured me, and I went cold. The look in his eyes sickened me. "When my business is finished here, I find you."

I swallowed the knot in my throat. Fear made me go numb, made me stare at him with wide eyes.

He lifted his hand and I flinched. He chuckled as he drew one blunt fingertip down my cheek. "You are sweet little rabbit." He leaned close until his big, broad face was a couple inches from mine. My heart thundered in my ears, and adrenaline spiked. His ashy breath ghosted over my mouth. "I like to chase my little rabbits."

Irina spouted off in a string of irritated Russian. The big man looked at her and laughed. Then he chucked me under the chin, turned on his heel and joined his companions. When he looked back, I was frozen in the beams of the headlights, held hostage by the awful power of his threat.

He tossed me a grin that made my skin crawl, then followed the other men into the same unit Irina had pointed at.

"Stupid girl!" Irina stopped in front of me, the gun pointed at me from the depths of her leather jacket. "Come." She gestured for me to follow her, and she headed toward the apartment. My steps slowed. I didn't want to go in there—not after that guy had threatened me.

"Why do you stop?" Irina whirled and gave me the evil eye. "Come, come!"

"That guy was…scary."

"Pah! Did I not teach you to be strong? We go now."

I reluctantly followed Irina into the apartment. A tall, thin man dressed in a cowboy shirt, denims and shiny black boots stood alone in the luxuriously decorated living room. Whoa. It was like walking through the door of a homeless shelter and ending up in a palace.

"My sister returns," he said, smiling faintly. "She has the soul?"

I hoped I still had the soul. I'd stuck it in my pocket as if it was a baseball instead of Sylvia's essence. It was disrespectful. I felt ill about what I'd done, and what else Irina might ask of me.

"Yuri, Molly. Molly, my brother Yuri."

Yuri executed a half bow. "A pleasure." He looked at Irina. "The box, darling sister."

"Are you a—um, you know?"

"A *you know?*" he mocked. "Such a silly little girl. *You* are the one the Oracle prophesied?" He laughed meanly.

I looked at Irina, but she was walking away, down the hall toward the far back bedroom. My heart leapt to my throat. I didn't want to be left alone with Yuri.

"You made quite an impression on my friends."

I nodded. I don't know where they'd gone, but I was glad I didn't have to see Mr. Arctic Eyes. He scared me. I shuffled my feet, unable to still my nerves. I wished Irina would hurry up. Ironically, I felt a little safer with her around. Yuri had a drink in his hand—a tumbler filled with amber liquid. He took a small sip then he grinned at me.

I didn't like that grin, or the feeling I got about what it meant.

Irina strode back into the room carrying a small obsidian box.

"Have you seen a soul box before?" asked Yuri. He put his drink down on the coffee table and took the box.

Irina snorted.

"Now, now, sister dear." Yuri stroked the obsidian square. "A soul box is rare and very old. Only a few ancient Egyptian reapers knew how to make them and for whatever reason, that knowledge has been lost. No one has been able to recreate a soul box—at least not one that works." He waved fingers at me. "Come. Give me the soul."

I couldn't bring myself to deposit what was left of Sylvie into that soul box.

"Incentive, sister, for our friend who is too burdened by her conscience."

Irina pulled out the gun. "I will shoot you."

"I know, I know, I know. You're *ruthless,*" I said. I unzipped my pocket, reached in carefully and extracted the purple teardrop.

Yuri laughed, obviously delighted by the oddness of my soul stashing. "Is it there?"

He turned to his sister, who held up a strange, diamond-shaped, milky gray glass to her left eye. She sucked in a breath. *"Da,"* she said in wonder. "She has done it, Yuri!"

"Into the box!" he demanded. He opened the lid. I was disappointed to see that it just looked like a regular box. Nothing was on the inside—not even carved spell work or reaper symbols.

I guided the soul into its new home. It was reluctant to go, but it obeyed me. When that which had been Sylvie dropped inside, I nodded to Yuri.

He snapped the lid shut.

"Good," he said.

"You're a traitor, Irina," I said in a shaking voice. "You're doing this for Set!"

Yuri laughed. "You said she was dumb."

"Not dumb enough," muttered Irina. She tossed the glass to her brother who caught it in the hand not holding the precious soul box. "We go."

"Go where?"

"Disneyland," she snapped.

"Beat that attitude out of her," suggested Yuri. "She must be more malleable." He patted the box. "We need only three more." He glanced at me. "You are valuable to us," he said. "So you will probably live. For a while."

I got it now. Irina had somehow tracked me when I hit Vegas. She'd known about Rick, too, I had no doubt. Why had she waited until I came here? Why not just kidnap me from Nekyia and be done with it?

"Come," she said. "I'll show you to your room."

"Get comfortable," said Yuri.

Irina escorted me through a door into a scummy little apartment. "The windows are barred. The front door is welded shut, and there is necro magic keeping you bound. You cannot leave." She shut the door behind us. Then she leaned in close and whispered, "Rest, Molly. And then prepare."

"For what?" I whispered back.

"Opportunity." She patted my cheek, and then turned. The door shut behind her and the lock snicked.

I couldn't figure out Irina. Was she friend or foe?

I didn't realize I'd fallen asleep on the bed until a backfiring car startled me awake. I rose up on my elbows and glanced around the darkened room. The door to the tiny bathroom was open; weak light splashed from the light that had been left on in there.

"Molly!"

Rennie was floating near the bed, panic in his gaze. "Get down!"

I heard the urgency in his tone, so I scrabbled off the bed and huddled on the floor. He squatted next to me, his velvet brown eyes wide with fear.

"How did you get here?"

"I followed you. From Nekyia. I've been invisible. Watching out for you."

"Why?"

"Because."

Another car backfired, and another, and then a barrage of *poppoppoppop*. Gunshots! My heart nearly stopped beating. I flattened onto the floor and covered my head. I pressed against the thin carpet and tried not to breathe in its stink. I felt Rennie's hand stroke my hair. I hadn't realized I could feel the touch of ghosts, too. It should've been obvious, I guess, since I'd felt Aunt Lelia's touch, too.

Then the terrible noises stopped. People were screaming and crying. I heard men yelling in Russian, then car doors slamming, and tires burning pavement.

"It's okay," said Rennie. "It's over."

I sat up, shaking, and scrubbed at my cheeks. More cars squealed away. The booming music turned off, and in the silence, I heard apartment doors slamming.

I accepted Rennie's chilly hug. I was still amazed that he felt real to me. But Rennie's odd comfort was better than none.

He pulled away and offered a half smile. He tilted his head. "There's been some kind of adjustment in the spell work around this place. It's weak. I think I can get the door unlocked."

I rubbed my arms to relieve the chill of Rennie's embrace. "Thanks, Ren. You're a good friend."

"I'm a ghost. You've got too much heart, Mol. You don't turn away no matter how bad it gets." He brushed the hair out of my face. "Leave the dead and the dying alone."

"I can't," I said. "I'm a reaper."

"You're a sucker." He straightened and waited for me to climb to my feet. "I'll make sure the coast is clear. Then we'll bail."

"I gotta go to the bathroom first."

"Really?" he said. "Now?"

"Sorry, dude." I went into the bathroom. When I was finished, I washed my hands. I stared at myself in the cracked mirror. I was too pale. Shadows bled under my eyes and my lips were chapped.

"Molly?"

Crazy as he was, Rennie was the only one around I could rely on. *The dead and dying.* They were mine, I thought, the dead and the dying.

"Mol? Seriously. You need to come out."

I opened the door and stepped into the room. Fear punched through me and I took a step back. Then I realized the man standing there wasn't Arctic Eyes.

He turned toward me, his blue eyes wide with shock. He was talking rapidly in Russian. I understood the pleading tone, but not the words. His hands were pressed against his stomach and doing very little to stave the blood burbling from the wound.

Horror filled me.

Yuri was begging for his life.

Only he didn't know he was already dead.

"Weary of utterance, seeing all is said;
Soon, racked by hopes and fears,
The all-pondering, all-contriving head,
Weary with all things, wearies of the years;
And our sad spirits turn toward the dead…"
~FROM "DEATH, TO THE DEAD FOR EVERMORE"
BY ROBERT LOUIS STEVENSON

"THOSE GUNSHOTS WERE PRETTY OBVIOUS. THE POLICE WILL probably be here soon," said Rennie. He stayed next to me, almost protective. "I got the lock jimmied. You need to go, Mol."

"In a sec." I walked forward and stopped before the devastated Yuri. He was silent now, his craggy face serious.

I noticed a gossamer line, as silvery and thin as moonlight, stretching from Yuri to…somewhere. It flowed through the door, shimmering. "You see that, Ren?"

"So?"

"I think he's still attached to his body."

"Not for long," said Rennie. "He's a dead man."

Yuri stared at me. Hope glittered in his eyes. "You will save me?" he whispered.

I didn't answer. Because I didn't want to save him. Was he supposed to die? Or live? I went with my instincts. I took his hand, which felt like clutching icicles. He clenched my fingers, his red with ghostly blood, and when I got to the locked door, it swung open easily.

Rennie came with us. "This is a bad idea!" he said.

I didn't respond. Because I knew it was a really bad idea. People didn't stop being people just 'cause they died. Irina's directive for me to be ruthless was a shout in my conscience. Unsurprisingly, the line went to Yuri's living room—into the floor behind the couch.

Rennie joined us and we all stared at the brown shag.

"See?" Yuri pointed at the line…no, at a crease in the carpet.

I squatted down and pressed my fingertips underneath it. "It's a trapdoor."

I lifted it, and we peered down into the hole.

"Ren, go take a peek."

"You're stupid," he said. "You know that, right?"

"Just go."

Rennie hovered above the escape hatch and lowered himself inside. When he reached the floor, or so I assumed, he looked around. "I see a light at the end of the tunnel."

"Very funny," I said.

Yuri used Ren's floating trick, and I followed the ghosts into the small concrete room. The gossamer line shone in the dark, and we followed it down a hallway to a closed door.

"Open it," said Yuri, excited. "Hurry."

I turned the handle and yanked open the door. I wasn't expecting the sumptuous room. Why suffer without luxuries while waiting out your enemies? Too bad Yuri hadn't gotten here before being fatally wounded.

Persian carpets covered the concrete floor. Most of the furniture was big and dark, from the leather couches to the towering cabinets filled with books, CDs and DVDs. Even the entertainment center with its huge flat screen was gigantic. I wondered how they'd gotten all this crap down here.

In the back corner of the room was a full-service bar. Booze and glasses were lined up on mirrored shelves. Overflowing ashtrays lined the marble countertop. Five barstools were tucked next to the brass footrest. The stale air down here smelled like cigarette smoke and mold.

"Here!" cried Yuri. He stood near the bar pointing at a wall. Rennie and I hurried to join him. I peered at the light switch that Yuri's ghostly finger was poking. I flipped it, and the lights above the bar flickered on.

"*Nyet!*" he shouted. He put his palm up and made a pushing gesture. I glanced at the gossamer soul string. It was thinning and getting a lot less shiny. Still, I didn't want to rush inside another mystery room without some info.

"This is getting seriously Scooby-Doo," muttered Ren.

"He's still acting human," I said, as though I knew what I was talking about. "Can you go through and see what's behind there?"

"Oh, I get it. *I'm* Scooby-Doo." He slanted me a look and grinned. "Guess that means you're Shaggy."

"Har."

Ren laughed as he walked through the wall. Yuri realized he could do the same thing. He tested the theory by sticking a hand through, then his arm. He shrugged and then he, too, walked through the wall.

About two seconds later, Ren returned. "It's like a surgical ward in there, but no doctor. Our dead friend is in there, on a table. His ghost is lookin' a little pale." Ren touched my shoulder, and I felt the chill of his fingertips through my jacket. "This guy ain't nice. You really think it's a good idea to try and save him?"

"He's in pain," I said.

"The whole world's in pain, Mol. Doesn't mean you gotta try to heal everyone in it."

Who said I was going to try and heal anyone? I stared at him. "Just get me in there, all right?"

He rolled his eyes. Then Ren disappeared. I heard a soft pop then a hissing noise as the wall in front of me slid back and revealed the surgery.

Yuri stood near his body. Ren hadn't been kidding about the ghost's paleness. His skin looked as though it had been bleached. The gossamer line that linked him with his physical form had lost its shine, and it was trembling. I knew it would break soon, and when it did, Yuri had no chance to live again.

"What are you gonna do?" asked Ren.

"Just give me a sec." I'd never seen a soul connected to the body like this before—that ethereal string wasn't part of the soul…um, was it? Not knowing what else to do, I reached down and poked it.

It felt silky and warm. My fingers tingled with heat, with power and as I touched the soul-line, for lack of a better term, it went all shiny again. Somehow I was strengthening the bond between Yuri's spirit and his body.

"Da," said Yuri, excited. "I'll give you a big reward, Molly."

Be ruthless. "How many souls do you have?"

Yuri's gaze narrowed. "It is no concern of yours."

His arrogance was amazing. I plucked at the string again, then I let go. "What are you going to do with them?"

He remained silent. I don't know if he was trying to wait me out or consider his options. Maybe he figured out that I was the *only* option, me being what stood between him and death.

"I have four."

"Why do you need human souls?" I asked again.

"You were right about Set," he said. "That is all I can say." Impatience crackled around him, and his expression went ugly.

I made scissoring motions across the string. "Those souls for yours," I said.

He took in my measure, probably trying to decide if I had enough courage to do it. Maybe he saw the resolve in my expression because his face went mulish.

"Fine!" He cursed briefly in Russian, and then crossed his arms. "In the other room. In my safe. You save me, and I get the souls for you."

"Yeah," I said. "About that." I grabbed the string with both hands. "I don't need you to get the souls for me."

"What are you doing?" he asked.

"Being ruthless." I pulled on the string hard and it broke. It turned into glittering silver, and Yuri the ghost disappeared. His soul, looking like a shiny black ball of goo, popped out of his chest.

I didn't see a blue light, nor did I hear the odd but welcoming music. Instead I heard a snapping sound, a growling, and then the black yuck that was Yuri was sucked down into the floor.

"Day-amn, girl," said Rennie. "You lied to him. That's brass balls."

"I didn't promise him anything," I said. My heart hammered in my chest. Where had Yuri's soul gone? What did that snapping and growling mean? I didn't want to be in this room anymore. I didn't want to be anywhere near Casa Villa—especially if Rennie had been right about the police being on the way. Maybe they were already here. I looked up at the ceiling, as though I could somehow discern if the place had been overrun by cops.

"I'm getting the souls." I went out of the room, expecting Rennie to follow.

He didn't.

He was a ghost, and I wasn't going to worry about him getting out of here.

The safe was obvious enough. What Yuri hadn't thought about was that I didn't need a combination. I was a reaper. I knew I was stronger than that stupid box. I would call them, much the way I had Sylvie's soul. And I knew, somehow, they would come. I'd never felt so sure of anything in my life. If that box was reaper magic, then it should do what I wanted and let them out.

I flattened my palms against the safe. I opened my senses, and the moment I did, I felt the fluttering of the souls in the box. Four of them trapped inside, including Sylvie's.

"Come to me," I whispered.

I could feel them trying, but the box kept them secure.

"Enough, you," I told the box. "Open. Those are mine, you know."

It sounds weird, but I could feel the box's reluctance to let them go. It was resisting me, but finally, I felt the lid pop open.

The souls flowed out like escaped butterflies. They popped through the safe and hovered before me.

"I suggest you choose the Light," I said. "Because the other option doesn't look all that fun."

They bobbed up and down, in agreement, I guess. It seemed almost natural. The blue light sparkled down from the ceiling. I wondered about the idea of heaven, or whatever people wanted to call it. What was it like? Did souls become people again there and hang out? Or did they just join up with some beam of energy and…I dunno, become stars?

All the souls drifted upward, and none separated. The right magic had to be uttered for that. You know, I wasn't all that sure anymore that making zombies was a good idea. Not that my dad would be thrilled about my new take on zombification. I couldn't help but wonder what happened to the souls whose kas had been taken to animate their corpses. Did they go into the Light? Or somewhere else? What happened if their zombie died? Did the ka rejoin the other soul parts, or was it forever an orphan?

I thought about Rick and my heart seized. I knew Henry had taken him somewhere safe. And I knew I had to figure out a way to save him. Again.

"Molly."

I jumped and turned around. My aunt Lelia's sheut detached

242 *Michele Vail*

from a darkened corner of the bar. "Go, darling. The spells that held you here are broken."

"What are you doing here?" I asked. It seemed like I was asking that question a lot.

"Trying to help you."

"How did you find me?"

She smiled. "I can always find you, Molly." She offered a sad smile. "But you should know that a sheut obeys its master."

"Was it Yuri?" I asked Aunt Lelia. I reached out, wanting to help. I was a reaper, right? "He's gone. Maybe I can—"

"No," said Aunt Lelia. "Yuri didn't control me."

"Then who?"

Pain crossed her face, and she sucked in a shuddering breath. "I belong to Set."

Shock arrowed through me. "He's here?"

"Not yet. But he will be, Molly." She shuddered. "I have to go."

"Wait! Who's my father?" I asked. "Where's Mom?"

"I can't answer those questions, Molly. I'm sorry." She cupped my cheek. "Be strong. I'll help however I can, but when Set comes—and he will—I won't be able to break free of his control. I need you to understand that. I won't be in control of what I do."

"Yeah. I get it. Will I see you again?" I asked, thinking of the first time we'd met. And I wanted to help her. I would find a way, some way to free her from Set.

Aunt Lelia smiled, genuine warmth crinkling her eyes. "Not if I see you first."

Then she sank into the floor, a puddle of ink that joined the shadows.

Sadness crawled through me, along with exhaustion. This had been the longest night of my freaking life. I wanted to go home—my actual real home, and just get a hug and some food, and be with the people I loved.

"Hey, babe." I turned and saw Yuri leaning against the wall, his arms crossed. "Hi, I'm Yuri," he said in a bad Russian accent.

I stared at the corpse of Yuri, but here's the thing: I could see the blue outline of the ghost who'd wedged himself inside. Gross. "Get out, Rennie. You're not supposed to be in there."

"No way," he said. "You know how hard it was to get inside this bloated thing?"

"He's not alive. You're walking around in a dead body."

"I just haven't figured out how to work all the parts yet," said Rennie. "It's like being inside a meat puppet."

"Yuck!" I marched over to Yuri and grabbed him by the face. "Get out. Seriously."

Rennie-Yuri shuffled and tripped toward me, as though he'd forgotten how to walk (maybe he had). He spun on a slick black heel and went down. When Yuri hit the floor, Rennie popped free.

"Dammit." Rennie looked at Yuri with some regret, and then glanced at me. "You all right?"

"Yeah."

"Police!"

I shrieked and raised my hands, my heart tripping over in my chest. Slowly I turned around. Two cops were pointing guns at us. Well, me. They probably couldn't see Rennie.

Rennie's ghostly hand clasped my shoulder and offered me cold comfort.

"What happened?" The cop asking the question had a gun trained on me. The other officer circled around the room and knelt to put his fingers against Yuri's carotid artery.

"My name is Molly Bartolucci," I said slowly. I kept my

gaze on the police officer. "And tonight, this man had me kidnapped off the Vegas Strip."

The cop eyed me, his gun trained at my chest. "All right, Molly. Just one question. Did you kill him?"

CHAPTER
23

"It is said that the gods have fathered many children among human females. Anubis was quite fond of his priestesses, and some believe that the first reapers were born of these unions."
~THE SECRET HISTORY OF REAPERS, AUTHOR UNKNOWN

HANDCUFFS WEREN'T PARTICULARLY COMFORTABLE. AS I WAS hauled across the parking lot, I saw Rennie on the sidelines, his gaze on mine as the cop marched me toward a police car. Unexpectedly, he unlocked the cuffs and led me to the passenger side of the car. I got in, feeling numb. My face still hurt from where Rick had hit me earlier in the evening.

"You kinda killed Yuri," said the cop.

As I looked at him, the blond, blue-eyed muscle-head morphed into the dark-eyed, dark-haired form of Anubis.

I opened my mouth to justify why snapping Yuri's soul string wasn't exactly murder, but what came out was, "Where the hell have you been?"

He lifted one eyebrow. "Set's influence is getting stronger, and Yuri was very high in his ranks. My uncle won't be happy that you not only released the souls he needs to free himself, but that you also facilitated Yuri's death."

"Um, you know all that?"

He pointed to himself. "I'm a god."

"But you couldn't break me out of Set's magic?"

"It's not as easy you'd think." His gaze searched mine. "Did you not see the path I laid out for you?"

"No," I said, feeling teary-eyed and exhausted. "I'm just a kid."

"Not anymore," he said kindly. "I see the changes wrought by your gifts. At least you had the ring."

"*You* gave it to me?"

"Yes. It's special, Molly. Like you." He gave me a long look. "I expected you to have had more training by now."

"I have! Rath taught me some moves, and so did Irina!"

"Irina?" Anubis laughed. "Is that what she called herself this time?" He shook his head. "You have something she gave you. I can sense it."

I pulled the diamond out of my pocket. "She said I could rely only on myself."

Anubis took the diamond and studied it, then handed it back. "Yes. That's definitely something she would say."

I was silent for a moment. "She's not Yuri's sister?"

"Maybe in form," said Anubis.

I remembered all the gunshots that had woken me. "Is she...dead?"

"Oh, there's no doubt Irina is dead—she'd have to be for her form to be taken by Anput."

"Who's she?"

He was silent for a long moment, and then he offered, "I think she's still trying to figure that out."

"Why didn't you tell me there are other Chosen? And that more than one of us thinks we're your champion?"

"It's complicated. You are my champion," said Anubis. "And you will need the other Chosen when it comes time. I know it feels too heavy a burden, but you were prophesied long ago." He took my hands. "What you will offer the world matters very much, Molly. I know what you must do seems challenging, but you're strong. You can handle all that will come your way."

"Sounds like a total bummer."

"It is, yes." He glanced over my shoulder. "A friend of yours?"

I followed his gaze to Rennie, who stood at the edge of the parking lot, looking morose and lonely.

"Yeah," I said. "He's my friend."

The next thing I knew, Rennie was sitting in the backseat, his narrow face filled with shock. "Dude. You did not tell me you had such badass connections."

"Just remember that," I said, "the next time you think about pissing me off."

Anubis laughed. Then he grasped my hand. "It's time to go home, Molly. To see your family." He smiled. "Just for a little while."

He meant Al, of course. The reality of going home to the family that used to be mine was here… Well, I wasn't sure I wanted to.

"He's not my dad."

"Yes, he is. He did not sire you, but he claimed you. You should honor that."

"Why did he lie to me? Why did everyone lie?"

"To protect you," said Anubis. "Until it was time to tell you the truth." He put a hand on my shoulder. "Go home, Molly. See your family."

Home.

I could hardly let myself believe it.

And then, in the blink of Anubis's eye, we had pulled up to my house on Grimsby Avenue.

Anubis returned to his cop form and pulled into my driveway. For the longest moment, all I could do was drink in the house I'd lived in my whole life. It was as if I'd been watching a movie for too long, and upon leaving the theater, I viewed the rest of the world as small and unreal.

"I called ahead," said Anubis. "They're expecting us."

We got out of the car, and Rennie followed behind me, staying quiet.

"Molly!" Ally bolted from the doorway first and wrapped

her thin arms around my neck. She squeezed me so hard my trachea nearly collapsed.

But I hugged her back. I was so glad to see her. To know she was okay.

I overheard the low voices of Anubis the Cop and my dad. Then Nonna was there, chattering at me in Italian, alternating between hugs and shaking my shoulders. She wagged her finger at me, tears falling down her weathered cheeks, and then roped me in for another hug.

Then my dad was there, and he stood in front of me, awkward, his gaze haunted. "I'm so glad you're okay, Molly," he said. "The school called and said you got separated on some kind of field trip tonight. I didn't even know you were in Vegas."

I wasn't sure I had forgiven him. But I did know that I loved him. And I didn't want him to hurt anymore. I stepped into his arms and he squeezed me hard. His sigh of happiness drifted right through me.

I held on to him, so happy to be home, to be part of my family again. He finally pulled back, his gaze so filled with relief, so shadowed with pain, I felt my own heart squeeze. "Oh, Daddy. I'm sorry. I got really, really lost."

"Nothing to be sorry about. You don't have to go back to Nekyia," said Dad. "You can stay here. We'll figure something out. I don't want to lose you, Mol."

"You won't, Daddy," I said. I glanced over his shoulder, and caught the blue-eyed gaze of the god in disguise. "I want to go to Nekyia."

"Okay," said Dad, though I could see he was less than thrilled with my decision. "If that's what you want."

"It is."

Sometimes, you choose your destiny, sometimes it chooses you, and sometimes...it's a little of both.

CHAPTER
24

"O, Anubis! Mighty Anubis!
As you take his measure,
And weigh his heart as he stands before you,
Know that he was loved by many,
And will be remembered by all."
~FROM PRAYER TO ANUBIS

ONLY HENRY KNEW THE FATE OF RICK. I HAD WORRIED ABOUT my ghoul and my boyfriend all night, although my exhaustion helped me sleep a little. By the time I arrived at Nekyia on Saturday morning, it was nearly 10:00 a.m. and I'd already promised to meet my friends at noon in my room so we could break down my wild Friday evening. I wouldn't tell them everything—I couldn't. One thing I knew for sure was that the Nekros Society did important, secret work. And I wanted to be part of it. At least until Anubis needed me to fulfill the prophecy.

No pressure there.

But now all I could think about was Rick. Rick who had been sick, and stealing people's essences.

I had done that terrible thing to him.

My heart felt heavy as I trudged to my room. The minute I shut the door behind me, I said, "Henry."

He appeared instantly, looking as sharply dressed and old as dirt as usual.

"Where's Rick?"

"I will show you, Miss Briarstock."

I didn't correct him. I was a Bartolucci and a Briarstock, after all.

I followed Henry, heartsick. Surely I could save Rick. Just one more time. Find a way to put his soul back together. I was a reaper. I could do it.

By the time we hit staircases, rounded curves, went through hallways, I was completely lost.

"Here we are, miss."

Henry gestured toward the ornate wooden door.

"What am I walking into?" I asked Henry, feeling suddenly nervous.

Henry inclined his head. "Whatever it may be, miss, I am confident you will prevail."

He executed a half bow, then he spun and opened the door for me.

The room was small and lit only by a fire crackling in a huge hearth. It was so big, three people could walk inside it and stand there without being crowded.

Rath stood before the hearth.

"Hello, Molly."

I gasped and stepped toward him. "What happened to you? Where did Clarissa...?" At the look on his face, my words trailed away. He nodded toward a table, and I turned and saw Rick lying there, utterly still.

"What did you do?" I cried. I touched Rick's forehead. It was cold. But I could see the shallow rise and fall of his chest. "He's not well."

"No," said Rath. "He hasn't been since the night of your party."

Rath nodded toward Henry. "Stand guard."

Henry's gaze met mine. "I obey only her," he said. "She is the Briarstock in residence."

"Sounds like a good idea," I said. "I don't want him left alone."

"As you wish," said Henry. He took position near the door and faced it, a sentinel that would protect us from any intruders.

Ghouls took their orders way serious.

I grabbed Rath's elbow and dragged him over to the hearth. It was then I noticed the flames were black and the fire emitted no heat at all.

"What's going on?" I demanded.

"I know what happened now. I figured it out. Rick's soul separated into the five parts, and you lost a couple of 'em. He's a thrall, because you didn't let him die."

"Thrall?" I swallowed the knot in my throat.

"Not human, not zombie…your servant. No reaper can do what you do, Molly."

"Not human." I felt the hot ache of tears and turned toward the fire while I gathered my emotions into a little ball and tucked 'em away. *Ruthless,* I told myself. *Be freaking ruthless.*

"Reapers used to have thralls a long time ago. It was what the Egyptians made after zombies… It turned out badly, which is why no one does it anymore." His voice softened. "I know you didn't do it on purpose, but Rick isn't really Rick anymore. He's not going to get better. Not with his soul shredded."

"Well, what can I do?" I asked. I looked over my shoulder. "How am I supposed to fix him?"

For a moment, Rath said nothing, and the silence between us stretched thin. "You have to go to Maat for his soul."

"Maat. *The* Maat?" I asked, my voice shaking. "The judge in the weighing of the heart?"

"Yes. They're not just stories," said Rath. "Humans didn't get everything right—how could they? But there is an afterlife, Molly. And there are gods. And there is judgment."

"I get it."

I knew all about the weighing of the heart ceremony. It was part of the History of Necromancy course that was a required high school credit for graduation. Every soul was taken before Maat and weighed against that of a feather. If the heart—or the soul, rather—was heavier than the feather, the crocodile goddess ancient Egyptians called "the gobbler" ate it and it was all goodbye afterlife.

"I can get you past the gates," said Rath. "But then you're on your own. You have to walk Rick's path. Take his journey. That's the only way to get to Maat."

"Shouldn't he go with me?"

Rath hesitated. Then he turned toward me. "You have to take his soul with you, Molly." He put a hand on my shoulder and squeezed. "Today Rick must die."

"But you said I had to go to Maat for his soul."

"This isn't a rescue mission." Sympathy flashed across his chocolate-brown eyes. "You're escorting Rick's soul to Maat so that he can move on to his afterlife."

Rath let go of me and stepped away. I guess he figured I needed to process what was unfolding. Or maybe he didn't care. Or maybe he thought I would punch him.

All three were viable theories.

I stared into the odd fire and tried to wrap my brain around what Rath was telling me to do. Was he still pissed off that I'd accidentally messed up his reap?

He was arrogant, and sometimes a jerk, but making me take the soul to Maat if it wasn't necessary for me to do it seemed an extreme move even for him. I figured I had to escort Rick's soul because I was the reason it had gotten all split up.

"Everyone dies, Molly," said Rath. "You serve a purpose within the realm of death. All reapers do. Yes, everyone dies." He paused and stared at me. "Even you."

And just because Rick was a hot, high school football star who'd given me my first kiss didn't mean he'd received some kind of get-out-of-death card.

What would've happened if I'd just let him die when he supposed to?

Would I be here now? Maybe if I hadn't messed around with my powers, I wouldn't have gotten into all the trouble.

Maybe. Maybe. Maybe.

That was the thing about life. There really were no do-overs. And there were always more questions than answers.

I had broken Rick. And now I needed to fix him—even if that meant taking back the gift of life I'd given him.

"Okay," I said. "Let's go."

Rath rejoined me and sidled a glance at me. "I know it's difficult—"

"Save it," I interrupted. "I don't need a pep talk."

Rath looked as though I'd slapped him. I know I sounded tough, but the truth was that I was scared. He wanted me to walk into the Underworld, get to Maat and somehow find a way to fit Rick's soul into one piece.

And, oh yeah, get him all approved for the Light.

"We do this now?" I asked. "What about school?"

"I'll write you a note."

I wanted to ask where Anubis was—why he wasn't tasking me with this because, hey, he's the one who spent so much time giving me the "life is difficult and so's death" speeches.

"Molly?" The gentleness in his voice threatened to unravel my control.

"Where do I put his soul?" I asked. No way was I going to stick it in a pocket.

"Here." He lifted his palm and I watched a glass orb appear.

"What is that?"

"A gift from Anubis to help transport the soul. It's not a reaper gift, if you were wondering."

I took it from him and then crossed the room purposefully.

Rick was still unconscious. He was breathing only because I'd stuffed three-fifths of his soul back into his body. He'd been living on borrowed time, and it sucked, really sucked, that I had to take him.

But it was the right thing to do.

I'd known for a while now. Honestly, somewhere deep inside I'd suspected things might end like this.

"I'm sorry," I whispered. I put my hand on his chest, and I felt the wiggling of his soul parts, the confusion, the feeling that something was missing. The soul knew that it was incomplete, and that it was sitting in a body it no longer belonged to. I had, as Rath had put it, superglued it back in there, however unintentionally.

It would listen only to me.

I was a reaper. I was the Underworld's champion. I was the girlfriend who would never be.

"C'mon," I said to the imperfect soul. "Let's finish your journey."

It sounds strange, but I felt its sigh of relief. Its happiness that it would no longer be imprisoned within the corporal form. How could Rick be Rick without his soul intact? How could I have justified what I'd done?

The soul, its vibrant blue color faded and its parts mashed together as though a toddler had twisted it into a weird shape, popped free.

"In here," I said. "You'll be safe."

It floated toward the orb, and then wiggled into it. Now it looked like a very warped lava lamp, bouncing around in excitement. It looked wounded. And wrong.

I held the orb in one hand, and kept my other hand on Rick's chest.

He didn't open his eyes. And that was okay. He would have an empty gaze anyway.

Rick took one long, slow breath, and died.

I sat there for a moment with an ache so big it squashed my

lungs, my heart. Then I put it all away. At least, I tried. Maybe later, I could take it back out again, examine these emotions, and figure out a way to deal.

"What will happen to his body?"

"I'll return with him to Las Vegas. I'll create a scenario where his death makes sense." Rath put a hand on my shoulder.

"Thank you," I managed. And then, "Don't tell me how sorry you are. Please."

We stood there in silence, and I felt horribly sad. At the same time, taking his soul had a sense of rightness.

"What do I do now?"

"We go into the Underworld." He let go of me and walked toward the hearth. He paused before the odd, no-heat fire and swept his arm forward. "After you."

My heart thudded. I walked to the edge of the hearth and peered into the wavering dark. "This goes to the Underworld?"

"Yes." He gave me a little shove and I was propelled forward, right into the flames.

Instead of burning, I felt like I'd been dipped into arctic waters. The darkness swirled like ink poured into crystalline water and then the world all around turned gray.

"The Shallows," said Rath. This time he didn't seem overly worried that I was alive and walking around in them. "C'mon."

We moved ahead, marching through the gray mists. There was nothing discernible about the Shallows—no landmarks, no landscapes, no sense of space.

It seemed that we walked that way forever in silence. The air eventually thickened, and soon it felt like I was trying to breathe in syrup. It smelled heavily of sandalwood and underneath that musky scent, I detected an ashy smell.

The gates appeared.

"Are those…"

"Bones," confirmed Rath.

The gates were huge, so tall and wide that it looked as though two giants could walk through side by side and not touch the bleached, gleaming bones.

"They say these are the bones of the old gods. The ones destroyed before Isis and Osiris brought peace to the world. Their magic is so strong they can bind in the dead—and trap immortals."

"Whoa."

I reached out and touched the strange skull that seemed to serve as the handle.

"This is as far as I can go," said Rath. "Once you walk inside, you'll travel down a corridor. At the end of it, you'll enter the chamber of Maat. There you'll plead Rick's case. If she finds him worthy, she'll repair his soul and guide him into the next world."

Terror bleached through my skin and threatened to paralyze me. I turned a wide-eyed gaze to Rath, unable to express how much I did not want to walk through those gates.

He put a hand on my shoulder and squeezed. This seemed to be the most comfort he could offer—and it was far too inadequate. "I'll wait for you."

I nodded, my gaze sliding away from his and to the massive bone gates. Then I pushed on the elongated, one-eyed skull of a nameless god and entered the Underworld.

The corridor was made of red sandstone that reached so far up, I couldn't see the top. The interior walls held gold-etched hieroglyphs that began to glow as I passed. In its glass barrier Rick's soul leaped around as though it had been electrified.

My heart thudded, and sweat slicked the curve of my spine. Then the corridor opened into a huge chamber. Above was a purple sky marbled by thin, golden clouds. Below the floor was interlocked red stones. And at the end of the chamber was a platform.

A gorgeous woman, who looked younger than I was, sat on a large throne made of beautifully carved and painted stone. She wore a white dress belted at the waist but no shoes. Her skin was the color of a caramel macchiato. Her long black hair gleamed like a raven's wing; a narrow gold circlet sat atop her straight, shiny locks.

It was the only jewelry she wore.

"Come forward," she said in a low, soothing voice. "And present yourself for judgment."

I approached Maat with knees shaking so bad, I thought I might collapse. I finally made it to the platform. When I stood before her, dry-mouthed and terrified, she rose.

She stood before her throne, her gaze on the soul that spun inside the orb.

There was a great sound—like the music and chanting I'd heard before when souls sought the light—and Anubis appeared on one side of the throne. Then a creature with a crocodile head and a woman's nude body appeared on the other.

And a man dressed in a simple black robe—and, oh yeah, he had the head of a bird, an ibis to be exact. He, I surmised, was Thoth, the scribe who would record the proceedings.

Anubis, FYI, had the head of sleek black jackal, his traditional form as the god of the Underworld. He stared straight ahead, not acknowledging me at all. He wore some kind of colorful skirt and held in his left hand a long, silver scythe.

That couldn't be good.

"Present the soul," said Maat. She waved her hand and a huge scale appeared. One side held a single, white feather.

Everyone turned to look at me, waiting for me to relinquish Rick's soul. I swallowed the knot in my throat, and cleared it a few times. "It's not whole," I said. "I was hoping you could repair it."

Maat stared at me with distant eyes. "Why is it not whole?"

I licked my cracked lips, my heart beating so hard I thought it might pop out of my chest. Sweat trickled down my brow. "I tried to save him. I didn't know…what I know now."

"I do not understand why humans struggle so against death. It is not an ending." She turned her gaze to mine. "You have done a great disservice to this being. What do you offer as penance?"

My gaze slid to Anubis, but he stood there like a statue, staring straight ahead. Obviously, I was on my own. I wanted to whine, to rail against the unfairness of everything, but all I heard in my head was Irina telling me to suck it up. *Be afraid if you must, useless one, but do what you must anyway.*

"What do you want?" I asked.

"Penance," she said simply.

Well, I didn't know what to do with that. What did penance constitute? Forty lashes? Laps around the football field? The removal of a limb? I wasn't sure what to say, so I stood there like a moron. And the goddess, who apparently had all the time in like, forever, to wait on my answer, didn't move while she waited for my answer.

"Goddess."

Maat turned, and looked at the god who'd spoken. "My lord Anubis?"

"Might I suggest that the reaper owe you a favor as her penance?"

Maat inclined her head and then faced me. "Three favors, Molly Bartolucci. One for the injustice of the soul you harmed, one for the healing now required of the one called Richard Widdenstock and one because I have honored Anubis's request."

I wasn't going to negotiate. "Okay," I said. "Three favors for you."

She smiled. Then she lifted her hand and the orb popped free of my grip. The glass shattered. The soul zoomed forward, as if eager to see Maat.

"Poor child," she murmured. She closed her eyes, and for the longest moment we stood there while she prayed or something. I was feeling deeply respectful of everyone in the room.

Especially the scary crocodile lady.

"Ah," said Maat. She held up her palm, and two wiggling blue lights appeared. She cupped the parts of Rick's soul in both hands, brought them to her lips and whispered.

When she opened her hands, Rick's soul was whole again. The blue circle floated into the empty scale and settled on it like a butterfly alighting onto a flower.

Maat considered the scale, which stayed even.

"I have found him worthy. Release him to the heavens." The scale disappeared instantly, leaving Rick's soul bobbing there all alone.

Anubis stepped forward then and sliced open the air with his scythe. Blue light and the music/chanting poured forth from the slit.

Rick's soul zipped inside and everything disappeared.

Maat returned to her throne. Thoth finished writing on his papyrus and poofed away.

Anubis crossed to me and gestured for me to leave. "I'll walk you to the gates."

We reached the corridor in no time. As we traversed its narrow, gold-flecked length, I held my breath. I couldn't wait to return to the real world. The Underworld, at least this part of it, was nerve-racking.

"Every soul goes through that?" I asked. "It seems like you guys would be sitting there all day."

"Some souls are so stained with their sins they are snapped up into the jaws of the gobbler. Others do not have to be judged—they go straight into the heavens." He looked at me, his snout twitching. "It's complicated."

We strode across the misty gray nothingness, and ahead, I could see the arch of the bone gates. I put my hand on Anubis's arm, and he stopped.

"You know who my father is," I said. I sucked in a breath. "It's why you choose me, right? It's why I'm kind of a Super Reaper."

"Yes," said Anubis. "I know who your father is."

My heart tried to climb out of my throat. "It's you, isn't it?"

Anubis's jackal face reverted into his human one. He took my hands into his. "I told you that you were prophesied." He squeezed my hands. "And yes, Molly, you are my daughter. Of my heart. And of my seed."

Ugh. *Seed?* Way to ruin a moment, Dad #2.

"So you and my mom…um, you know…hooked up?"

"It wasn't quite that simple, Molly."

He didn't say anything else, so I said, "Aaaaaand…?"

"It's not relevant right now," he said. "You need rest. And to reconnect with your human father. You're my child, too, Molly. It makes you very special, but there is a price to be paid, too. Knowing that I'm your father—that has to be enough for now."

"Yeah. Okay."

And you know what? It was pretty cool to finally know.

MOLLY'S REAPER DIARY

What to Do if Your Bio-Dad
Turns Out to Be Anubis

First, relax, because even if you are a reaper, Anubis probably isn't your real dad. I mean, maybe some of the other Underworld gods played nookie with your mom, but...unlikely.

Second, if Anubis is your dad, you're not supposed to ditch your human family. It's not cool, even if they LIED to you for your whole entire life.

Third, you'll probably be special in a way that requires you to work hard and do things you don't want to do. Like be responsible.

Fourth, you have to grow up. You have to be brave. You have to give up stuff you want because who you are is more important than malls and cute boys.

Finally, if Anubis is your dad, your life will suck. But you know what? It will also rock.

EPILOGUE

I WOKE UP ON MONDAY MORNING TO HENRY LEANING OVER my bed. His expression held vague concern. "Your presence is requested."

"Ugh!"

After killing my boyfriend, escorting his soul to the Underworld and finding out my freaking sperm donor was Anubis, I had returned to my room and crawled into bed. My friends had arrived en masse to offer comfort, movies and chocolate, but after a while they'd all drifted back to their own rooms.

I'd spent the night crying and sleeping until finally, I was just sleeping.

"I'm not going to class," I said. *Ever again.*

"It is Ms. Chiles who requires your time. I'm afraid it's urgent—and not something you can reschedule."

Really? Gah. I sat up and threw off the covers. "Fine. Whatevs."

I got dressed and brushed my hair, and then followed Henry around the castle until we ended up somewhere on the second floor. Henry led me to a large, ornate door that had necro symbols carved all over it.

"You're still my go-to guy, right?" I asked, as I stared at the door. I felt like I shouldn't go in there. A bad feeling lodged in the pit of my stomach. "Maybe we could go live in Mexico. Or Canada."

"Destiny is not so easily escaped," offered Henry. "I will come whenever you call me."

"Thanks."

I entered the room, feeling exhausted. I just wanted to go back to bed and sleep. Or maybe eat some of that chocolate stash and then sleep for a hundred years.

The room was small and held only a long, dark wood table in front of it, and sitting at the table, three people.

Medusa Chiles sat in the middle, her expression grim. A plump woman dressed in an alarming shade of purple sat to her right, and on the left, a man with a long, gray beard. He wore glasses and a checkered jacket. He looked confused, as though he wasn't quite sure how he'd gotten here.

Me, either, buddy.

"Please come forward," directed Ms. Chiles.

I didn't like this. It felt weird. Maybe it was another Nekros Society thing? "Molly," said Ms. Chiles. Her expression was as smooth as glass. "We've convened a council of three, as outlined in Nekyia Academy's bylaws." She stretched out her hands on the table and threaded her fingers together. "This is done when an accusation of forbidden necro magic is levied against a student."

I had been slowly walking toward the table, and I stopped about a foot away. There was no place for me to sit, so I stood before the table of judges feeling awkward and unsure.

"Um, okay. Why am I—" I heard Irina's voice in my head telling me to stop babbling. *Shut up. Listen. Assess the situation, Molly. Prepare yourself.*

I pressed my lips together and stilled.

"We've become aware of a situation where you took a soul from a dying woman and gave it to an enemy of Anubis."

Ms. Chiles's quiet accusation chilled the air. The people on either side of her eyed me with some amount of trepidation.

I said nothing.

"We have evidence of this," she continued. She nodded toward the checkered jacket man. He lifted his arm and muttered something.

The black soul box that I'd last seen in Yuri's possession appeared on the table. I had taken it with me...put it in my room.

And this council of three somehow had known that I had the box.

How?

"Do you recognize this item?" she asked.

"Yes."

"And you're aware of its purpose?"

"Yes."

"And you've used it?"

I nodded.

"She admits to the use of forbidden objects and magic," said the lady in purple in a clipped tone. Her brown eyes filled with worry. "No necro has yielded such power since..." She trailed off.

"We do not render judgment," said the man in a deep, lazy tone, as though he were merely commenting on the weather. "Until we have all the facts and hear from all parties involved."

Gah. What was going on here? I just couldn't catch a break.

Ms. Chiles stood up, her robe rustling. "Molly Bartolucci, you are hereby charged with illegal use of necromancy and the use of forbidden objects. You will be taken into custody by the Guardians and confined until your trial."

★ ★ ★ ★ ★

Look for Molly's next adventure
UNCHOSEN
Book 2 of THE REAPER DIARIES, *in 2013!*
Only from Michele Vail and Harlequin TEEN.

THE GODDESS TEST NOVELS

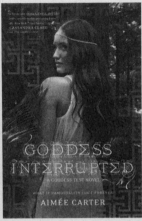
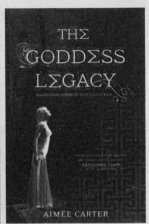

Available wherever books are sold!

A modern saga inspired by the Persephone myth. Kate Winters's life hasn't been easy. She's battling with the upcoming death of her mother, and only a mysterious stranger called Henry is giving her hope. But he must be crazy, right? Because there is no way the god of the Underworld—Hades himself—is going to choose Kate to take the seven tests that might make her an immortal...and his wife. And even if she passes the tests, is there any hope for happiness with a war brewing between the gods?

Also available:
THE GODDESS HUNT, a digital-only novella.

Be sure to look for THE GODDESS INHERITANCE coming April 2013!

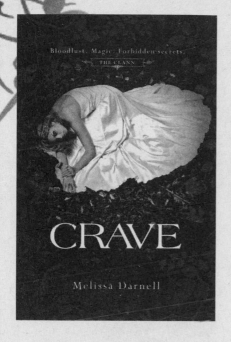

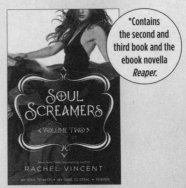

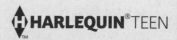

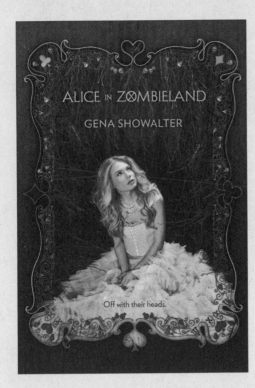